Leader
of the Pack

The Dogfather · Book Three

roxanne st. claire

Leader of the Pack
THE DOGFATHER BOOK THREE

Copyright © 2017 South Street Publishing

978-0-9981093-5-0 – ebook
978-0-9981093-6-7 – print

COVER ART: Keri Knutson (designer)
and Dawn C. Whitty (photographer)
INTERIOR FORMATTING: Author EMS

Critical Reviews of
Roxanne St. Claire Novels

"St. Claire, as always, brings a scorching tear-up-the-sheets romance combined with a great story: dealing with real issues starring memorable characters in vivid scenes."

— *Romantic Times Magazine*

"Non-stop action, sweet and sexy romance, lively characters, and a celebration of family and forgiveness."

— *Publishers Weekly*

"Plenty of heat, humor, and heart!"

— *USA Today's Happy Ever After blog*

"It's safe to say I will try any novel with St. Claire's name on it."

— *www.smartbitchestrashybooks.com*

"The writing was perfectly on point as always and the pace of the story was flawless. But be forewarned that you will laugh, cry, and sigh with happiness. I sure did."

— *www.harlequinjunkies.com*

"The Barefoot Bay series is an all-around knockout, soul-satisfying read. Roxanne St. Claire writes with warmth and heart and the community she's built at Barefoot Bay is one I want to visit again and again."

— *Mariah Stewart, New York Times bestselling author*

"This book stayed with me long after I put it down."

— *All About Romance*

Dear Reader:

Welcome back to the foothills of North Carolina where the Dogfather, Daniel Kilcannon, is once again pulling some strings to help one of his six grown children find forever love. On these pages, you'll find my favorite things in life and fiction: big families, great dogs, and lasting love. And, I am delighted to inform you that a portion of the first month sales of all the books in this series is being donated to Alaqua Animal Refuge (www.alaqua.org) in my home state of Florida. That's where these covers were shot by photographer Dawn Whitty (www.dawncwhitty.com) using *real* men (not models, but they are gorgeous!) and *rescue* dogs (now in forever homes!). So you don't only buy a terrific book...you support a fantastic cause!

I couldn't publish a book without my amazing crew, so huge thanks to my editor, Kristi Yanta, who knows how to make my voice sing; copyeditor Joyce Lamb, who is wonderfully picky and detailed; proofreader Marlene Engel, who makes sure every page is clean and shiny; cover designer Keri Knutson, who gave me Liam and Jag; and veterinarian Linda Hankins, who helps me get the dogs right. Thanks to all of them, along with my family, my best writing friends, and my dear little puppers who wait patiently for a walk while I finish a scene.

Sign up for my newsletter on my website at www.roxannestclaire.com to find out when the next book is released!

xoxo
Rocki

Dedication

For Nemo, a precious, protective *Schutzhund* who helped inspire this story. (Doggie kisses to his owner and my dear friend, Gena Showalter, who taught me about these amazing dogs!)

Chapter One

Two Months Ago

It would have been so easy to leave. Liam's brothers already knew the decibel level coming from the crowd and music in Bushrod's was enough to make him itch for air, silence, and solitude. They knew he hated the bar scene that never, not once, resulted in him meeting anyone worth seeing again.

So, when Andrea Rivers walked in, laughing with another woman, Liam knew that no one would have blinked twice if he'd slipped out into the night.

Including Andi herself.

Regret, disappointment, and the stale taste of rejection made him reach for his beer and down it the way a man would if he was about to leave a bar.

Not so his younger brother Shane. Unencumbered by any regrets, disappointment, or personal experience with rejection, Shane was up and beelining to the bar to buy the women drinks. He made no effort to hide his interest in Chloe Somerset, the woman Andi was with. Chloe was on Shane's radar, which meant the town's new tourism expert didn't stand a chance.

Now they'd all come back to this table to have their drink. With Liam. Unless…he left.

Or he could stay and talk to Andi. How would that go, he wondered.

Andi and Liam would say hello and give each other an awkward hug. She'd congratulate Garrett and Jessie on their engagement when they came back from the dance floor. Then Shane would persuade Chloe to dance the next time a slow song started. Garrett and Jessie would suck face or go back to dance again.

And that would leave Andi and Liam inches apart and forced to say something to each other. Dead air was not his favorite thing.

But Andi was.

His gaze slipped to the door, an escape just fifteen feet away.

Still, he stayed rooted to his seat, watching through the crowd as Shane put his hands on Chloe's shoulders and saved her from some guy who'd already moved in. Shane received a warm smile as his reward.

A few feet away from them, Liam caught a glimpse of Andi's long blond hair, but then Shane blocked his view.

Liam looked away, moved his empty glass an inch, shifted in his seat, and swiped slightly damp palms on his jeans. Then he checked his watch.

When he looked up, he saw her again. Closer now. Moving through the crowd. Coming straight toward this table. Her gaze was downcast, avoiding eye contact with guys who stepped aside to let her through, one of them staring at her backside like a Rottie ready to hump. Instantly, Liam sat up straighter, fisted his hands, and glared at the moron.

But then Andi reached the table and offered a tentative smile. Everything in the bar faded to background noise and colors. All he could see was hair the color of wheat blowing in the wind and eyes like a Carolina summer sky. Lips he'd kissed enough times to know exactly how sweet they tasted. A silky blue top rose and fell with a breath before she spoke, drawing his attention to her body, which was delicate, feminine, and, oh man, so perfect.

"Hello, Liam."

"Andi." One word, and he couldn't get it out without it sounding like the bark of a sick dog.

"I hear there are open seats at this table." She gestured toward the one catty-corner from him, hesitating when he didn't move.

Because his frickin' brain just went dead.

"Unless you'd rather I..." She pointed her thumb at the gathering of goons behind her, and one side of her mouth lifted in a smile.

"No, God, no. Please." He started to stand and get the chair, but she slipped into it before he even made it to his feet.

She angled her head toward the bar. "She's too kind to ditch me, but Chloe got distracted by your brother."

"Yeah," he said, trying so hard not to stare into her eyes. Failing, though. *Talk, Liam.* "He has that effect on unsuspecting victims."

She laughed easily, a sweet sound that made her tip her head enough so that he could see the fine line of her jaw. "Oh, I don't think she's unsuspecting. Plus, he gave her a dog."

"Yeah, I heard she took Daisy in." He glanced down at his empty beer, gathering his thoughts, which were pretty much scattered to the four winds and lost because…Andi.

"Did you—"

"Have you—"

They both laughed at the awkward, simultaneous questions.

"You first—"

"Go ahead—"

And again.

Andi shook her head, putting an easy hand over his, probably unaware that just that slight touch of her long, feminine fingers felt a little like a live wire on his skin. "How are you, Liam?"

Besides being shell-shocked by the woman he never, ever got over? "Great. You?"

He could see her relax instantly. "Really good. Christian just finished kindergarten."

Of course her first report would be about her little boy. The kid was her whole life, which was another thing he liked and respected about her.

"Wow, that was fast," he said. Not that it seemed fast to him, but he grabbed the first thing people said when they talked about kids. Truth was, it seemed like forever since he'd held her and said goodbye and tried to make her believe he understood her decision.

But it hadn't been forever, only about three years, during which time he'd trained a hundred dogs and tried to date a handful of women, none of whom were Andi Rivers. But here she was, inches away and as beautiful and magnetic as ever.

"You have no idea how fast," she said. "And how

are all your dogs? I hear Waterford is the largest rescue and training center in the state now."

"That's true."

"And I remember when it opened and I brought Christian to that grand-opening event for the town? Remember?"

Did he remember the day they'd met? Was she kidding? She'd stood in the sunshine at Waterford Farm, like an angel with a glow of goodness around her, a tiny tow-headed boy hiding behind her leg, desperate to get closer to a German shepherd Liam had on a leash, but terrified of the dog, too.

"We've come a long way since then. I mean, Waterford has." Because he and Andi had made it slightly more than one month before he got pushed aside for someone else. Someone who happened to be the father of her child, but still.

"I hear nothing but good things about Waterford," she said. "And you're the leader."

"Only where K-9 training is concerned," he said. "My dad runs the operation, really."

"The Dogfather."

He chuckled, inexplicably happy that she remembered inside jokes his family shared. "That's what they call him."

"That's what they call who?" Shane held two beers and put one in front of Liam, then pulled out a chair for Chloe, who held two glasses of wine and gave one to Andi.

"Oh, thank you," Andi said.

"Thank Shane," Chloe replied, lifting her glass to toast Liam. "Nice to see you again, Liam."

With Shane back, the talk wasn't small or awkward

anymore. In a few minutes, he was telling a story about how they had four new puppies all getting leash-trained at the same time, making everyone howl with laughter.

Liam only made dogs howl, or at least he could train one to do so on command. Fat lot of good that skill did him with a beautiful woman next to him, frequently glancing at him. Quite frequently, unless that was his imagination.

"So we send Darcy out there," Shane continued, talking with his hands and mesmerizing everyone. "Which was a huge mistake, because adding our little sister to a group of puppies is kind of like adding one more crazy puppy."

Except Andi wasn't that mesmerized. She took a sip of wine and shot another look to Liam over the rim. Her blue eyes held his, the tiniest smile behind the glass.

Just enough to slam him with hope.

Unless his third beer had made him dumb.

Was he *imagining* her gaze on him?

No. It was real. Every time he looked to his right, he'd catch her eye, and before he could look away, he read something in her expression. An invitation? An open door? Another chance?

After three years? Two since her ex was killed in a car accident. Liam had visited Andi after the guy died, to give his condolences, and she'd been understandably distant. He'd seen her around town, of course, but every encounter was brief and uncomfortable.

She certainly had never looked at him *like that*. Like she wanted something. Like she wanted him.

"Oh no." She pulled out her phone on a sigh. "The text I've been dreading."

"Everything all right?" Liam asked as she read.

"My sitter is wondering when I'm coming home." She looked at Chloe. "I didn't expect our dinner would turn into a night out, and I told her I'd be home by ten."

"Totally understand," Chloe said, reaching for her purse.

"No, you don't have to leave," Andi replied. "You're having fun. My house is on the other side of Bushrod Square. I'll be home in ten minutes."

"I wouldn't think of letting you leave alone," Chloe said.

"Please." Andi put her hand on Chloe's and looked from her to Shane. "You don't have a six-year-old, and it's Saturday night. Enjoy yourself."

Chloe shook her head, and Liam interjected before she could argue, "I'll take you home." He hoped he didn't sound too much like a hungry dog who'd glimpsed a bone. "Let me walk you."

Andi opened her mouth to answer, and he braced for the rejection. But she stayed speechless for a split second, then sighed softly. "Okay. That would be great."

"Are you sure?" Chloe asked.

"Only if you have someone to take you home," Andi said.

Shane held up his hand. "I got this."

"Then I'm sure." Andi turned to Liam. "Let's go."

The two words were like music to his ears.

Part of Andi knew exactly what she was

doing…the part that resided in the lower half of her body. Because if she had been conducting business with her heart tonight, she would have made polite small talk with Liam Kilcannon and left with the girlfriend she arrived with. Or, if she'd actually used her brain, she would have made up an excuse and slipped out the back of Bushrod's the minute she saw Liam, insisting that Chloe stay and have fun.

But her actions were driven by that knot low in her belly, the white-hot ache that she'd learned to ignore during her two years of self-imposed celibacy, also known as loneliness. One look at a man who never failed to shake up her hormones and she couldn't ignore anything anymore.

Couldn't ignore the need to put a casual hand on the masculine forearm with a dusting of dark hair. Couldn't ignore the thrill of a three-seconds-too-long lingering look over a glass of wine. And she sure as heck wouldn't ignore the text from her sitter, which was like a message from the great beyond saying, *Let Liam walk you home and see what happens.*

A few minutes later, he held the door for her, and they stepped into the hot summer night of Bitter Bark, North Carolina.

"I have my truck if you'd rather ride," he said.

She angled her head, considering the choice, but she already knew exactly what her answer had to be. "Walk, I think. It's the coolest part of the day, and I don't want to miss it."

"True," he said, setting a hand on her back and then moving it again, as if it burned to touch her. "It's been so hot that the only time we're really training in July and August is early morning and after sundown."

"Are you still training German shepherds for sale as protection dogs? What's it called again? *Schutz*..."

"*Schutzhund*. High-protection guard dog training. Yep, still doing it. Turns out it's the most lucrative aspect of our business, so I've got one dog going at all times," he said.

"And K-9 training?"

"Sure. I'm still working with law enforcement and military trainers who bring their dogs to us, but the market for high-end, specially trained German shepherds is booming. We've gotten a reputation as one of the best in the country."

"I'm not surprised, Liam. You have an uncanny ability to coax fearlessness out of an animal."

He nodded a silent acknowledgment of the compliment. "That's all thanks to being a military dog trainer in the Marines, and believe me, I have help," he added with that soft note of humility always present in his tone. "It's insane what people will pay for these dogs. One of our biggest clients is a security firm up in New York who shells out fifteen grand a dog."

"But it takes a long time to train one, right?"

"Some longer than others," he said. "Like I got one about a month ago, Jag. He's protective as hell, but easily distracted. Might not command the big bucks." He shook his head. "Sorry. You probably don't care about the details."

She smiled up at him as they crossed the street and headed toward the square. "I'm all about the details, remember? I'm an architect."

"Yes, I remember," he said with a slight laugh that told her he hadn't forgotten a thing. "An architect who wants to be a professor someday."

Of course Liam would remember the personal tidbits she'd shared over dinner dates with him. How ironic that Jeff Scott, the man Andi chose over Liam, never took that second-career dream seriously, but Liam remembered how important it was to her.

"I'm taking baby steps toward that now," she confided. "Teaching an adult-ed class this summer at Vestal Valley College."

"Wow." He drew back and looked impressed. "Professor Rivers. Like your dad, huh?"

And he remembered that, too. Her heart hitched that she'd meant so much to him that he bothered to retain all those little facts.

"Not exactly," she assured him. "He's teaching urbanism and foundational computation to MIT graduate students, and I'm leading discussions on European architecture to some retirees and a few lost fortysomethings having midlife crises and taking college courses."

"Still," he said. "It's a step toward what you always wanted to do, and I respect that."

She sighed softly, appreciating his respect, but knowing that wasn't why she'd jumped on the opportunity to be alone with him. Not tonight. Tonight she wanted…

Him.

"Look how pretty it is here," she said, gesturing toward the parklike square lit by gas lamps and hundreds of twinkling white lights in the trees.

"This town sure likes to string lights in Bushrod Square," he said.

"It's probably what ol' Thaddeus Bushrod imagined when he founded Bitter Bark and named it after a tree that's really a hickory tree." She gestured toward the bronze statue of the man whose name graced the square, standing next to the landmark tree that rose at least thirty feet in the air, the spot somehow beloved and sacred to all the residents of Bitter Bark. "I'm on the tourism committee, and Chloe informed us of that fact in her first presentation."

"Sounds like town heresy."

She laughed, watching a few people stroll through the square, several getting in their evening dog walks and a runner or two. Bushrod Square always felt safe, and never more than when she was with a man as big and protective as Liam.

Walking next to him, she wanted to slide both her hands around his arm for the sheer pleasure of hugging that solid bicep and feeling the warmth of his body. Just the thought of it tightened everything in her that was already pretty darn tight.

"So, how's your little guy doing?" he asked.

She smiled, of course, at the mention of Christian. "He's good. So, so good."

"He's, um, over the tough stuff?"

"Pretty much," she said, recalling that when Liam had visited her a month or so after Jeff's death, she'd shared some of the sleep and social problems Christian had because his father had been gone, come back, then disappeared forever. "He's a quiet kid, so it's hard to figure out his feelings." She glanced up at Liam, who was also quiet and challenging to discern.

"And how about you?" he asked, the question tentative enough for her to know he was inching into personal territory with great care. "Over the tough stuff?"

She didn't answer for a few seconds, long enough to decide he deserved honesty. "I survived," she finally said. "Maybe a little too easily."

He slowed his step, looking down at her, his expression a mix of surprise and something else she couldn't quite read. Confusion? Hope? Admiration? "You're stronger than you realize," he said.

"I was also not as in love with Jeff as I, well, as I would have liked."

He choked softly, but didn't say anything. Considering all he could say at that, it was a true point in his favor.

"Is that an awful thing to admit?" she asked, hoping the conversation didn't veer off into a discussion about how much Jeff had changed after he returned to her life. It would only make her feel worse about what she'd done to Liam.

"No," he said.

"Even though he cost us, well, us?"

He swallowed visibly, taking a moment to collect what he was going to say, making her get a tiny bit closer, because experience had taught her that when Liam said something from the heart, it was right and real and worth listening to.

"You didn't make that decision because of us, Andi. You made it for Christian."

She stopped completely, looking up at him, the little white lights on that tree in the center of the square blurring in her eyes for a second. "I did, and it's very sweet of you to remind me. Very sweet of you to talk to me at all."

"Sweet isn't something I'm accused of too often," he said, a smile taking his strong-boned face from handsome to heart-stopping. "You know I only wanted you to be happy."

"I know." And she knew he'd been disappointed when she broke off their budding relationship to give Jeff a real chance. Liam being Liam, however, she had no idea the extent of that disappointment, or if he harbored resentment toward her. "I know I hurt you."

"But you were really nice about it," he said, turning to face her.

She sighed at the way he said it, placing a hand on his shoulder for the pleasure of feeling how strong it was.

Somewhere across the square, a dog barked. A dove hooted. Conversations from other people drifted by like the scent of jasmine on warm summer air. But Andi didn't hear much beyond the steady pulse in her head. Heat and need thrummed from those veins down, down, down to the center of her, everything warm just from looking at him.

She closed her eyes and pressed a little harder, loving the breadth and muscularity of his shoulder.

As if it were the most natural move, he put his hand on her waist, inching her closer. "Didn't make it hurt any less, but you were nice."

Exhaling, she dropped her head back a little bit, her eyes shuttering.

Just one kiss. One.

"It's good to talk to you, Liam," she whispered. "To..." Very slowly, she put her free hand on his other shoulder, dragging her palms down a bit, each move like a choreographed dance getting them closer and closer. "It's good to be with you again."

She let her fingers hold the thick cords of his biceps, thumbing under the sleeve of his T-shirt that just about covered a tattoo of a bulldog and two German words.

Teufel Hunden.

Devil Dog. It popped into her head along with a memory of a night she'd run her fingers over that tattoo and Liam had told her Marines had the nickname because they were so fierce that they were considered dogs from hell. And as a military dog training specialist, the image and nickname meant even more to him.

She also remembered that she'd almost slept with him that night as things had grown from heated to desperate on her living room sofa, but since she had a toddler who'd wake up at sunrise and expect his mommy to be sleeping alone, Liam had been far too considerate and controlled. Without spelling it out, they'd both silently agreed they'd find a better time and place...but Jeff Scott had shown up at her front door a few days later asking for a second chance, and Andi had been forced to make a sudden and difficult decision.

"It's so good to hold you again," she said, tipping her head back so there could be zero doubt what she wanted.

"Andi..." He barely whispered her name as he closed the space between them and kissed her.

She felt the heat of his mouth just before it touched her lips, tentative at first, then with a little more demand. She melted into the kiss. Parting her lips to breathe him in, she slid her hands up and over the breadth of his shoulders, squeezing the hard and masculine muscles, already imagining how his skin would feel against hers.

It had been so long. So long. So lonely.

He tasted delicious, like a tangy beer and sweet, hot man. Like the Liam she remembered and had long ago told herself to forget.

Large, hot hands coasted over her back, lingering every few inches as if he wanted to appreciate each new place he touched.

"Liam…" She broke the kiss but not the full-body contact, leaning against him for the rush of his hard chest against her sensitive, aching nipples. His heart was beating like hers, pounding with the same kind of need. And lower, more need was evident as she felt the pressure of a man seconds away from full arousal.

He trailed some kisses down the jaw she offered, while she inhaled the musky, sexy scent of him, an aroma that made her anxious and desperate for more.

No. One kiss was not going to be enough. Not for a woman who had spent way too many nights utterly and completely alone and empty. She didn't want to be alone tonight. She didn't want to be empty.

She wanted Liam in her bed and in her body, and she'd wanted it the minute she walked up to the table and saw him. She attempted a ragged inhale and kissed him again, with even more intent and a clear message of desire. Finally, she loosened her grip and inched away. His eyes were black with the same arousal that rocked her.

"I knew this would happen," she murmured.

He looked stunned by that. "Was that why you let me walk you home?" He eased farther back. "Because I'm pretty surprised by it all."

"Mmm." She gnawed on her lower lip, hard enough to hurt.

"Hey." With one finger, he gently eased that lip from under her tooth. "Use that lip for better things."

That made her smile, a nervous, shaky smile, as she searched his face. Was he going to make her ask him to come home with her?

During their few weeks together, Liam and Andi's kisses had hummed with an undercurrent of electricity, but he was patient, easing her closer every time they were together, a man one hundred percent comfortable with taking his time.

Of course, he hadn't known time would be cut short.

But that was then, and this is now. Liam might be patient, but Andi wasn't. She dug around for a way to invite him home without sounding like the sex-starved, celibate-for-too-long, single woman she was.

"Christian's asleep," she finally said, and from the look on his face, she was certain he knew exactly what she meant. And she could have picked a leaf off the ground and knocked him over with it.

She laughed a little. "I know it never happened before, Liam, but it was about to."

Until her ex-boyfriend showed up and wanted to be a full-time daddy. And then she'd made her choice, and it hadn't been Liam.

"I haven't said more than ten words to you in two years," he said.

She gave a teasing smile. "Hey, that's a big conversation for you."

He choked softly, as if he really couldn't believe this was happening. "Look, Andi…"

16

Oh God. That didn't sound like, *Hell yeah, let's go.*

"Have you thought this through?" he asked.

She didn't want to *think* tonight. She ran her fingers over the nape of his neck, slowly, knowing she owed him some kind of rationale besides *I want you.* Except, that was the truth.

"When I saw you tonight, I thought…well, yeah. When I saw you tonight, I started thinking it through pretty hard."

He stared at her, silent.

Really? Didn't people just hook up nowadays? Yes, she had a six-year-old who'd taken her off the market, but she shouldn't have to persuade him to have sex with her, should she?

"I trust you, Liam. I know you. I've…" She wet her lips. "I'm not with anyone, ever. I'm celibate, is what I'm saying. And when I saw you, it hit me so hard how much I want to…change that. Tonight. With you. Don't you?"

"Pretty sure how I feel about it is five minutes from obvious."

"Then let's try this again." She gave a meaningful look. "*Christian's asleep.*"

"Then what?"

Now she choked an uncomfortable laugh, echoing his. "Then…" He wanted her to spell it out? "He's a good sleeper. You could stay…for a little bit."

"A little bit?" The question came out rough. "How about the night? Another month? Longer?"

Exactly the very reason she was the lonely sex-starved celibate woman. "No, Liam. No." She shook her head. "I can't do that. I won't do that. I will never do that again."

"Like actually date someone and have a relationship?"

"No," she said, drawing back to make her single-word statement stick. "I can't ever take that chance again. Christian struggled when Jeff left."

He had nightmares, and tears, and so many questions. She'd *never* do that again.

"Jeff *died*."

"I know, but..." Would Liam even be standing here if Jeff's car hadn't gone off an icy mountain road? She couldn't be sure. She might have stuck it out with Jeff for Christian's sake. But what difference did that make? He was gone and Andi was alone. So alone.

"So this is different," he said. "We have another chance."

She shook her head again. "Things don't always work out. They usually don't work out. Heck, they almost never work out. One minute, you have a plan, and the next, wham, life throws you a curve ball. Nothing is certain in this life, Liam. And I have learned the hard way to protect myself—and my son—from that reality."

"So that would keep you from taking a chance on..." He swallowed, and for a moment, she actually thought he was going to say *love*. "Happiness?"

"I can't risk that instability in my son's life again, Liam. Especially now. He's six, and while he was always a quiet kid, he really retreated into a shell of painful shyness after Jeff died. I vowed I'll never bring a man into my life while he's growing up."

"But you'd have sex with one while he's asleep?"

She felt the blood drain from her face. "Ouch."

"I don't say that to hurt you, Andi. You can do

what you want, you're a grown woman, and I…get it. But I…" He took a slight step back, not even an inch. But it felt like a football field of space between them. "I'm not going to be that guy for you."

She looked up, certain she looked as stricken as she felt. "I guess I deserve this after what—"

"No." He cut her off. "I'm not *punishing* you. That's not what's going on here."

"Then what is, other than my failed seduction?"

"Look," he said on a rough exhale. "Maybe I am the lug nut Shane says I am, because I should probably be dragging you home by way of the nearest drugstore right this minute. Or maybe I'm a few months shy of forty and I know there's more to this than sex. Don't get me wrong, I wanted to have sex with you since the day I saw you at Waterford, but not…like this. Not a hookup after seeing you at a local bar."

She winced, knowing he didn't mean to make her feel bad about the offer, but she did anyway. Bad, rejected, and a little embarrassed she'd asked.

"This is all I can offer you," she said softly. "I will not open my heart or my life up for any man but the one I'm raising."

"Well, I want more from you," he said simply. Of course, Liam was never one for fancy words or declarations or verbal sparring. He said what he thought and meant what he said.

And as much as she appreciated what he was saying, *more* was never going to happen.

"I won't settle for a few hours with you while Christian's asleep," he said. "I deserve more than that, and so do you."

She eased away from him completely, wrapping

herself in her own arms now. "Wow. I honestly forgot men like you existed."

"Idiots? We're all over the place. We just keep a low profile."

She tried to smile, remembering how much she liked his self-deprecating humor. "I'm sorry."

"Don't be. Just go out with me. Have dinner with me. Come to Waterford, bring your son, and let's pick up where we left off."

Oh. She stared at him for a long, long time. With each heartbeat, she knew what she had to do. Who she had to protect from hurt. Not her, not Liam. But the boy who owned her heart and soul.

"I can't do that, Liam. I won't do that. I've made this decision, and I'm not changing my mind."

He blew out a breath. "All right."

"My house is right there," she said, pointing to the three-story brownstone on the corner.

"I know where your house is."

"Then you can watch me to make sure I get in okay. I know you will anyway." She blinked, and her eyes misted over again. "Goodbye, Liam."

He just looked at her, silent. Liam would never say a word unless it was the right one. And this minute, there was nothing left to say.

She turned and crossed the street, heading into her home still knowing that nothing in life was ever certain…except the fact that she'd be sleeping alone tonight.

Chapter Two

Present Day

"Is this something I can install myself?"

The clerk took the keypad electronic dead bolt and turned it over, reading the package as if Andi hadn't already done that three times. "With some tools. You got a spade bit to drill a hole in the side of your door?"

She was an architect, not a contractor. She had pencils and drafting triangles, even a toolbox? What she needed was the phone number of a handyman.

Next to her, Christian dragged his finger along of row of unmade keys, making them all jingle. And two keys clanged to the linoleum floor of Bitter Bark Hardware. Well, *Better* Bark Hardware, now that the town had voted to change its name for one year.

Already, the effects of the tourism campaign could be felt. A few businesses had hired Andi's architectural firm to draw up plans for updates or new locations. And, thanks to the genius idea of Andi's good friend Chloe Somerset, there were more and more dogs showing up—with their owners—as the tourism committee and business owners worked together to make "Better Bark" famous as the most dog-friendly town in the country.

But more people in Bitter Bark meant more crime, too. Which was what brought this single mom to a hardware store instead of a toy store on a Saturday afternoon.

"I can figure out how to install it," she said as she bent down to scoop up the keys and put a hand on her son's shoulder to draw him closer.

"'Cause we sell the bits," the clerk said. "Right in aisle six."

"Or you can get one of my sons to come over and install that lock."

Andi turned at the sound of a man's voice behind her, her eyes widening at the sight of a tall, handsome, older man with a regal-looking Irish setter on a leash. "Hello, Dr. Kilcannon," she said, greeting him with a smile. "I haven't seen you for a while."

"Since that last Tourism Advisory Committee meeting before Shane took my place." He gave her a friendly hug.

"And I understand congrats are in order with Shane and Chloe's engagement," Andi said. "Guess it worked out very well that you gave him your place on the committee."

"Don't tell me you've heard that rumor that I'm trying to pull strings and get my kids married off."

She laughed. "I've become good friends with Chloe. Something tells me it's not a rumor."

He leaned a little closer. "Truth is, I was trying to get Liam to take my place, not Shane."

She felt a little heat crawl up her chest at the mention of his oldest son. She hadn't seen him since the night she'd humiliated herself in Bushrod Square two months ago. But Christian curled his hand around her legs, half hiding, half fascinated by the dog Dr. K had with him, and that saved her from answering.

"Oh, hello, big guy." Dr. K grinned at him. "Would you like to pet Rusty? He's real friendly."

Instantly, Christian's cheeks turned pink, and he inched closer to Andi.

"You can say hi, honey. Dr. Kilcannon is a friend. I'm sure his dog is sweet."

Christian nodded and hid again. Andi opened her mouth to say her usual *he's shy* excuse, but stopped herself. It wasn't helping Christian to point out his social challenges in public. And she shouldn't answer for him anymore, either. First grade started in two days, and she wasn't going to be with him every minute to help navigate the waters.

"I had a kid like that," Dr. K said, giving Rusty's leash an infinitesimal tug to encourage interaction between his dog and her boy.

"You had a kid like everything," Andi teased, knowing that with six children, there probably wasn't a type Daniel and Annie Kilcannon hadn't raised. And they'd all turned out great. Some even greater than others.

"I think Rusty would love if you'd pet him," Dr. K said in a soft, encouraging voice to Christian.

She felt little hands grip her hips.

"Do you have a dog?" Dr. K asked.

"Oh, no. I work all day," she said quickly, knowing this kind veterinarian loved nothing more than making sure every dog in the world had a home.

"Do you want the drill bit or not?" The man behind the counter did a fairly poor job of masking his impatience.

"Oh, I'm so sorry. No, I have a drill. I'll figure something out. I'll just take that lock."

Finally, Christian slipped out and came one step closer to the dog, who lifted his russet-colored head for love.

"Go ahead," Dr. K said gently while Andi got her wallet out to pay for the lock.

"He's soft," Christian whispered as he touched the dog's head.

Andi looked over her shoulder, smiling at the look of rapture on Christian's face. Dr. K glanced at her, then the lock that the clerk was putting in a bag for her.

"That's a serious dead bolt," he noted.

She nodded and checked Christian, who was deeply involved with the dog now, giggling as Rusty offered a paw.

"I think I need it," Andi whispered.

Dr. K looked surprised and worried. "Something wrong, Andi?"

She glanced at Christian again, making sure he wouldn't hear. "My house was broken into," she said quietly, tapping the credit card pad and taking the bag.

"Really?" His brows, so much darker than his salt-and-pepper hair, furrowed. "That's unusual in Bitter Bark."

"I know." She glanced again at Christian, still a

few feet away, now on his knees with Rusty. "But I live right off the square, and there are a lot more tourists in that area, which is the whole idea of that committee, right?"

"Tourists aren't thieves."

"They didn't steal anything." Except her sense of security.

He drew back. "Are you sure? Have you reported this?"

"I did, and I replaced the door lock but want to add this for extra security. And, yes, the Bitter Bark police came and wrote it up."

"Any leads?"

She shook her head. "No and since nothing was stolen, it probably isn't a high priority. But the door was ajar when I got home, so I know someone was in there. But they didn't take jewelry or electronics."

"You sure they weren't still in the house when you arrived?"

She shuddered as she remembered how scared she'd been walking in that day and searching the house, trying to stay nonchalant so Christian wouldn't freak out. "Something must have spooked them and they left before I got home." She threw a smile at Christian. "And someone conveniently lost his toothbrush, but I think he was just taking advantage of the situation."

"He knows it happened?"

"He knows I was trying to find out if anything was missing, but I didn't tell him we'd had a break-in."

Dr. Kilcannon's deep-blue gaze grew dark and serious. "You need a dog, young lady. Something protective."

"I can't take care of a dog, and I don't think it's fair to leave one alone all day. This will do the trick." She held her bag up. "If I can tackle that drill bit."

He gave her a look she couldn't quite interpret, but there was caring in his expression. And some wheels spinning. He didn't say anything, though, then shifted his gaze behind her to Christian.

"You should come to Waterford and see our puppies, young man," he said. "Would you like that?"

Christian's baby blues widened, and he stood, immediately coming back to Andi to press against her.

She gave an apologetic smile. "He's shy," she whispered.

"Did pretty well with my dog, though," he noted.

"Yes, thank you for letting him play with Rusty."

He opened his mouth to say something, then closed it again, nodding. "Really nice to see you, Andi. Holler if you have a problem with the drill. I have plenty of sons who could help you."

One in particular. Did he think she couldn't see *that* wheel turning? "Thanks, Dr. K. I can manage."

After buying the lock, Andi headed home, listening to Christian chatter endlessly about Rusty and thinking, as she so often did, about Liam Kilcannon. Which she suspected was exactly what the Dogfather wanted her to be doing.

Liam wiped the sweat from his brow with the bottom of his filthy T-shirt, grabbing a cold bottle of water on his way into the kennels. His brother Garrett was right behind him, still making a point that Liam wanted to ignore.

"He's ready, and we have an offer for ten thousand dollars, Liam."

"He's not ready," Liam argued. "He needs more time with me."

"It's a good and fair price for that dog."

If you could put a price on Jag, which Liam was starting to think he couldn't. He hustled around the corner toward Jag's kennel.

"You've been working with him for months, Liam," Garrett said, catching up. "We've got four more puppies lined up, ready to come here for training. It's time for Jag to move on."

"I'll be the judge of that," Liam said, gulping the water and nearly finishing the bottle. "He is not ready."

"Not for an elite police department," Garrett agreed. "And he'll never work in the military. But this owner is top notch and made of money. He wants a highly trained German shepherd now. He's willing to fly you down to Miami for the handoff, or come up here in a private plane. We need to take this offer."

"Jag will hate Miami." He tossed the bottle into the recycling bin.

"He has an aversion to paradise?" Shane popped out from around the next corner, a few leashes strung over his arm. "This dude lives on Star Island, Liam."

Just what Liam needed—two of his brothers breathing down his back to persuade him to part with Jag. "I don't care if he lives on Fantasy Island, Jag's not ready to leave me yet."

"Not supposed to get that attached," Garrett said in a warning voice.

Liam whipped around. "Protection-dog training is my business, little brother." Maybe a little more emphasis on *little* than was necessary, but Liam hated this conversation. It was the second time they'd had a potential buyer for Jag and the second time Liam fought the sale. "I'm taking him home."

"He lives here," Shane said.

Liam swore under his breath. "He works all night. It's his job to stay awake and prowl. He can't do that in the kennels. When he stays here overnight, he's miserable the next day."

"Kinda like his handler."

Liam didn't dignify Shane's needling with a response.

As soon as he reached Jag's kennel, the big guy immediately responded, jumping up and letting his oversized tongue hang out, something he did only for Liam. His pointed ears popped up with interest and intent, and his bushy black tail swished with happiness. And, of course, he barked at Garrett and Shane, rather than holding Liam's gaze as he was supposed to.

Which was why he wasn't ready.

Garrett leaned against the wall and crossed his arms. "It would be a pretty lousy investment if you kept him."

"Again, Garrett. I *know* the high-protection canine business. I started it, remember? My idea, my skills. And my dogs to decide if and when they're ready."

"Don't push him," Shane said. "He's been in a bad mood for months."

"He's been in a bad mood for forty years," Garrett muttered.

Liam blew out a breath, shaking his head, so sick

of these two. They were worse than ever now that they went home to their brides-to-be and Liam went home to…nothing.

"Jag. *Hier*." The dog obeyed the command to come to Liam, one that only the *Schutzhund*-trained dogs would know, then waited for the next. "*Aus*," Liam said with the biting precision that made the German commands so effective.

Instantly, Jag stepped out of the kennel, and Liam rewarded him with a good scratch on the head.

"You know what you need, Brother?" Shane asked, clamping a hand on Liam's shoulder.

"A shower and a beer."

"A shower and a *babe*. Preferably at the same time."

Liam rolled his eyes, and even Garrett snorted at Shane's ridiculousness.

"You know I'm right," Shane said.

Yeah, he was. Which pissed Liam off even more.

"We want you to be as settled as we are," Shane continued, since knowing when to shut up had never been his strong suit.

"Quit telling me to get rid of this dog." Liam snapped his fingers at Jag. "*Vorwärts*!" The dog marched "forward" on the command, past his brothers, and out to the late afternoon sunshine—and damn near slammed directly into his father.

Who would side with them, of course.

"Liam, so glad you're still here." He beamed down at Jag, putting his hand on the dog's big head. "And Jag. So glad *you're* still here."

He was? Probably because he had another offer, and this one for more money.

Shane and Garrett came out from the kennels behind him, and he braced for a full-out war.

"I've found the perfect solution for the problem of Jag," Dad said.

The *problem* of Jag? Liam looked down at his dog—yes, *his*—and saw his ears rise at the mention of his name.

"Don't bother, Dad." Garrett came up next to him. "Liam's not parting with Jag."

"Not even for ten grand," Shane said, a little disgusted.

"He needs more training," Liam said, tired of explaining the same thing to them. "He's easily distracted and wouldn't take commands from a new owner with enough ease."

"But he's protection ready," Shane argued. "I've been out there in that training field with you for at least forty hours with that dog, and I know he's ready. He'd bite a baddie in two seconds flat. Won't kill, but he'll stop an intruder in his tracks."

He'd bite, yeah. Assuming the baddie didn't throw a brightly colored chew toy in the opposite direction. He needed a little more time.

"We'd never ask you to give a dog to the wrong family," Garrett assured him.

Dad held his hand up, probably not aware that the Dogfather had "trained" his own sons to stop bickering with just that one hand. And they did, instantly.

Liam shot him a grateful look for stopping the conversation. "Listen, it's been a long day, and I need a shower and a *beer*." He threw the last word at Shane and started walking past all of them. "I'll see you tomorrow afternoon for Sunday dinner."

It had been a long Saturday, with ten sheriff's trainers and dogs that Liam had worked with since eight this morning. He had no time or energy for—

"Andi Rivers needs that dog."

Dad's words stopped him cold. He didn't turn around, because he wasn't sure what his expression would show, but whatever it was, Shane would interpret it. And Liam would never hear the end of it.

"Someone broke into her house."

He pivoted, his brother's teasing forgotten. "*What?*"

"I talked to her today at the hardware store, where she was buying a new dead bolt."

Liam stared at his father, while the possibility that Andi, and Christian, could be in danger slithered through his veins and made them icy cold.

"She needs a dog," Dad said. "We can find her one, or…let her have Jag."

"Is she okay?" Liam asked.

"Yes, she's fine, and she played down the incident," Dad said. "But all the way home, all I could think of was how much she needs a dog, a protection-trained dog."

Shane stepped forward. "I doubt she'd pay ten grand for a highly trained German shepherd, but we could—"

"She could have Jag." The statement was out before Liam even thought about it, because…Andi and Jag. Yeah, there was a match made in Liam's own personal heaven.

"Give him to her?" Garrett said with a soft choke. "After all the time you've invested in Jag? He's a major asset."

"Shane just said he's protection ready, and he'd stop an intruder. Andi would need some training…"

"Which wouldn't suck for you," Shane said under his breath.

Liam ignored him. "If she needs a protection dog, Jag is perfect."

Garrett shot a look to Shane. "Now he's ready to part with him."

"'Cause Dad brought kryptonite," Shane joked.

Liam didn't bother to argue with that.

"Why don't you take Jag to her and see how it goes?" Dad suggested.

Because last time…didn't go so well.

Behind his father, he could see Garrett fight a smile and Shane do the same. If Liam were the smiling type, he'd probably be doing battle with a grin himself.

"You're not even trying to hide it anymore, are you, Dad?" Shane asked on a chuckle.

"Hide what?" Dad said defensively. "That a member of our community might be in danger and we have the perfect dog to protect her?"

"Never argue with the Dogfather," Shane said.

"Yeah," Garrett agreed. "Look how it worked out for us."

Engaged, both of them.

Liam cleared his throat. "If that's your end game, Dad, you can give it up right now. She's not interested, and I'm not going begging like some kind of lovesick hound." He narrowed his gaze at Shane, fending off whatever ill-advised joke he was ready to lob. "Not a word out of you."

"I didn't say a thing."

Then Liam turned his attention to Dad. "She can have Jag, and I'll personally cover the investment Waterford made in him. Or I'll find her another dog if she wants one. But that's it. That's all that's going to happen between Andi and me."

Dad tried to look serious, but the twinkle in his eye was impossible to hide and, like everything else in the past few months—hell, few years—it pissed Liam off.

"Why don't you invite her for Sunday dinner tomorrow?" Dad said, like Liam hadn't just made a freaking speech. "She can bring her little boy, and they can play with Jag."

And his whole family could observe firsthand that Andrea Rivers wanted no part of him except when she'd had some wine and felt lonely. No, thanks. He could humiliate himself without an audience.

"I'll handle it," he said.

He grabbed Jag's collar, got the dog's attention off a butterfly, and headed to the air-conditioned comfort of a big-ass 4x4 that would take him home to that shower and a beer. And a few hours to think about how to help someone he cared about without falling down that particularly painful slippery slope again.

Chapter Three

"Watch me, Mommy! Watch me climb to the top of the pirate ship!" Christian broke free from Andi's hand the minute they reached the playground area in Bushrod Square. He headed straight for the multilevel wooden structure that, to her architect's eye, had been placed a little off center and needed a slightly longer top platform and something to fix that particularly hideous circular tube slide.

But Christian didn't see the design flaws in the playground equipment. To him, it could be a pirate ship, a medieval castle, an army fort, or a jungle hideout. Her son's imagination was a beautiful thing that never failed to give Andi a burst of maternal pride and joy.

Letting him run free on the soft rubbery surface, she made her way to a bench nestled under some oak trees, settling down with a sigh to appreciate a quiet Sunday morning in Bitter Bark, her home for six years now.

She was a long way from Boston, where she'd grown up, and an even longer way from Europe, where she'd thought she'd be living now back when she made her Big Life Plan. And that plan had blown up, as plans so often did. Now her life plan was focused on a sweet, precious, delightful little human being who was currently channeling his inner Blackbeard.

Yes, plans changed, but not all of life's surprises were *bad*, she mused, even when they might seem that way when they first hit so hard you couldn't breathe.

She tipped her head back to feel the early morning sun, closing her eyes, listening to the birds and breeze and Christian's playful chatter. If only he talked to other people the way he talked to himself.

She stole a peek to see where he was, finding him on the top platform. He took a few steps and tripped, grabbing the railing and making her jump up to be sure he hadn't hurt himself.

"Be careful up there," she called.

"This thing is sticking up!" He tapped his foot on what looked like a loose board.

"Then stay off the top level, Christian."

He made a face. "This is the lookout tower, Mommy. It's the best place to see." He cupped his hands into the shape of a telescope and turned slowly to scan the "waters" around his ship.

"Christian, I don't like the top level if a board is loose. Until it's fixed, come down to the lower level."

"I can fix it. Do you have a nail?"

She laughed softly. "Not on me. You can still play one level down."

Making a face, he scooted to the ladder, came down, and resumed his lookout position, clearly not quite as happy as he'd been at the top. Still, he was in a great mood today, thanks to a peaceful night's sleep uninterrupted by the nightmares that had plagued him on and off for two years. And there wasn't another kid in sight, which, sadly, put Christian right in the middle of his comfort zone.

Christian had never been a super-outgoing child, but his bashfulness had been precious as a baby and toddler. When Jeff came back from Europe, Christian had been almost four, and the best part of that year of living with Jeff was seeing Christian come out of his shell. Then the unthinkable…his daddy was dead.

He didn't understand that daddies could die, but he understood that the man in his life was gone, that the piggyback rides to bed were over, that, unlike other trips Jeff frequently took, this time he wasn't ever coming back.

"Ahoy, matey, I see a spy!" he called out, pointing ahead. "Mommy, look!"

She smiled and waved in his direction. "You keep an eye on the spy, Captain."

"No, Mommy. A spy and a really big dog. At our house. Look."

His pretend-pirate voice was completely replaced by his high-pitched child's tone, with an underscore of seriousness. Andi instantly turned and followed his gaze across the boulevard that separated her side-street row of brownstones from the square. From her vantage point, she could see her three-story home on the corner and, at the bottom of the steps that led up to her front door, a man and a dog.

Instantly, a shot of adrenaline, hope, and a little horror ricocheted through her at the sight of Liam Kilcannon and one of his watchdog German shepherds. An involuntary shudder rippled through her as she stood to walk closer to get a better look. Yep, it was Liam. She'd recognize those shoulders anywhere.

Liam was as still as the dog, looking up the three stone steps to her door. After a moment, he walked up the stairs, rang her bell, and stayed still and strong, like the steadfast Marine he'd been.

What the heck was he doing ringing her doorbell at eight thirty on a Sunday morning? With a dog?

But deep inside, she knew *exactly* what he was doing there. And why he had a dog.

Oh, Daniel Kilcannon. The Dogfather did *not* take no for an answer. She took a few steps toward the edge of the playground, watching Liam wait for a response to the ringing doorbell that, of course, wouldn't come.

Would he be disappointed? Try again? Call her? Leave a note?

For a moment, he did nothing, as if he was running through the same litany of possibilities.

And what should she do? While the road that separated the residences from Bushrod Square was usually busy, traffic was light on a Sunday morning, and he'd hear her if she called to him. And then what? He shifted from one foot to the other, his broad shoulders rising and falling with what she imagined was a frustrated sigh.

Was he doing this as a favor to his father? Because he cared about her? Wanted to take her up on that offer she'd foolishly made right here in this square a couple months ago?

Even at this distance, it was no damn wonder why

she'd practically begged for sex that night. Liam Kilcannon was like a six-course gourmet meal to a woman who'd subsisted on bread and water for two years.

Christian suddenly screeched, his attention no longer on the "spy" but on another pretend pirate. The sound carried and made Liam turn toward Bushrod Square.

She couldn't exactly hide now. She lifted a hand in acknowledgment and watched him draw back, ever so slightly. She had an impact on him, and knowing that gave her a heady rush. Along with a reminder that toying with Liam Kilcannon's feelings simply because she needed a physical release would be wrong.

Nothing had changed since that night.

He said something to the dog, moved the leash a centimeter, and, of course, the animal responded with the kind of military precision Liam expected from his trainees.

Both of them were headed right to the square now.

Only then did Andi realize her heart was beating a little too fast and her palms suddenly felt damp. She brushed hair off her face, aware that she'd skipped even cursory makeup this morning and wore a plain T-shirt and cutoff shorts.

Not that she cared how she looked to Liam, but...yeah, she cared.

"I know that spy," she called to Christian, watching man and dog cross the street, knowing she had a few minutes until he got to the break in the shrubs and walked to the far-end playground. A few minutes to prepare for the impact of seeing him again. "He's my friend, Liam. Do you remember him?"

From his lower-level perch, Christian frowned and shook his head. "No."

Of course not. Christian had been the ripe old age of three when she'd dated Liam, and though he'd been wonderful the few times they'd met, they hadn't done a lot together. Andi had been testing the waters, still unsure of dating as a single mother, and *wham*. Before she could slide all the way into that relationship, Jefferson John Scott had upended everything.

Jeff's own father had died while he was in Europe, and while they hadn't been particularly close, losing his father had had a profound effect, as if he'd suddenly realized his own mortality. Jeff had said he didn't want to live separated from his son or, he'd claimed, his son's mother.

Dating another man when Jeff had moved into her house to be near Christian was too complicated, so she'd broken off the month-old relationship with Liam and made every effort to be a "family" for Christian.

It hadn't been a perfect year by any stretch, especially since Jeff never really settled into a life with her. They tried to make it work, but it had been difficult. Maybe it had been his father's death, or that Bitter Bark was a huge letdown after the capitals of Europe, but Jeff never seemed completely happy or relaxed, though he put on a good show of it for Christian.

But, he'd taken off repeatedly for freelance jobs, and when he'd get home, he was short-tempered and preoccupied. She often found him pacing the house in the middle of the night, fighting insomnia.

She suspected it was that very inability to sleep that made him lose control of his car on an icy road in the Blue Ridge Mountains, careening into a ravine two years ago.

Two long and difficult and lonely years, she thought as she finally caught sight of Liam headed toward them along the stone path.

"Ahoy, matey! I see a dog! A big, bad dog!" Christian stood on the play structure, his hand over his eyes, his gaze fixed on the new arrivals.

Really? Because I see a man. A big, good man.

Liam stood six-two with broad shoulders in a plain white T-shirt and faded jeans and moved with the same grace as the animals he trained. His short hair, so dark it qualified as black, gleamed in the morning sun and, even though he was far away, she could imagine those dark chocolate eyes narrowed as he focused on her.

Every single shriveled-up, lonely hormone hiding in the sad corners of her body woke up, stretched out, and moaned for attention. *His* attention.

But Andi wanted sex, and Liam wanted strings.

Taking a deep breath and digging for a stability she didn't quite feel, she started walking toward Liam to greet him. He slowed his gait, and his big German shepherd did, too, no doubt trained to keep perfect time with his master.

"Hey," she said, coming closer, hating that he looked better and more delicious with each step she took.

"You're probably wondering what we're doing hanging out at your house."

She laughed lightly, stopping a few feet away. "Not at all." She gestured toward the animal, who instantly dropped to his haunches and sat at perfect attention. "Because that would mean I underestimate the power of your father."

He laughed, too, a rare, masculine, and genuine laugh that still had the ability to send a shiver down her spine.

Christian squealed as he spun around a pole, making them both turn, and the dog got up and pulled in that direction.

"Jag!" Liam tugged the leash. "*Bleib.*"

Whatever he'd said, the command worked, and the dog sat back down, giving Liam a quick look.

"So this is one of your special dogs?"

"This is Jag, and he is just about finished with his *Schutzhund* training," he said.

"And you brought him here because…"

He lifted a shoulder and angled his head, glancing back at Christian before answering. "My dad told me your house was broken into."

She knew it. "Liam, I don't want a dog, and I did tell your father that."

"Wanting and needing are two different things." His eyes flickered a little, as if the possible double entendre in that sentence hit him. He looked away, at the playground, where Christian had made his way back up the slide ladder and perched on the top rung, clinging to the bars, watching them talk.

"You need to be safe, Andi." Christian was too far away to hear their conversation, but she appreciated that Liam kept his voice low.

She wasn't going to argue. "I appreciate your concern and the fact that you showed up here, but I'm not equipped to own a dog, Liam. I'm out all day, and Christian—"

"Can I pet him, Mommy?"

She hadn't realized he'd come down the slide and walked toward them, his blue eyes wide with interest and intimidation.

"Of course," Liam answered for her, immediately crouching down to get on Christian's level. "His name's Jag."

Christian stared at the dog and then Liam, silent.

"And I'm Liam." He held tight to Jag's collar, but let the dog approach for a sniff. "I remember your name is Christian."

He looked from Liam to the dog, up to Andi, and back to the dog. "I like dogs," he whispered, the words so soft they were nearly carried away on the morning breeze.

Andi's heart shifted a little. "Mr. Liam said you can pet him, honey."

He swallowed, frozen, at war with his shyness and desire to get closer, while Andi waged a different internal war. Her battle was with a mother's instinct to encourage, even push him, but a sixth sense told her he had to start to break through those fears himself.

Liam loosened his hand, and Jag got closer to the boy, poking his nose against Christian's chest and belly, making them all laugh.

"*Setzen*, Jag," Liam ordered, his hand on Jag's massive head, stroking from the top down the back. The dog sat, but looked alert and waited for the next command. "This is all you do," he told Christian. "He won't bite, I promise."

Christian took one step closer. "He's big."

"Very," Liam agreed. "But he's really nice to people he likes. Well, people I tell him to like. See?"

Still not quite there, Christian held back. "Can he do tricks?"

Liam chuckled. "He can catch a Frisbee."

"Really?" His eyes lit as he came a little closer and gave Andi another look, seeking reassurance.

On the other side of Jag, Andi got down, too, and the dog turned to her, barking once, making her suck in a breath and draw back.

"Jag," Liam said without reacting, still petting him. "He gets distracted, but we're working on that."

Petting the dog, Andi was surprised that his fur was an unexpected combination of wiry and soft, a blend of deep honey tan and stark black around his eyes and snout.

"Good dog," she said.

"Does he roll over and play dead?" Christian asked.

"He doesn't do those kind of tricks," Liam explained. "He's being taught to be a guard dog to protect people he cares about. He answers to special commands in another language."

Christian's eyes popped with curiosity.

"I'll show you," Liam said as he rose to his feet. He glanced around and grabbed a six-inch branch of the oak tree, snapping it off with ease. "Ready?"

Christian nodded, and Liam got in front of the dog, reaching down to unclip his leash.

"Jag, *achtung*!"

Instantly, Jag snapped to attention, standing and staring up at Liam.

"*Voraus*!" He tossed the stick, sending it sailing across the playground, and Jag took off, shooting toward the goal and grabbing it with his teeth.

"*Bleib*!" Liam shouted, and it was as if Jag still

wore a leash. He jerked to a stop, staring across the expanse at Liam, motionless.

"Why doesn't he bring it back?" Christian asked.

"Because I told him to stop. That's what *bleib* means. Now he won't move unless I tell him to." Liam waited a few beats, letting them see how obedient his dog was. Then, "*Hier!*"

And Jag shot off again, bounding toward them and stopping right in front of Liam, holding the stick up between his teeth.

"Good boy," Liam said, bending over to reward the dog with affection. "*Gib laut!*"

Jag barked as if answering him.

"What did he say?" Christian asked, mesmerized, as Andi was.

Liam chuckled. "Probably 'again,' but I gave him the command to speak."

His intimidation forgotten, Christian came right up to the dog and put his little hand on the Jag's mighty forehead. "Down, boy," he whispered.

Jag didn't move.

"He's trained to answer to special words," Liam explained. "You need to say *setzen* to him. It sounds like zet-zen. Use your strongest voice."

Christian studied the dog, visibly working up nerve with little fisted hands and a frown drawing his pale brows together. "*Setzen!*"

Jag dropped to his haunches, the response delighting Christian. "Good boy!" he said, fluffing his fur and laughing. "Good boy, Jag."

Liam smiled, rubbing Jag's head affectionately.

Jag responded with a friendly pant, letting out a tongue the size of a slab of ham.

"How did you make him bark, again?" Christian asked.

"Can you say *gib*?" Liam asked.

Christian nodded. "*Gib*."

"Good, then you say *laut*, like loud, only it ends in a t sound."

"*Laut*," he repeated.

"Put them together," Liam instructed.

Christian stared at Jag like he was about to ask for magic. "*Gib laut*," he said softly. Jag didn't do a thing.

"You have to use your command voice," Liam told him. "You have to make sure he knows you're in charge."

Christian laughed a little, the sheer size and obvious strength of Jag making the idea seem crazy.

"You can do it," Liam encouraged. "Just be strong and loud."

Nodding, Christian took a step closer. "*Gib laut*!" he hollered.

Andi's laugh at Christian's enthusiasm was drowned out by the deep, low bark of a dog that, she had to admit, would scare anyone. But Christian giggled with delight at this new trick.

"*Gib laut*!" he yelled again and was rewarded with another bark. He laughed from his belly, and Andi and Liam looked at each other, momentarily enjoying his pleasure.

Whoa. Wait a second. This was not supposed to be happening.

"Well, that's fun," she said, pushing up and searching for all the reasons she shouldn't allow Christian to fall for that dog and she shouldn't be sharing looks with Liam and—

45

"What else can he do?" Christian asked, holding his little hands together in front of his chest as if he couldn't contain his excitement. "Can you teach me more of those words, Mr....what was your name again?"

"Liam." He threw a look at Andi, as if he sensed she was ready to rein in all this fun in the sun.

"Teach me another one, Mr. Liam!" he pleaded.

Andi opened her mouth to argue, but there wasn't a single thing she could say.

Christian had climbed out of his shell, and nothing in her wanted to stop that progress. It didn't mean she had to take the dog. It didn't mean she was dangling any strings that Liam would want to tie. It didn't mean anything but a few minutes of pleasure at the playground that Christian would talk about all day.

But even as she nodded, she knew it meant something. She just wasn't sure what.

Chapter Four

This was dangerous territory, and Liam knew it.

This sunny morning at the park. This precious little child. This gorgeous woman who looked all natural and morning soft, her hair a hundred different shades of golden blond pulled back in a sloppy ponytail with a few stray strands around her face.

Very, very dangerous for the man who vowed that no matter what transpired this morning, no matter if she took the dog or sent him packing or told him one more time how lonely she was, he would not fall down the Andi Rivers Slippery Slope to Misery.

Man, he'd have to hang on tight to avoid that particular ride. Because, this moment, sitting in the sun on a park bench, listening to Andi's sweet laugh and Christian's "command voice" and Jag's tireless bark in response, he knew down to his last strand of DNA that he could do this all day. Longer.

And he had to remember, that was the problem with Andrea Rivers. She didn't do *longer*.

"Can I walk him?" Christian asked, lifting up the leash Liam had dropped. "Then I can tell him to *setzen* and *bleib*."

"If you stay close," Liam said. "Okay with you, Mom? Or we can go with him."

"No, I want to go alone," Christian insisted, glancing around at the empty playground. "I'm not a baby."

"Yes, but Liam's right. Stay where we can see you," Andi said. "You can circle this play area, but no farther."

"Okay." He held the leash out to Liam with a question in his eyes.

"You can put it on him," Liam said.

Self-doubt flashed in his pale blue eyes, instantly touching something deep in Liam. Something he couldn't name, but it felt familiar.

"You can do it," Liam assured him. "Tell him to sit and stay, and then squeeze that little clip and put it right on the silver ring on the collar."

Christian swallowed, then nodded, mentally reviewing the instructions before using his little-boy yell to get Jag to sit. It worked well enough.

Christian got him to stay and used his tiny fingers to clip the leash. Liam could practically feel Andi inching forward, ready to assist, but she restrained herself and let her son learn a lesson Liam knew before he was two: how to leash a dog.

"Where I can see you, Christian," she reminded him.

"I promise." He gave Jag's leash a tentative tug. "Come, boy. Oh, I mean...what's the word for walk?"

"You can say *vorwärts*, but you don't have to. He's trained to go with whoever is walking him on a leash if he senses that's okay with me," Liam explained. "Just take off, and he'll stay right next to you."

Christian beamed. "Okay. Thanks. Bye!"

"Wow," Andi whispered as they watched the two of them walk away.

Liam glanced at her, trying to figure out what that response meant.

"That's the most I've heard him talk to someone who's not me in a long time," she explained. "He's normally so shy."

"Dogs are magic like that."

She turned to him, her smile relaxed and warm. "It's not *just* the dog."

He took the compliment with a nod and studied her for a moment, mostly because he was unable to look away. It was like pouring ice water down the parched throat of a man who'd been wandering the desert for years.

"Does that mean you'll take him?" he asked.

She sighed. "Liam, I don't even know where to begin with a dog. I'm at work all day and in meetings with clients and can't be sure I could come home to let him out or feed him. Christian is at school and after-school care most days. And I don't..." She turned to watch Christian, who was making poor Jag sit, stay, and bark like there was no tomorrow. Every success made the little boy clap or giggle. "I have to think about it. It's a huge, long commitment owning a dog."

"And you don't do huge, long commitments."

She closed her eyes like he'd hit a target. "That didn't take long."

"Just want you to know I'm not here trying for round three, Andi. You need a dog and I have one."

"I didn't know I needed a dog until your father told

me I did." She fought the slightest smile. "And I'm sure he has ulterior motives."

"Maybe he does," Liam said. "But I don't."

She wet her lips, still watching her son, thinking. "You never were one to mince words."

"Don't see a point in it," he said. He rubbed his chin, the morning whiskers rough on his fingertips. He could have shaved, almost did, but that would have meant he cared too much. And he didn't want to care at all. "You might be helping me, too," he added.

"How's that?"

"Jag needs some practical experience," he told her. "He's not my best work to date."

She laughed softly. "Then he can't protect us?"

"Of course he can. He's a great protection dog for a home and situation like yours. But that's honestly not what he's trained to do. The *Schutzhund* dogs are for very elite security purposes, which is why we get a small fortune for each one I train. But they have to meet stringent requirements, and Jag has passed all but one."

"What's that?"

Jag barked, and Christian let out a simultaneous yelp, making them both look at him.

"Distractions." Liam leaped immediately at the sight of a woman in running clothes coming closer. "Tell him to sit," Liam said as he got closer.

But Jag's barking and a little bit of pull on the leash threw off Christian's game, and he looked from Jag to the approaching jogger with fear.

"Nothing to be afraid of." Liam got right down in front of Jag, held his gaze, and gave one order, under his breath, in the dog's ear. Of course, it was enough. Jag stopped barking, looked at Liam, and sat.

"What did you say?" Christian asked.

"It's our code word," Liam said. "It makes him stop whatever he's doing."

The woman stopped to run in place when Jag's barking quieted, looking at them with a mix of wariness and something else Liam couldn't quite interpret. Interest? Expectation? Something lit her dark eyes as she brushed a few brown hairs off a sweat-dampened face.

"He's beautiful," she said with a bit of wonder in her voice. A dog lover, then. "May I?"

Liam took over the collar, gripping tightly but nodding. "He'll want to sniff you," Liam warned.

"He likes bellies," Christian added, making the woman look at him and smile.

"I bet that's fun for you," she said, talking in that high-pitched voice that some people used around kids.

"He won't bite if Liam says you're okay," Christian said confidently, clearly enjoying this small authority about the dog.

She came closer, letting Jag have a good sniff, then offering her hand for a lick. The move struck Liam as odd, but some people liked to prove they weren't scared, and maybe she knew how to establish a bond.

"What's his name?" she asked.

"Jag," Christian offered proudly.

"And what's your name?" she asked him.

He looked up at her, not answering. All that doggie bravado disappeared as if he suddenly realized he was in the middle of a conversation with a stranger.

"It's okay," the lady said, using that just-licked

hand to pat his shoulder. "I was shy, too, when I was your age."

Christian backed up as Andi joined them, her mom radar probably sensing where this encounter would go.

"You can say hello, Christian," she said sweetly.

"Christian." The woman beamed at him, Jag apparently forgotten. She pressed her hands together, a few diamonds and gold glittering on fingers with red-tipped nails. "That's a nice name." She looked at Liam. "Named after your daddy?"

"Oh, uh, no…" Liam said, but Christian turned and pressed his face into Andi's legs. "I'm not his father."

Andi offered an apologetic smile, but the woman angled her head, looking from one to the other with enough judgment or curiosity that it was uncomfortable.

Then she gave a tight smile. "Your doggie is very handsome, Christian." She raised her voice as if the child was hard of hearing as well as shy around strangers. "And so are you. Thanks for letting me pet him." She started jogging in place again, then her gaze settled on Andi. "He's a nice boy."

"Thank you."

"He's, what? Six years old?"

Andi nodded, her hands on Christian's shoulders. "Yes, six."

The woman's expression grew wistful, almost sad, and she visibly swallowed. "That's a sweet age." She held Andi's gaze for a moment, looking as if she had more to say. Then, suddenly, she waved and yelled, "Bye!" as she took off down the path at a quick clip.

"It's okay, Christian," Andi said, easing him away from his hideaway against her hips.

He turned slowly to the dog and started to retrieve the leash he'd dropped, but Liam had picked it up. "Can I walk some more?" he asked tentatively.

"Of course," Liam said.

"Will you sit down again, Mommy? I liked walking him alone."

She sighed and nodded. "We'll be right on that bench."

"Mr. Liam, will you tell me that secret word?"

Liam shook his head. "Right now, I'm the only person who can use it with him. That's a very important part of his training. Only the person or family he's trained to protect can know that word. If someone else makes Jag bark, I'll be right there to help you."

Satisfied with that, Christian guided Jag back to the brick path, tugging the leash and walking again.

Andi watched after him, closing her eyes as if something had hit her hard.

"I was the same way," Liam said softly. "In fact, I still am. It's hard to explain what introverted feels like to someone who's outgoing and talkative."

"But he wasn't always this shy," she said softly. "He was quiet, but now it's literally painful for him to talk to people."

"You told me a little bit about that," he said, remembering some of the things she'd said right here in the square a couple months ago, a conversation he'd replayed in his head many times. Christian struggled when his father died, she'd told him. That's why she said she'd never take a chance like that again. Christian was the only man in her life.

53

She didn't say anything, but headed back to the shady bench, sitting down again, her gaze on her son.

"This is why I can't take your dog." She turned from her son to level her sky-blue eyes on Liam. "But thank you for the offer."

A frown tugged. "I can be pretty dense, Andi, so help me out here. Not sure how you're getting from point A to 'I can't take your dog.'"

She smiled. "Because you and I both know exactly what it will lead to."

Liam knew what he hoped it might lead to in a perfect, blissful, ideal world, but he certainly wasn't sure. "What do you think it will lead to?" he asked.

"Well, let's see. You'll have to help Christian learn how to handle Jag. I seem to recall that there's a fairly official order of events when you give one of your highly trained protection dogs to a new owner. Right?"

"Absolutely. There is a handover process that takes some time. I have to teach Jag that you two are his handlers now, and he's taking orders from you. I'd have to teach both of you to learn the German commands. There's obedience and response training and getting him acclimated to your house."

"Exactly."

"Exactly...what?"

"We'd be together. A few days, some nights. Feelings would...emerge."

He laughed softly at her choice of words. "My feelings are all emerged and managed, Andi. I know you don't want what I want."

"And you don't want what I want."

He was quiet for a moment, and she looked sharply

at him. "Or have you changed your mind, Liam?" she asked.

"I'd be lying if I said I didn't kick myself a few times for being a high-road-taking blockhead who didn't accept a dream offer."

"You're not a blockhead," she said, reaching over to touch his hand. "You're a good, considerate, kind man who won't take advantage of a woman even when she begs for it after three glasses of wine."

Had it been only the wine, then? Disappointment thudded, harder than he'd expected. "You didn't beg for anything, Andi."

She slid him a look. "Like I said, kind. You're letting me off the hook, of course, but we both know what happened. Or what *didn't* happen, as the case may be."

He didn't argue that. "And I still don't follow how you taking Jag is going to lead to some dark and dangerous liaison that will ruin your life."

"Not dark, not dangerous, not ruinous," she said. "Which is why it would be so tempting, and if I spend enough time with you, *something* is going to happen, and that would probably turn into more than one *something*—"

"Which would suck," he said, slathering on some sarcasm and making her laugh a little. Pretty sound, that.

"Of course it would be amazing," she said. "And then you'd be around all the time, and Christian would get dependent on you because you'd be the father figure missing in his life, and then…wham."

"Wham." He felt a smile tug. "Can't wait to find out what that means."

"It means heartache and unhappiness and explaining that you're not the daddy that strangers like that woman think you are."

"Andi." He turned completely to look at her. "Your logic is faulty. It's a dog, not a proposal of marriage."

Just then, Jag barked, and they both looked to see him focused on a squirrel, pulling Christian hard.

"Damn," Liam muttered, getting up. "Gotta work on that distraction problem."

She joined him, both of them heading toward Christian, who shouted a sit order with enough command in his voice that Jag reacted immediately, staring at his new little friend.

"Oh," Andi said, putting her hand to her chest. "Look at that. He did it."

"And we didn't even have to have six months of training that turned into heartache and desolation."

She elbowed him. "You know what I mean."

"I do, but I don't agree."

"Which is precisely why I'm saying no to this dog."

He nodded toward Jag and Christian. The little boy plopped on his bottom with two arms around Jag's neck, talking to him with the most serious face, his mouth moving nonstop. "Sure doesn't look like something that would be bad for a kid struggling with shyness," Liam said.

Andi let out a long, slow sigh, and he could practically feel her inner battle. Any second, she'd say yes. Then she looked up at Liam, opened her mouth, and closed it again.

She stared at him, hard and long and seriously conflicted. "No, I can't," she said. "It's too much of a risk."

"So's not having protection after someone broke into your house."

She nodded. "I have a new lock. I mean, I will when I get it installed."

"I can do that for you right now, Andi." At her look, he added, "Unless that's the first step to wedding plans in the Andi Rivers Convoluted Logic of Relationship Progression."

She laughed. "Okay. You can install the lock."

Of course he could. But how could he get rid of the one on her heart? He'd spent two years trying to figure that out, and as much as he told himself to quit trying, he knew he couldn't.

Hell. Maybe she was right about the dog.

Chapter Five

By nine o'clock that evening, Andi still hadn't quite shaken the little buzz that spending a few hours with Liam had given her. And that only made her one hundred percent certain she'd made the right decision. He might not agree with her "logic," but one look at him and she knew exactly where a dog, borrowed or bought, would lead.

Not that more buzz-inducing hours with Liam wouldn't be lovely, because they would. But that would also go against every vow Andi had made after Jeff died and she was left to pick up the pieces of a broken little boy.

She closed the dishwasher and wiped off the counter, taking inventory of the Captain America backpack and school supplies laid out on the kitchen table. The first day of first grade was tomorrow...the start of a new era.

Before she knew it, that little boy would be off to middle school, then high school, then college.

Would she let herself fall in love then? Was she doing the right thing by waiting for—

A soft tap on her front door startled Andi, pulling

her from her thoughts. Who would be here at nine at night?

Her first thought was Liam, followed by a jolt of happiness and a kick of excitement and a sudden desire to throw caution and those vows of solitude to the wind. Maybe he'd come back to try things the way she had wanted them…purely physical.

And as she walked to the door and smoothed her hair, Andi was already certain of what her answer would be.

Christian's asleep.

Which meant—

A figure shifted, barely visible through the stained glass of her Victorian front door. She couldn't see who it was, but her visitor was too small and narrow to be who she hoped.

She peered through the peephole into the light spilling over a dark-haired woman who looked from side to side and then knocked lightly again. A complete stranger at her door at this time…

No, that wasn't a stranger.

Andi's pulse kicked up as she fisted her hands, staring at the woman she recognized as the lady who'd talked to them today in Bushrod Square. Why on earth would she be knocking at Andi's door twelve hours later? A cascade of chills and goose bumps rushed up her arms as she placed her hand on the massive lock Liam had installed that day.

But something, a deep, protective, maternal instinct, kept her from touching the keypad she'd coded mere hours ago.

Andi remembered thinking the woman had looked oddly at Christian that morning and even had a fleeting thought that maybe she'd lost a child or something tragic. There was such a longing, melancholy look in her eyes but, honestly, Andi had been so wrapped up in Liam, she'd never thought about it again.

Why was she here now?

Frozen, Andi tried to decide if she should call out or pretend not to be home.

The woman knocked again, harder this time. "Andrea?" she called. "I know you're home."

Andrea? She knew *her name*?

Andi swallowed, her questions morphing into real concern now. Who was this woman?

"I know you're there, Andrea. Please open the door. We need to talk."

A low-grade trembling rolled over her. "Who are you?" Andi asked through the door.

"You mustn't have looked at me very hard if you don't know."

What? Andi peered out the peephole again, straining to see the glass-warped features of a woman who appeared to be about Andi's age, mid-thirties, stick-straight dark brown hair falling past her shoulders, a sharp aquiline nose, and a slash of high cheekbones.

There was something vaguely familiar about her. Something unsettling to Andi, also.

"How can I help you?" Andi asked, her voice tense. "Tell me who you are."

"My name is Eleanor, but everyone calls me Nora."

Nora? She didn't know anyone named Nora.

"Nora Jean Scott."

Andi swayed a little, pressing her hands on the door as the name hit home. "You're Jeff's sister." He'd mentioned her a few times, with disdain and disgust, mostly. Nora was the blackest of black sheep who had broken off communication with Jeff and his parents. What would *she* be doing here?

"I am," the woman confirmed. "His twin sister. And I'm also Christian's aunt, so I would appreciate it if you would let me in."

Andi fought for a steady breath. Why, two years after Jeff died and six years after his son was born, would his sister—his *twin* sister—show up in Bitter Bark? And why talk to them in the square that morning and not identify herself?

"Andrea, please. I'd like to come in and talk to you."

"Why?" The question was strangled in her tight throat.

"Because I don't want to have this conversation through a closed door."

"I...can't. We'll talk tomorrow. I'm not coming out there, and I'm not letting a stranger into my house."

"I'm not a stranger. I'm Christian's blood relative."

The way she said *blood* made Andi's own veins go cold. Jeff's family had cut Andi and Christian off in the cruelest, coldest way. His mother had called to tell her Jeff was dead because Andi, who was legally no more than a roommate, hadn't been listed as his next of kin. Then Nadine Scott had informed Andi that they would handle all the arrangements and, worst of all, Andi and Christian were not welcome at the funeral service. She'd made it clear that she suspected

Andi would be looking for a piece of the family money and that she had her doubts that Jeff was really Christian's father.

Yes, it had been ugly and heartless for Andi, but not having an official goodbye had been much worse for Christian, who was too young to understand any of it. She'd heard him whispering in his room, using the word *Daddy*, and he no doubt harbored childish fantasies about a reunion that would never happen.

"Why are you here now?" Andi asked. "Why didn't you come when he was alive?"

"I came to tell you that my mother has passed away."

"Oh, I'm sorry." But the words felt disingenuous. The bitter, cold woman who didn't care about meeting her own grandson? Andi didn't feel a drop of grief for Nadine.

"Which means I have no one, only Christian. He's the last Scott alive."

Except he was a *Rivers*. "Nora, let's set up a time to talk tomorrow. I'm happy to tell you everything about Jeff and—"

"I don't care about Jeff. It's Christian I want."

Suddenly, her legs felt weak. "We can talk tomorrow, Nora," she said, fighting for air.

"You can't put me off, Andrea," she said. "I have all the paperwork, a lawyer, and a family arbitrator on my side. I'm seeking custody of Christian, and I'll get it by proving you are an unfit single mother who has purposely kept Christian from his father's family and will undoubtedly try to steal his trust fund."

"*Excuse me*?" She almost opened the door to be sure she'd heard right, but the words *lawyer* and *custody* and *unfit mother* and *trust fund* paralyzed her.

"You heard me."

Fury bubbled up like a hot volcano, making her whole body shudder. "You're out of your mind," Andi ground out, inching away from the door to find her phone to call the police and get rid of her.

"Andrea, maybe Jeff never told you how much his family was worth, but as of two weeks ago, when my mother died, Christian inherited a trust of six million dollars, and without a Scott to supervise that money, I know you'll steal it. I will not let that happen."

She froze midstep, blinking as though this were all a dream that she had to clear out of her head. "You need to leave."

"You need to listen," she shot back. "I can prove that you work long days and spend your evenings with college students and in bars. He's with a sitter as much as he's with you, and anyone can break into your house, and I do mean anyone. I paid someone to do it, retrieved his toothbrush, and now have a DNA match if you think you can get away with saying he's not my nephew."

She started to shake. Hard. "Go away," Andi said in a harsh whisper. "You need to go away and go back to whatever rock you've been hiding under."

"Have it your way. I'll leave the paperwork right here, and you can call me when you're ready to discuss the case."

There is no case.

Andi backed away from the door and slipped to the front window in the living room, inching the drape wide enough to see the bottom of the front stairs that led up to her door. She gasped softly when the woman came down the steps and turned toward the house, the carriage light spilling over her face.

Now she could see it so clearly. The same intense eyes, the same wide mouth, the same angular bones. The female version of Jefferson Scott.

This couldn't be happening. It wasn't possible. A stranger, an estranged relative, could *take her son*? Or even suggest that it was possible?

Six million dollars?

People would do anything for that kind of money. She watched the figure disappear down the street and into the shadows. For a long, long time, Andi didn't move. She stared out the window, too stunned and terrified to open the door and get what the crazy woman claimed to have left behind.

While she stared, she knew she needed help, and deep inside, she knew exactly where to get it.

When Liam came in from drug-detection training, he was hot, starved, and sick of talking. He was finally finished with the four TSA agents and their dogs for the day, and they'd done amazing work in the rubble pile. It was time for all of his students—two- and four-legged—to break for lunch. The dogs would sleep in cool kennels all afternoon, and the trainers would listen to a lecture from Waterford's resident dog behaviorist. That left Liam free to head into the main house, ready to eat in air conditioning and speak to absolutely no one for a while.

The hardest part about training wasn't the dogs, it was the small talk and conversation, his least favorite thing to do with strangers. The four agents weren't really strangers after a few hours of digging through trash and rewarding dogs for finding drugs. But they wanted to chat about dogs, kids, bad guys, Waterford, *stuff*.

He loathed chatting.

In fact, he was a little pissed off to find his sister Molly and his brother Shane having their lunch at the kitchen counter, laughing about something they were both watching on Shane's phone. Great. More freaking chatting.

"Hey, Liam." Molly greeted him with her easy smile. Her long, wavy hair was pulled up in a knot, and she wore white vet scrubs, both of these things telling him she'd been seeing patients and their owners all morning. Shane looked as sweaty and tired as Liam felt, no doubt because the civilian dog training class he was teaching had reached the agility phase, which was hard as hell in this heat and frustrating because owners had much higher expectations than the dogs could usually meet.

He grunted, "Hello," hoping that told them he had no interest in joining their little lunch party.

"Crystal made chili," Molly said, gesturing to the stove. "It's weird how eating something hot cools you down, but that's what they say."

He made another noise meant to sound grateful and headed to the sink.

"I'm sorry." Molly leaned forward. "I'm not fluent in caveman. What did that mean?"

He shot her a look. "Means I'm hot, tired, and not in the mood to talk."

She rolled her eyes as he washed his hands and Shane sniffed noisily. "Shower would be better."

Molly snorted. "You should talk, Shane."

He was in no mood for family joking. "I'll eat in the family room," Liam said, glancing at the expansive sitting area that was blessedly empty. The staff, guests, trainees—human and dog—rarely came into the house during the workday. The main house was reserved for Kilcannon family who'd all been raised in this homestead and still had their own "places." His was at the end of the big couch, with a cushy hassock, under the AC vent, next to the remote.

Being the oldest had its privileges.

"Don't leave, Liam," Molly urged. "We all smell like dogs. I had two in surgery this morning, and we ended up putting Cinnamon on an IV. It's been a rough day in the vet office."

He paused in the act of scooping chili into a bowl. "That long-haired doxie? She going to be okay?"

"I think so. Pancreatitis."

"Your specialty, Moll," Shane said. "No better vet in North Carolina for that. Liam, did you hear Garrett might have an adoption for that Saint Bernard, Seymour?"

Liam's shoulders dropped as they piled on the small talk. "Yeah. Good. I'm going in the family room to eat alone."

"Are you in a bad mood?" Molly asked.

"He's awake and breathing, isn't he?" Shane jabbed.

Liam glared at him, then started to walk out, carefully holding his bowl of chili and a spoon.

"Oh, look, we have a guest pulling in." Molly stood to peer out the kitchen window to the drive.

"Isn't that Andi Rivers's SUV? She drives a silver Acura, right?"

And Liam froze, jerking to a hard stop and almost spilling the chili. Then he exhaled, refusing to look when he realized what his siblings were up to. "I'm not taking your bait, Molly."

"It is Andi," Shane said. "And look at that. Dad is on her like a fly on honey."

Liam gritted his teeth. They were yanking his chain, which was a favorite family pastime. He continued to the family room.

"They're hugging," Molly reported. "And talking."

"Ten bucks he's inviting her to Wednesday night dinner to sit next to you, Liam," Shane said with a laugh. "Dogfather doin' his matchmaking thing."

Liam still didn't turn to look, because he did not trust them to be telling the truth. Or himself, if they were.

"Oh, she's talking." Molly continued her play-by-play. "A lot."

"She looks serious," Shane said, adding the color. "Dad's frowning and putting an arm on her back. Pointing to the kennels."

"I bet she came for Jag!" Molly exclaimed.

"Son of a…" Liam slammed down the chili bowl on the coffee table and marched back to the kitchen, swallowing the damn bait whole. Which wasn't bait at all, but the truth. "Holy crap. She is here."

"You think we'd lie?" Molly asked, feigning shock.

"Dude, you better get out there before Dad plans *your* wedding." Shane cracked up, and so did Molly, the two of them sharing a ridiculous high five like a couple of ten-year-olds.

But Liam ignored them, staring at the woman who was, indeed, in the middle of a serious conversation with his father. She wore white jeans and a pale blue top, and while the outfit looked summery fresh and beautiful, there was something about her expression that didn't look happy.

Not that he could tell the nuances of her features from this distance, but...actually, he could.

She wasn't happy. And the minute he knew that in his gut, he headed out to the yard. He stepped out into the steamy afternoon and, as if she sensed his presence, Andi turned to the house. He could have sworn her shoulders dropped a little, as if she was relieved to see him.

"Hey," he said, trotting down the stairs from the back porch to the expanse of the yard. "You change your mind about Jag?"

She gathered some of her thick, flaxen hair, lifting it off her neck and pushing it behind her shoulder. "I changed my mind about everything."

He paused midstep, not sure he'd heard that right. "Everything?"

She came closer, and Dad was right beside her, he noticed. "I need the dog, yes, Liam, I do. And I might need more than that."

He frowned, angling his head, searching her face to figure out what she meant. "You can have anything you want," he said softly, vaguely aware that his father was observing the exchange.

Let him. He had nothing to hide where Andi Rivers was concerned. They all knew he was crazy about her.

She got close enough that he could see the pain and agony in her cornflower blue eyes as she held out a thick white envelope. "Someone is trying to take my son away from me."

"*What*?"

"Andi's got trouble, Liam," Dad said. "But we're going to circle her with Kilcannons, get her all the help possible, and we'll be the family she needs right now."

Liam wasn't sure what he meant by that, but he really didn't care about anything but the fact that Andi looked like she'd been through a war since he last saw her.

Without saying a word or even thinking about it, he reached for her hand, and she let him pull her closer.

"I'm scared, Liam."

"Don't be," he whispered. "I won't let anything happen to you or Christian."

He felt her collapse a little in his arms and knew that no matter what had happened, he would never let her get hurt or be scared. He'd do whatever it took, sacrifice anything, to protect her.

No matter how much it hurt him in the end.

Chapter Six

Andi had never experienced anything quite like the tidal wave that was the Kilcannons on a mission. There was a palpable energy in the room when these people joined forces, laser focused, to address a problem that needed to be solved.

For a few minutes after Liam led her inside and into the family room, Andi just took it all in. She momentarily wondered if this was what it had been like on that well-documented day after this family buried their beloved mother. That was when Daniel proposed that all his kids pick up their lives and move back to Bitter Bark and transform Waterford Farm into a world-class canine training and rescue institute.

She remembered Liam telling her about the morning that the grieving Daniel came out to the backyard and presented his idea and how they spent the rest of the weekend planning the project and had it built, running, and profitable less than a year later.

Did they gather in this room that day to open the floodgates of family power?

An only child with a professorial father and passive mother, Andi had never experienced this much heart and brainpower in one family. She'd learned at a young age to solve her own problems and hoped to be teaching that to her son. All these opinions. All these voices. All these powerful individuals dragging her along made her both uncomfortable and relieved that she didn't have to navigate the white water of Nora Scott alone.

She'd tried that overnight and slept little, barely able to hold it together when she took Christian to his first day of school and finally spewing her troubles to Dr. Kilcannon when he met her in the driveway.

Alone wouldn't work in this crisis, so she'd have to ride the tsunami of Kilcannons and see where it took her.

Right now, it had taken her to the middle of an overstuffed sofa, with Liam sitting on her left, as close to her as he could without putting her on his lap for comfort.

"I know you said Christian's at school," Liam said, "but are you one hundred percent sure it's secure? Isn't it a new school?"

"New grade, same school he's been in since pre-K. I don't think anyone could get past the office into the classrooms, and I have an approved pickup list."

"But you said Nora was the woman from the square," he reminded her. "What if Christian thinks he recognizes her or sees her on the playground?"

She closed her eyes. "They still wouldn't let her take him since she's not on the list."

"Call the school now," he said calmly. "Talk to the principal and tell him or her that no one, without exception, no matter who they claim to be, can be allowed in his classroom or near him on the playground or wherever he might be. If they are not on the list, they can't get him, no matter who they say they are."

She silently agreed, slipping her phone out of the side of her bag.

"So how was he today?" Liam asked. "Excited or nervous on the first day?"

She slowed her finger on the keypad and looked up, a kick of warm emotion that he'd even asked the question. "He was a little of both. He was still talking about Jag all morning."

A smile pulled at his lips. "He'll be so happy when we bring him home today."

She opened her mouth to respond, but knew he was right. She needed Jag.

As she talked to the school, more and more Kilcannons showed up as if a secret SOS had gone out to the entire clan. Shane had taken ownership of the papers Nora had left, reminding Andi that he was an attorney with quite a bit of experience. She gladly let him take over the fine print of Nora's shocking news.

Molly sat on her other side, her hand on Andi's back in single-mother solidarity. Tiny Gramma Finnie came down from her third-floor apartment, got quietly briefed by her son, and took her place in a rocking chair next to the sofa, her eighty-some-year-old eyes alert but warm when she smiled at Andi.

Daniel Kilcannon paced the floor, his loyal setter, Rusty, keeping up with every step. "And you say you've never met Jeff's sister except for the encounter in the square?" Dr. K asked, a tinge of confusion in his tone. A family like the Scotts was probably hard for a Kilcannon to understand.

"The entire time I knew Jeff, both in architecture

school and when we worked together and after he came back from Europe to live here, he had no contact with his twin sister. All I knew was that she had done something the family felt was unforgivable, and I got the impression it had to do with a romantic entanglement, and she moved away to the West Coast and cut all ties with his parents and him."

"And his parents? You knew them?"

"I met them once in Boston, when we both got our master's degrees."

"No contact since then?" Liam asked. "Not even with Christian?"

She shifted uncomfortably. "Jeff was already gone to Europe when Christian was born, and we'd split up. They really had no interest in their grandson."

"They had enough to put six million in a trust," Shane said dryly.

Which still stunned Andi when she thought about it.

Just then, the youngest sibling, Darcy, still wearing a dog-groomer's apron and holding her phone as if she couldn't believe the text she'd received, came sprinting into the room, instantly falling onto a hassock next to Gramma Finnie.

"Garrett and Jessie are on their way in from the training area," she announced. "And Chloe texted to the family group chat that she could be here soon, too. You're friends with Shane's fiancée, right, Andi?"

"Very good friends," Andi said. "It'll be good to see her." Chloe had often spoken about the incredible life force that was the Kilcannon clan, and she, also an only child like Andi, had thrown herself right into the clan with her whole heart and soul. The Kilcannons were the family Chloe had never had.

Andi scanned the room, not even sure she'd know what to do with this many type As in her life. One of the reasons she'd been attracted to architecture, other than her father's influence and the pleasure the process gave her, was that it was essentially a solitary endeavor. Just Andi, the pencil, the blueprint, and the idea. Andi controlled the lines and vision, and she was certain of the outcome.

With a life among a group like this? Nothing could be certain except plenty of noise, opinions, and, yes, love.

Next to her, Liam threaded her fingers with his, the touch so comforting it reminded her that not everything should be done alone.

"You're going to get through this," he assured her during a moment when the chaos calmed down. "No one is going to touch Christian, no matter how much he has in a trust fund. You have my word."

Which she knew was a word she could count on.

She glanced at him, seeing Liam differently with his family. Oh yes, he was still the attractive man who drew her in like a magnet, but here he was without a doubt the leader of his pack. Daniel Kilcannon might be the patriarch and Gramma Finnie the dowager grandmother, but there was something about Liam's military-trained steadiness and his role as the oldest of a big family that gave him a quiet, assured authority.

"I hope you're right," she said, vaguely aware that he ran his thumb over her knuckles in steady strokes that brought her heart rate down. "Those papers would say she has a fairly strong argument."

Shane, seated in a chair across from them, the pages spread out on the coffee table, ran his hand through thick chestnut hair. After a moment, he looked up, pinning Andi with his hazel gaze.

"Strong-ish," he said. "But far from airtight."

"Can she take Christian from me?" That was all that mattered.

Shane didn't answer immediately, and the hesitation was enough to make Andi's stomach grip. She tightened her fingers around Liam's for support.

"Can she?" Shane repeated Andi's question slowly. "Technically, legally, with the right lawyer and the wrong judge? Yes. Will she?"

"Not if we have anything to say about it," Dr. K chimed in.

"I know a great family law attorney," Shane said. "You'll need to build a case that shows she's wrong about your capabilities as a mother and your intention to touch a penny of Christian's inheritance. She's never seen the child, so that won't work in her favor. The grandmother who left the money had no interest in him, so that…will be something a judge has to take into consideration."

Andi shook her head. "I had no idea Jeff's mother had even died."

Gramma Finnie looked up from her phone, the sight of a woman her age thumbing an iPhone with dexterity quite the anachronism. "Was her name Nadine? She died two weeks ago at the Scott family home in Charlottesville, Virginia."

Everyone stopped talking and moving to look at Gramma Finnie, who squinted through bifocals to read the screen. "It says she's survived by one daughter, Eleanor—"

"So not *that* estranged," Liam murmured.

"—and that Nadine was married to a retired bank executive who died a few years ago."

Andi nodded. "That was why Jeff came back from Europe so suddenly. He was very affected by his father's death." Changed, really, she thought. He was never the same person after he'd been in Europe.

"But still never took Christian to meet his mother?" Liam asked, his disbelief evident in the question.

"They didn't have a great relationship," she said softly. Jeff had complained about his family, his mother a social climber and his father unavailable. He said many times he didn't want to be like his father but wanted to be present for Christian. And that had been one of the saddest things about Jeff's death.

"Will that affect the case?" Dr. Kilcannon asked Shane, who was still perusing the demands Nora had left.

"The case is going to be about money," Shane replied. "And the control of Christian's trust."

"I don't care about money," Andi said.

"But it belongs to Christian," Liam replied, his voice gentle. "You have a responsibility to see that he gets it."

"Not if it means some protracted court case that tears him—and me—apart. He's already a painfully shy little boy. If he finds out some stranger wants to…to…." Her voice cracked, and she shook her head. Instantly, Liam's arm was around her.

Dr. K knelt in front of her, Molly slid closer, and Gramma Finnie put down her cell phone to rock nearer into the little group.

They might be a tidal wave, but they wouldn't let a person drown.

The kitchen door opened, and Garrett, the middle brother who ran the dog rescue operation, walked in holding hands with Jessie, the spunky redhead he'd fallen for a few months ago. They both wore serious expressions that told Andi they'd been briefed on the "family group text" that Darcy had mentioned.

They greeted her, but before the conversation picked up again, someone knocked lightly on the kitchen door, then pushed it open.

"We're here," Chloe called.

Shane's face instantly brightened at the sound of his fiancée's voice. "'We' means Chloe *and* Ruby," he said with a smile.

Andi automatically got up to greet the woman to whom she'd gotten so close over the past few months.

"Chloe," she said, meeting her friend halfway into the family room for a hug, getting her legs nuzzled by Ruby, the sweet chocolate-colored Staffy Chloe had adopted. "I'm so glad you're here."

The two women had met on the Tourism Advisory Committee when Chloe first came to Bitter Bark to offer some of her tourism marketing expertise. As Chloe and Shane's relationship blossomed into love, Andi had become friends with the lively brunette, too.

"This is ridiculous, Andi," Chloe said, squeezing tight. "We're all going to help you."

Of course, Chloe, not yet officially in the family, was a cog in the industrial-sized problem-solving machine of the Kilcannons.

She realized that Liam had gotten up, too, as if he didn't want Andi to get too far away from him, and that made her heart lighter. Without thinking too much about it, she slipped her hand into his as he led her and Chloe back into the family room.

Taking a steadying breath as she sat back down, Andi looked from one family member to the next. The siblings, father, and grandmother all shared something in their eyes, despite the color, as if God had imprinted them all with an invisible "Kilcannon" label.

"Where were we?" Dr. K corralled the conversations that started to break into smaller groups as questions and comments got thrown around. "On the legalese?"

"No," Liam said. "First, protection. Andi and Christian need round-the-clock protection, and I'm taking Jag over there today. We'll start the process to train both of you to know exactly how to handle him so no one, and I do mean no one, gets close to you or Christian."

She exhaled and nodded, already having accepted this as the first line of defense. Nora had *hired someone to break into her home*. How cold did a woman have to be to not care how frightening that would be to a single woman and a child? "Yes, of course."

"Will that be enough to stave off one determined, greedy aunt?" Molly asked.

"Enough that she won't try to kidnap Christian," Dr. K said.

Andi closed her eyes and put her hand on her chest. "I can't believe she'd do that."

"She likely won't," Shane said. "She wants custody and guardianship because of the money involved, not because she wants to bond with him. Kidnapping him would ruin her case."

And Andi's life. She gripped Liam's hand as the very thought of it rolled through her.

"I still don't want anyone to get near their house or the people in it," Liam said vehemently. "What about a restraining order?"

"She hasn't done anything to physically threaten Andi or Christian," Shane replied. "That actually might go against us, as if we're purposely trying to keep Nora from getting close enough to see what kind of mother Andi is."

"A good one," Liam said under his breath. "A stunningly good one."

Andi gave him a grateful look, then turned to Liam's father, feeling his gaze on the two of them.

"That doesn't solve the bigger problem," Dr. K said. "We have to demonstrate that Christian has a human hedge of protection around him."

"I'll stay with you," Liam said. "I'll come with you when you drop off and pick up Christian at school. When that woman sees you, she'll see me."

"Will that help the case?" Chloe asked Shane, glancing over his shoulder at the papers. "Another stable force in Christian's life?"

"It can't hurt, but..." Shane flipped the paper. "Family friends are supportive, but it's not legal and binding."

Andi stared at him. "What would be?"

"Well, obviously you're not going to give nonparent custody to this stranger without a fight, and the fact that she is a stranger really works in your favor. This woman has no long-term relationship with Christian. And courts tend to side with parents. Even single parents."

She heard the subtext and knew being a single mom would definitely be used against her, no matter how archaic and ridiculous that was. "That's what I thought. I'm worried," she admitted.

"As you should be," Shane continued. "It's safe to assume she has some money, estranged or not, and can bring in deadly legal guns. She's already been observing you and documenting facts, like your work hours, how often Christian is in day care or with a sitter, which she states is mostly for full days during the workweek."

"Well, I run a business and try to take him to the office, but yes, I arrange for care."

"Also how frequently you go out—"

She choked back a dry laugh. "Out? Never."

"She said she has photos of you at Bushrod's drinking with Chloe."

"The night last week?"

"I took her to Bushrod's to ask her to be my maid of honor," Chloe said with a soft choke of disbelief. "Not for a night of wild drinking."

Andi's shoulders sank. "It was the first time I stepped in that bar in months."

"Ugh." Chloe groaned. "This could get ugly."

"Ugl*ier*," Andi muttered.

"Shane, what will it take to get rid of this woman once and for all and quickly?" Liam asked, his voice taut. "Money? Threats? A countersuit? Tell us what our options are, and we'll do them."

Us. Our. We. The inclusive words were like kisses on Andi's cheek, welcoming and appreciated.

"The best thing Andi can do is demonstrate beyond a shadow of a doubt that Christian has stability and his every family need is being met," Shane said. "Put this woman's arguments that Andi is an unfit mother, or that Christian is somehow not being taken care of, so far out of the realm of possibility that she knows she'll lose the case. And if it goes to a judge, she *will* lose the case."

"How do we do that?" Andi asked on a whisper.

Daniel stopped pacing right in front of Liam and Andi, his crystal-blue gaze shifting between them, suddenly flashing like a literal bulb had turned on in his head.

"We make Christian part of our family. You and him. Legal, binding, and indisputable."

Andi blinked at him, confusion and questions swirling in her.

"How?" she and Liam barely whispered the word in perfect unison.

"Well, you marry each other, of course."

Everyone reacted differently with a mix of gasps, disbelief, groans, nervous laughter, and one loud bark from Rusty. But all Andi heard was the thumping of her pulse in her head, because she knew marrying Liam was the last thing she should do to protect her son...and the best way to protect her son.

Chapter Seven

He'd lost his damned mind.

Liam stared at his father, aware that Andi's hand had slipped from his and her jaw had fallen open in a perfect O of disbelief.

"Just hear me out," Dad said quickly, holding up both hands. "Hear me out."

"Dad—" Liam started to stand to end the madness, but Dad stopped him with a furious shake of his head.

"It makes perfect sense, Liam. You and Andi—"

"Are *not* getting married." He got to his feet to make his point before Andi started wailing or running off or somehow letting them all know how heinous that idea was to her.

"It would put an end to this Nora Scott's claims," Dad continued as if Liam hadn't spoken. "It would give Christian a legitimate last name."

"Dad!" Liam's voice boomed. "He *has* a legitimate last name—his mother's."

Dad gave a half shrug in acknowledgment of his error. "But it might not be enough to keep him safe from this woman," he insisted. "If Andi's married, part of a big family, surrounded by support? No one can get near her or Christian. In fact, we could have the three of you live here, like your mother and I did when you were a baby and—"

Liam's head spun at the idea, and he shut his dad up with a single hand ordering silence. "That is not the answer."

"Yes, it is." At the sound of Andi's voice uttering the three words, every single person in the room turned to her, including Liam.

She had her hands folded in front of her face, the knuckles pressed hard against her chin. She stared straight ahead, as if her gaze was locked on some distant target and nothing could or would stop her from getting to it.

Christian was that target. She'd do anything for him, including marry a man she wouldn't even consider having anything beyond sex with two months ago.

"You make perfect sense, Dr. Kilcannon."

"Andi." Liam sat back down. "Don't you think it's...drastic?"

She finally looked at him. "It wouldn't be forever," she said softly, the whisper of words like a kick in his gut. "We can get it annulled after I secure Christian, right?"

Annulled?

"Actually," Garrett said, stepping closer into the fray. "Shane happens to be a bit of an expert on annulment."

"You are?" Andi looked from Garrett to Shane, an expression of hope in her eyes.

Hope that this solution could be used and then...discarded. Hope that felt like a ten-inch nail shoved through Liam's chest.

"Yeah, actually, I have some experience in that area of the law."

"So, we could get married legally and long enough to appear before a judge or whatever, and then not be married?" she asked.

"You may never have to appear before a judge," Shane said. "Nora Scott might back off."

"That's what I'm talking about!" Dad exclaimed. "The perfect answer."

Liam shot him a look. Sure, his matchmaking lunatic of a father thought he'd hit pay dirt on this one. But wasn't he *listening* to her? She wanted it annulled before...before they even discussed this as a couple.

"What about Christian?" Liam asked as the question popped into his head. She'd said she was terrified of introducing a man into her life because it might hurt her son if it didn't work out. Didn't this marry-and-annul plan fly in the face of that?

"What about him?" she asked, as if she'd forgotten the excuse she'd offered for not wanting to date Liam. Because it was exactly that: *an excuse*.

"What will you tell him?"

She stared at him as if the question didn't even compute in her head.

"That you got married to someone you barely know because his long-lost aunt wants to take him away from you?" Liam prodded. "Wouldn't that terrify him?"

"Yes," she whispered. "So we'll tell him that...we decided to get married."

"And when it's annulled?"

She closed her eyes as if *maybe* the impact of that

84

hit her. "He'll survive," she finally said. "It's better than living with some stranger."

So marrying Liam was the lesser of two evils. Great.

"Then it's settled," Dad said.

Liam gave him a pleading look, then sent another to his siblings who, except for some mumbling among themselves, hadn't offered one word of support for him.

Of course not.

Because this wasn't about Liam's tender and unrequited love for Andi Rivers. A child's well-being hung in the balance, and he would no sooner think about his own feelings than one of his dogs would hesitate to attack on command to save a life.

He needed to buck up and play this game, and do it well.

Andi leaned back and sighed as if she'd experienced an adrenaline dump and needed to figure out what had just happened.

"Would you like to take a walk?" Liam asked her.

"Why would you go anywhere?" Dad asked. "We have to make a plan."

Shane shifted the papers on the table, nodding. "If this is going to work, the entire town has to buy into it being real. One word slips from the wrong mouth that this is a fake marriage and Nora Scott will have way too much ammunition."

"We have to hold a wedding and fast," Molly announced, maybe a little too excited to jump into this. "We should have it right here at Waterford."

"During the engagement party!" Darcy said, clapping her hands with glee.

"But that's for Jessie and Garrett, and Shane and Chloe," Andi said. "I don't want to—"

"It's perfect," Chloe interjected. "All the friends and family will be here Saturday for our double engagement party. I'm fine if that turns into a wedding. Aren't you, Shane?"

"Of course."

"Oh, us, too," Jessie said, sliding her arm through Garrett's. "If it would help you, Andi, we should definitely do this Saturday night."

"This Saturday?" Liam croaked.

"The sooner the better," Shane said, tapping the paperwork.

"Couldn't agree more," Dad boomed, practically unable to wipe the smile from his face.

What was he happy about? This wasn't a notch in his matchmaking belt. This "marriage" would be annulled the minute the mysterious Nora Scott backed off. Andi would be happy. Christian would be secure. And Liam would be by himself, licking wounds he didn't want her to know he even had.

He exhaled, resigned to the idea. "Come on, Andi," he said, reaching for her hand. "Let's go."

"Where?" she asked.

He shrugged. "Kennels? See Jag?"

She blinked at him. "That's what you want to do now? See Jag?"

Garrett snorted softly. "Better get to know your new husband, Andi," he said. "Dogs over people every time."

"I don't want to go see Jag," he countered.

"Then why do you want to leave?" Molly asked.

"So I can be alone with Andi for five minutes," he

86

said. "And so I don't have an audience when I propose."

"*Propose*?" At least five of them repeated the word at the same time in a teasing, shocking tone.

But Andi didn't smile, not one bit. "That's not necessary, Liam," she said softly. "We both know this isn't, you know, real."

Not to her. And it better not be to him. So they needed to set some damn ground rules before he got so tangled up, he couldn't breathe. "I know. But I want to talk to you anyway."

After a second, she nodded and stood. "Thank you," she said, directing the words to everyone in the room. "I'm blown away by your kindness and strength. I'm honored and grateful that you would all do this for my son and me."

Dad beamed and put an arm around her. "You don't worry about a thing, young lady. Your son will be safe. You're a Kilcannon now."

Liam could see her nearly sway at the words.

Putting a hand on Andi's shoulder, Liam led her toward the kitchen, knowing that if they didn't stop to have a private rules-establishing discussion right this minute, the fake marriage might spin entirely out of control.

As he passed Gramma Finnie's rocker, she reached up a weathered hand and grabbed his, getting his attention. With her other hand, she crooked a finger so he'd lower to let her whisper in his ear.

"Down on one knee," she said softly. "That's how Kilcannon men do this."

That's how Kilcannon men proposed to women who actually wanted to get married. When they were doing a favor for a friend? No way.

He merely nodded and headed outside with Andi…his fiancée.

When he thought about how much he'd once wanted that, it was another kick in the ass. He'd gotten what he wanted…but he didn't have her at all.

The moment they were alone outside, Andi put her hand on Liam's arm and squinted up at him, blinded by the sunshine and some unshed tears she'd had no idea were threatening to spill. Maybe it was the crush of that tsunami that had swept her away. Maybe it was the lack of sleep and pressure of worry. Maybe it was Liam's total disgust at the idea of a sham marriage to fend off lawyers.

Something had her literally trembling with emotion.

"I'm not exactly sure what just happened," she said. "But you don't have to do this."

He didn't even look at her. Well, he'd barely glanced at her since his dad had the idea. All he did was…fight it. Throw out excuses for why it wasn't a good idea. Call it "drastic" and look at his father like he'd absolutely lost his mind. And when he said he'd "propose"?

He sounded like the very word strangled him.

"I want to help you, Andi," he replied. "And this…this *idea*…is temporary. Extreme, yes, but if it keeps some nutcase away from Christian, you know I'll do it in a heartbeat."

Speaking of heartbeats, hers kicked at her chest when he said *this idea*. He couldn't even utter the word.

Married.

Yeah, well, it wasn't a word she uttered too often, either.

She exhaled as they walked around the training pen, keeping her gaze on a few dogs that were running around one of the staff trainers, a young woman who looked like she was having a blast.

"Hey, Liam," she called. "Can you give me a hand with the therapy dogs in a few minutes?" She put her hand on the head of a dog that looked a lot like a German shepherd, but was so much smaller and thinner than Jag. "Harley is giving me fits in obedience training, and you're so good with these dogs."

He nodded, taking a few steps closer to the fencing, as if he wanted to seize on any distraction from the big, fat problem he'd just been handed. And she'd been warned: He loved dogs more than people.

"Maybe later, Allison," he said. "I'm dealing with a situation."

A *situation.*

No, she certainly didn't expect Liam to jump up and down and be thrilled at his father's solution, but did he have to act like it pained him?

The dog in question came trotting over to the fence, barking in acknowledgment of Liam, who bent down to get face-to-face with him. "I'll straighten you out, Harley. And you'll make someone a happy therapy dog."

There was something in his voice—a wistful note, maybe frustration. Something that said his emotions and comments were not about the dog.

Puzzled and still coming to terms with what she'd

just agreed to do, Andi waited until he chatted for a few seconds with the trainer, then returned to the path to continue into the kennels.

"Why are we going into the kennels?" she asked.

"It's where I go when I need to escape them."

"Them? Your family?" She gave a soft laugh. "They are a force to be reckoned with."

"A good force," he shot back, his voice defensive.

"Oh, of course, Liam. They're amazing and supportive and unlike anything I've ever known. Remember, it was only me, my quiet opinion-free mother, and my dad, a college professor whose strongest commentary was on the modernist bias against traditional architecture."

That made him smile. A little.

"We didn't have family meetings and tackle other people's problems or build a family 'hedge of protection' around someone."

He shrugged. "That's what we do. En masse."

She didn't say anything, but took a deep breath of cool air when they stepped inside the air-conditioned kennel that could house thirty or forty dogs. Instantly, Liam seemed to somehow relax as soon as they were inside.

It wasn't the change in temperature or setting, she guessed, but the constant barking that echoed over the white walls and clean tiles, and the faces of different dogs as they looked up from sleep or food, warmth in their gazes.

"You really are at home in here," she mused.

"I love them all," he replied. "But sometimes I have to escape the onslaught of the whole bunch of Kilcannons."

She understood that. "Guess they weren't kidding when they said your dad is trying to marry you all off," she joked.

"*Real* marriages," he said, no joke in that edgy voice. "Not...this."

"Of course." She couldn't forget that.

They walked down the wide hallway, her sandals tapping against the cream-colored tile, listening to the cacophony of different-pitched barks. They turned a corner, and she glanced at a few of the local four-legged residents, some greeting her with a bark. Most of them slept, with a rumble of snoring, all happy for the air conditioning and quiet in the middle of a blistering North Carolina summer.

Liam was stone silent, naturally. She usually liked how quiet he was; it never bothered her that he wasn't a big talker. When he said something, it was worth listening to.

He finally cleared his throat. "Andi, you don't have to worry that I'll try to make it real."

When he said something like *that*.

"I'm not worried about anything except keeping my son," she said, barely loud enough to be heard over the noisy greeting of a golden retriever in a large kennel.

He nodded. "Yeah, of course. But I want you to know that I'm not going to, you know..."

She didn't know. And wanted to. She looked up at him, narrowing her eyes, trying to get past his silence to know what he was really thinking. "You're not going to what? Try to pretend this is something it isn't? Insist on sleeping in my bed? Create a bond with Christian that will hurt when it breaks? Fall in—"

"None of that," he said sharply, turning to her. "I won't do any of those things."

Shockingly, shamefully, she realized that disappointed her.

"That's why I brought you out here," he said. "To set some expectations and guidelines."

Guidelines? And foolishly, she'd thought it was to at least pretend like he was proposing, maybe to be amused at the whole charade. Make it something bearable, since it seemed they'd be stuck together for a while.

Of course, what man wanted to be roped into a fake, temporary marriage to help out a woman who turned him down cold when he asked for more than a one-night stand?

Sure, she'd been ready to climb into bed with him that night, but that had been a moment of midnight madness.

This was a different kind of madness. Desperation. And deep down, all that mattered was Christian, so she should be grateful for Liam's help and quit going all mushy about what it meant or didn't mean.

Because it didn't mean a thing.

"Yes, I think guidelines are a great idea," she said. Whatever the hell guidelines there were for a fake marriage.

He rounded the last corner to a separate section of the kennels, and the first thing she noticed was an oversized illustration on the wall of a bulldog with *USMC* under it and above it the words *Teufel Hunden*. Devil Dog, like the tattoo on Liam's shoulder.

"Now we're in Liam Kilcannon territory," she said with a laugh, glancing around at the pristine kennels and the tools of his trade. "German commands only."

He spared her a quick smile. "You'll be learning them, too."

Three of the four kennels were empty, but Jag bounded toward the gate of his as they arrived, barking in greeting and, she assumed, hope that he could get out and be with his master.

"Hey, boy," Liam said softly, unlocking his gate.

Immediately, she noticed a change in his tone, even his posture. The tension of their bizarre situation seemed to dissolve from his squared shoulders, and a slight smile tugged at his lips when he looked at his beloved dog.

He got to his knees, crouching to get eye to eye with Jag, murmuring something, using his large, masculine hands to rub the dog's head and neck until an animal trained to scare off predators and threats nearly melted into the ground from the love and attention.

Andi stayed outside his kennel, staring at the exchange with a mix of admiration for his genuine connection with the dog and trepidation. Could Christian handle this big, protective, dangerous animal?

"You ready to head to a new home?" he asked Jag. "Big day for you, buddy."

"You really think we'll be ready to take him home today?"

He looked up at her. "Would you two like to move into my house? I have a three-bedroom house halfway between here and town, and you're welcome to live there."

"Oh." She considered that and the effect on

Christian. "I don't want to upend his life any more than necessary, and I'm not sure how that would affect him. I'd prefer to stay home with him."

"And Jag."

She answered with a sigh as the impact of just how much her life was about to change hit hard.

"Andi, look, I don't really care about optics, as you might guess, but if you're worried about your, you know, reputation and don't want me at your house overnight, I get that. But you are not going to be without this dog for one minute when you're home. When does Christian get home from school today?"

She blinked at him, the question throwing her when she was still stuck on *optics* and *overnight*. "I had originally arranged for him to go to the little after-school-care program that's adjacent to the elementary school, but this morning I canceled it so I could pick him up at two o'clock."

He nodded, considering that. "Bring him home at two, and I'll be there with Jag and everything you need. We'll spend the afternoon getting both of you up to speed on handling this dog and training Jag to know you'll be his masters, too. That's a big part of the handover, and if it's not done right, we could have problems."

She studied him for a minute, the whole conversation sinking in. "We do have problems," she said softly.

"And we're solving them." He stood, keeping one hand on Jag, but looking down at her over the five-foot gate door. "It may not be the ideal solution for either one of us, but it makes perfect sense, and you have my whole family on board to assist."

"What about Christian?" she asked.

"We're doing this for Christian."

"But you were right in there." She gestured in the general direction of the house. "We have to tell him some version of the truth."

"Yes, we do. And I know that your biggest fear is that he's going to have the same kind of setback he had when your husband—"

"He wasn't my husband," she corrected.

"I know, I'm sorry, I wasn't thinking. But you know what I mean. His father."

"He wasn't my husband for a reason."

Liam drew back, clearly not expecting the conversation to go in that direction.

"I didn't love him," she said simply. "I felt that it would be disingenuous to marry him just because he was Christian's father. I considered marrying him when I got pregnant, and I did have very strong feelings for him, but when he refused to give up Europe, I knew where his priorities were."

"Why didn't you go with him?"

Because Jeff didn't want a baby in Europe, she thought, but something made her protect him, even in death.

"The job was hard, full time, and involved a lot of travel, all over the continent. I—we—couldn't envision doing that with a newborn or leaving my baby for long periods of time. The opportunity to run Bruce Williams's Bitter Bark operation was the perfect answer for a single mom and young, relatively inexperienced architect. But I also didn't marry Jeff when he came back to live with us and be in Christian's life."

"But you did live with him."

And she'd chosen that over what Liam surely would have offered her eventually...permanence. "But I didn't *marry* him," she insisted. "Because I don't take marriage lightly, and I want you to know that."

He didn't answer, but held her gaze with a hundred different unreadable emotions in his dark brown eyes.

"So, while this is a great solution for the threat I'm facing now, I want you to know that..." She paused, looking for a way to tell him that even though this technically didn't matter, it still mattered to her. "The vows mean something."

"But not like this."

"Oh, no," she agreed instantly, getting his drift. "Not like this."

"Then cross your fingers when you say them."

She gave a light laugh. "Are you serious?"

"Sure." He lifted a shoulder. "The people who matter know it's not a real wedding. You, me, my family, and..." He frowned. "I guess Christian is awfully young to try to understand a temporary marriage of convenience."

She almost smiled at the archaic phrase. "Yes, he is too young to understand," she agreed.

"Also, if you tell him the truth, he might mention it to someone."

"He doesn't talk to many people, as you may have noticed."

"Still," Liam said. "What if he confides in a teacher at school? And he or she walks out of the building right into Nora Scott and whispers the truth? Bam. You're screwed."

She cringed at the truth of that. "So I should tell him we're getting married on Saturday?" She reeled a little, thinking of the impact that would have on Christian. "He might not be able to handle or understand that. He's seen you one time."

"You said he'd survive." There was a little edge in his voice, as if he was tossing back her words to remind her that, really, it might not be so easily survivable. "Just tell him we're getting married, Andi. He's too young to understand that people have a relationship long before they're married. It's safer. Then I swear I won't worm my way into his heart if that's what worries you. When you have him safe and secure, when this thing is over, when we can annul any vows we made with crossed fingers, then he won't even care that I'm gone."

Jag barked once, loudly. Maybe because he was bored and wanted to leave, or maybe because he understood and agreed with everything his master had said. Maybe because that was a helluva long speech for Liam Kilcannon.

But she got the most important phrases: *When this thing is over. Vows made with crossed fingers. Won't care that I'm gone.*

Words to live by, Andi told herself. He was offering her everything she needed and wanted. A way to protect Christian from an outside threat and an easy way out when it was over.

"That's what I want," she said softly.

"Then that's what you'll get."

He bent over to rub Jag's head again. "I'll be back in a little bit, big guy. I'll take you to your new house."

"Temporary house," she added. "I don't know if we can keep him…after."

Liam straightened slowly, a dry smile on his lips. "You don't have to keep reminding me of how temporary this is, Andi. I know exactly what we're doing."

She swallowed. "It was said in the spirit of, you know, setting guidelines."

He stepped out of Jag's kennel, locking it behind him and putting a light hand on her shoulder. "We forgot something," he said.

"More guidelines?"

"I think I'm supposed to ask you if you'll marry me."

She gave a dry laugh, the unexpected punch of emotion making it come out strangely. "Sure," she said, holding up her crossed fingers. "Till annulment do us part."

Chapter Eight

iam climbed out of Rin Tin Tin, the Jeep used by Waterford Farm to deliver dogs to new homes, after parking in front of Andi's narrow three-story home. He was early, but would use the time to get Jag acclimated to the neighborhood, maybe walk up and down the street and learn the smells, and wait for Andi to come home with Christian.

Following the world's lamest proposal—and the pitiful "sure" he got in reply—Andi had spent a little more time with the family. There were some chaotic discussions with Molly taking the lead on the wedding plans, promising to keep it simple, fast, and authentic.

Liam couldn't take that. He left and went out to work with Jag and do some paperwork in his office. He also made one quick call to Paul Batista, a detective friend at the Charlottesville, Virginia, police department, but had to leave a message.

When he came back to the house, Andi had disappeared into Dad's office for a brief call with Shane's family law attorney friend, who would be in town later in the week for the engagement party—which was now Liam's wedding.

After making plans to meet with the attorney in person, Andi seemed to be a lot more optimistic and encouraged than when she'd arrived. She obviously didn't love the idea of a fake marriage any more than he did, but Shane's lawyer friend thought it was a stroke of genius.

Oh, there'd be no living with the Dogfather now.

With a promise that she'd meet Liam at home at two, she finally left. And Liam felt like he wanted to throw his body in a river of ice and not think about how he'd volunteered to throw himself down the Andi Rivers Slippery Slope to Misery instead.

This was not real, not on any level, not in any way. He could never forget that.

Heading down the street with Jag, he studied her house, a rich-looking brick structure that had some kind of cool architectural history, if he recalled a conversation they'd had on a date many moons ago. He didn't remember the details, but always thought the house fit her so well. It was classic and balanced and flawless, but had unexpected curves and surprisingly sweet angles, and all he'd ever wanted to do was climb up those stairs, walk in that door, and never leave Andi's side.

He'd known so fast that she was the woman he wanted, the one he'd waited his whole life to find. The first date, maybe the second. He didn't know how, didn't know why, didn't know what to do about it, but in his gut, there was no doubt that she was the extraordinary woman he'd always believed he'd find.

Then she dumped him for a guy who hadn't stayed with her when she was pregnant with his child. She made a decision to give Jeff Scott a second chance, but that hadn't changed how bruised it left Liam. He'd tried to forget her. Tried not to compare every woman to Andi Rivers.

And he failed miserably.

He shook off the thoughts, forcing himself to look for potential security weaknesses, like shrubbery too close to a window or well-hidden side entrances that could be broken into even during the day.

The street off Bushrod Square was one of the oldest in town, with rows of iconic rust-colored homes built smack up next to each other, all dating back more than a century.

When Bitter Bark was founded by Thaddeus Ambrose Bushrod back in the 1800s, Liam recalled from his local elementary school education, shops had popped up around the square and all of the roads that led into that hub were developed into residential areas. The result, a hundred and fifty years later, was a lot of charming real estate on tree-lined streets leading right into the heart of a small town that was currently enjoying gentrification and a push to build tourism.

And that meant more than a few people strolling the area, putting Liam on a slightly elevated alert. He glanced at a man in running shorts with earbuds in who darted by him, probably on his way to the trails in the square. An older couple with a dachshund on a leash strolled slowly, looking around like they were the very dog-loving tourists his soon-to-be sister-in-law Chloe had been working so hard to attract. A young woman who looked like she probably attended the local college walked briskly while talking on the phone, a backpack hooked over one shoulder.

Any of these people could be working for Nora

Scott, who paid someone to break into Andi's house and steal Christian's toothbrush to do a DNA test.

The very thought made him tense, tugging Jag's leash a little. Immediately, the dog glanced in anticipation of a command, ready to obey.

"Good boy, Jag," he muttered, happy that the distraction issue seemed to be waning. He turned at the next intersection and headed back to Andi's house.

But would Jag be enough protection? Would he obey the commands of a woman and a child he barely knew in a moment of distress? With the right handover training, yes, but that could take hours, sometimes days, depending on the new owners' comfort level and dog skill, and leave Liam worried that something could go wrong.

He wasn't that confident of Jag's ability to take on a new owner yet. He was close, almost there, but—

A woman pushing a baby stroller crossed the street, coming from the square, slowing down as she neared Andi's house. He was five or six houses away and she wore sunglasses and a ball cap with a sandy blond ponytail spilling out the back. She was too far to make out her face, but not so far that he couldn't sense her interest in the house.

He watched her come to a complete stop in front of Andi's brownstone and take out a phone. To call, text…or take a picture?

Was that Nora in a wig? An accomplice? Or simply a tourist who liked the looks of the local architecture and wanted a picture? But would a tourist be pushing an old-fashioned pram? Liam was no baby expert, but he was observant and he spent a ton of time in the square with dogs he was socializing. Baby strollers didn't really look like that anymore, did they?

Picking up his pace and notifying Jag he was on duty with a single flick of the leash, Liam walked briskly toward the woman. Yes, she appeared to be texting with two thumbs, but her attention seemed to be more on the house than the phone. And she had the same narrow build as the jogger, but he couldn't be sure.

When he was still fifty or so feet away, she turned and saw him, reacted to Jag with a quick blink, then tucked the phone back into her bag and turned the stroller to go in the direction she'd come from, away from him. Scared of Jag? Or did she know she shouldn't be there, taking pictures? In a matter of seconds, he'd almost reached her, seeing her glance over her shoulder and pick up her pace even more.

Should he stop her? Ask why she was taking pictures of Andi's house?

No, that would alert her of his suspicions. Instead, he kept his pace but got as close as he could while she waited to cross Bushrod Avenue, then, giving up on a break in traffic, she made a sharp turn and continued down the street without crossing.

As she did, Liam got a look inside the stroller. He didn't see a baby, but she could have had a newborn covered in blankets.

His chest tightened, and he resisted the urge to run after her and demand to know why she was taking pictures and walking an empty stroller. But he knew making a scene wouldn't change anything. She'd lie, anyway. Better she didn't know he was on to her.

He walked back to Andi's house and sat on the top stair with Jag to wait for her and Christian, thinking of how she'd take the news that she was no longer sleeping alone in this house.

Probably not well. Too bad. He wasn't going to leave her for one minute until Nora Scott was no longer a threat.

Sometimes, Andi thought that words were actually pent up inside Christian, deliberately withheld around anyone who wasn't her. Then, when they were alone, the words came spilling out so rushed and impassioned that she could hardly keep track.

That was the case on the drive home from Jackson Elementary on the afternoon of his first day at school.

"Ms. Rossetti said we would have homework every night starting next week and there is a reading corner with books for us, but Mommy, I already know how to read the baby books. Plus, we get to go to the library every Tuesday afternoon, and there's going to be a fire drill soon, and maybe a real fireman will come, and did you know I get to take a science class?"

She glanced into the rearview mirror to where he sat buckled into a booster seat. She wanted to be sure this was an actual break in the stream, still not at all certain how to tell him that life was about to change pretty drastically.

So she stuck with typical first-day-of-school questions. She wished that was all they had to talk about today—normal things, easy things. "Did you make any friends, Christian?"

"I like Ms. Rossetti. She's really nice."

"But no kids?"

He lifted a shoulder and turned to look out the window. "Nobody takes naps in first grade." He sounded a little disappointed in that.

"Well, you're a big boy now. Use that time to play with new friends."

"Can we go to the square today? After the hardware store?"

Frowning, she looked in the rearview mirror. "The hardware store?"

"For that nail to fix the pirate ship."

She laughed. "You really want to do that yourself? I could also call Mayor Wilkins's office and report it."

"I can fix it, Mommy. I just need a nail."

"And a hammer and strength, but..." She grinned at him. "I like your pluck, young man. Good to solve your own problems in life." She turned onto Bushrod Avenue, peering toward the edge of her brownstone, now visible. "No hammer and nails today, though, because I have a surprise for you."

His eyes widened, and his hand fell to his lap. "Did you get the new Star Wars Death Star Lego set, Mommy?"

She laughed, a wistful ache for yesterday when his world was that simple. "Nooo...." Drawing out the word, she drove closer and spied a bright yellow Jeep that anyone who lived in this town recognized.

Forget the fact that Christian's mother was getting married to a virtual stranger in five days. He was about to find out that a dog was moving in with them. A big, tough, protective, hard-to-handle, speaks-a-different-language dog.

And Jag.

"What's that?" Christian asked as she turned onto their street and he saw the Jeep.

"That's Rin Tin Tin. At least, I think that's what they call the Jeep."

He sat up, scowling, and then Liam stepped out in front of the Jeep with Jag on a leash.

"Jag! Jag is back!" If Christian could have ripped the seat belt off himself, he would have, the sound of his excitement like a kick of joy to Andi. This whole situation was tenuous and scary, but Jag would make Christian so happy. There was that. "Mommy! Mommy! Jag is here!"

"And he's staying," she announced, pulling into her small reserved parking spot. Climbing out, she waved to Liam, who gave her a slow, sexy smile.

No. Not sexy. Don't think like that, Andi.

A *friendly* smile. A *platonic* smile. A *dog trainer's* smile. A *fake husband's* smile.

She might not have to remind him, but she sure might have to remind herself frequently.

"He's about to explode," she called as she opened the back door. When she did, she met her son's beaming Christmas-morning kind of joyous expression.

"We're keeping him?" he asked, doubt in his voice, because it really was a little too good to be true.

And the first question was about permanence, of course. She hadn't even thought about the aftermath of getting—and losing—a dog.

One problem at a time, Andi.

"For a little bit, at least," she said, hoping that was vague enough. "Mr. Liam thinks it would be a good idea for us to help with Jag's special training by having him living in our house for a while."

He didn't care about the rationale, she guessed, by the way he started kicking his legs like the excitement couldn't be contained, practically pushing her aside as she unlatched the childproof seat belt.

"Jag!" He ran to the dog, and immediately, Jag barked and tried to take off to meet Christian. Liam gave an order, which the dog ignored, but not the next command, which was delivered in German with biting authority.

Jag instantly sat on his haunches and braced for the onslaught of little-boy love.

Liam stayed close, still holding the leash, but his gaze was on Andi as she came over.

"I think he likes this idea," she said softly.

"So does Jag."

"Yes, he does," she said on a laugh. "I think he would have plowed Christian down if you hadn't held him back."

Liam made a face as if he wasn't happy about that. "I have some dog food and supplies in the back of the Jeep. But let's take him inside and get him acclimated while I do a site check, and then we'll start the handover process. There's quite a bit for both of you to learn. And...we have to talk."

The low and serious tone in his voice snagged her attention away from Christian, making her frown at him. "Is anything wrong? Did you change your mind? A problem?"

"Of course I didn't change my mind." He ushered her toward the house, as if he wanted them all off the street, but she noticed he hadn't answered the other two questions.

"Let's start this transition so Jag will at least take

cursory commands from you," he said instead. "I'll want to teach Christian a little more slowly."

"All right. And, you know, I didn't really prepare anything. I don't have a dog bed, no toys."

"Jag doesn't need a bed," he assured her, glancing both ways down the street as he added some pressure on her shoulder. "He'll find a place to rest, but at night, his job is to patrol this house and make sure you're safe. He'll know that instinctively. Let's go inside."

Sensing an undercurrent of urgency in the request, she corralled Christian, and Liam gestured for the dog to go up the three steps to her door.

"Christian." Liam held out the leash. "You can walk him in, but here's what you do."

He crouched down to deliver the instructions. "When the door is open, you tell him to heel, or stay right next to you. Do you remember that command from yesterday?"

"*Fuss*," he said softly.

Liam nodded. "Good. Now you always want him to go in before you, but not until you give him the command to do that. So after he stops next to you, wait a second, then say, *vorwärts*. Remember that one?"

"It sounds like forward with a z," Christian said, taking the situation with such seriousness that Andi's heart cracked with love.

"Yes, exactly. It means he can keep walking."

"Okay, I can do that." He glanced up at Andi, his little face so solemn. "I can do that, Mommy."

"I'm sure you can. Let me unlock the door for you."

"Once we're inside, we'll walk through the whole house together," Liam added. "We want Jag to know every inch of the place. Sound good?"

Christian looked up at him. "Will you teach me the secret password now, Mr. Liam?"

"Not yet. But you can drop the Mr., if that's okay with your mom. It's too formal for your, um, dog trainer." He glanced at her with a touch of deer-in-headlights as he probably realized everything he said now could be questioned later when they told Christian about this weekend's wedding.

"That's fine," Andi said as she got her keys out. "Liam is my friend, too, Christian. A really...good friend."

He couldn't have cared less, with all his little six-year-old boy attention locked on Jag, who was giving it right back.

Once Christian flawlessly executed his first lesson, they were all inside. Liam instantly looked around with a sharp gaze that told her he wasn't assessing décor. He'd been here before, of course, years ago, but only in the first-floor living area. She had no recollection of him going up to the second floor, where Christian's room and Andi's office were located, and he'd certainly never made it to the top floor, which was dedicated entirely to her master suite.

But she looked around, seeing the house through his eyes. A comfortable home, with muted shades and soft sofas, and...her gaze fell on an eight-by-ten framed picture of Christian and Jeff. It was one of several around the house, kept as part of her effort to be sure her son didn't completely forget his father.

And maybe those pictures were a reminder to Andi, too. Life wasn't *certain.*

"Do you want to start by walking Jag around down here?" she asked. "I can—"

"I'll do the tour, Mommy," Christian announced.

She blinked at him, the statement so unexpected, she was momentarily stunned. "Okay."

"Come with me, Jag! *Vorwärts!*"

"I better come, too," Liam said. "I want to be certain he listens to both of us."

"Or you can just tell me the password," Christian said brightly. "Then me and Jag will have a secret language!"

Andi let out a soft breath of disbelief as Christian raced up the stairs with the dog at his feet.

"It's okay, Mom," Liam said, obviously misreading her surprise as exasperation. "I'll go with them." Liam followed Christian and, after a moment, Andi started to go, too.

It was out of habit, of course, knowing she'd have to speak for her quiet son and lead the tour. But she stopped herself before she climbed the first step, hearing Christian tell Jag how nice his room was and ask Liam if Jag ate Legos.

No, he had this. And the last thing she wanted to do was squelch Christian's enthusiasm and chatter.

"I'll get your cookies and milk," Andi called. "Chocolate chip today."

"Can Jag have one?"

"No," Liam answered instantly. "No chocolate, ever. No table food. I brought him food. Christian, let me show you…"

His words faded as the two of them entered his

room and Jag barked a few times. Andi stood stone-still at the bottom of the steps, her whole being still humming from the day, the changes in her life, the troubles in her world, and the unknowns she faced.

She liked things clear and defined and, like the architect she was, had created a blueprint for her life that had both form and function. With Christian as her plumb line, she had sketched out an existence that might be a tad lonely for a thirty-five-year-old woman, but was certainly satisfying in every other regard.

And suddenly that house was shaken to its very foundation, with walls crumbling and the whole structure threatened.

Which was always what happened to her life. Draw your plans and watch them get torn apart by some unexpected storm of change. Pregnancy. Jeff. Death. Now this.

The uncertainty of life rocked her, scared her, and made her long for something that would be dependable. Like Liam.

No, no, *no*. Like Christian. Her child was dependable. Liam was…doing a favor.

Heading into the kitchen, she set out a plate of cookies and a glass of milk, listening to the unusual sound of Christian's nonstop talking, followed by Jag's occasional bark, and then Liam's baritone in short, calm sentences of instruction.

For a moment, she leaned on the counter, closed her eyes, and let this new normal roll over her. A dog, a man, a happy child. A moment of domestic bliss.

All obtained under false pretenses, like building a house on shifting sand.

A single bark from a few feet away shook her out of her reverie as Jag led the way into the kitchen.

"Jag!" Liam called. "*Setzen*!"

"*Setzen*!" Christian echoed.

Jag sat, almost immediately, at strict attention, but it was obvious the smells of the kitchen and the floor intrigued him.

"Is he never allowed to just be a dog?" Andi asked.

Liam exhaled softly. "Not until he knows that this is his workplace. If we relax and let him dog-out for an hour, we risk him thinking of this as a resting place."

"Dog-out." Christian repeated the phrase with a grin that showed the gap from the tooth he'd lost a few weeks ago. "Is *that* the secret code word, Liam?"

Liam laughed. "No. But all you need to know is how to keep him at attention. Go ahead, do it."

Christian nodded, standing in front of the dog. "Jag, *achtung*." The German word rolled off his lips, and Jag obeyed by looking right at Christian the way he looked at Liam.

"Why are they trained in German?" Andi asked.

"*Schutzhund* training started in Germany, with German shepherds. It's always done in German, which is handy since the vast majority of bad guys don't know it. Some people train these dogs to compete and always use the German commands. I only train them to protect, but stick with the proper language. Christian, by the way, is a very fast study."

Andi beamed at the compliment. "He is bright," she agreed.

Liam notched his head toward the back door that led to a small patio. "This is completely enclosed, right?"

"Yes. Do you want to see?" Andi twisted the dead bolt lock so he could go out to the grass and small patio, which wasn't more than forty square feet, but had a vine-covered wall and shrubs to offer complete privacy from Bushrod Avenue that ran along that side of the house. "The wall is high for security, and there's a little grass that Jag can use for a bathroom."

"Good, but step out there with me now." He angled his head for her to go first. "Alone."

She glanced at Christian, who was at the table gobbling cookies. "I'm sorry you can't eat chocolate, Jag," he said with a mouthful. "But I can't eat dog food, so we're even!"

"They're okay alone together?" she asked Liam.

He nodded. "They're going to be just fine. It's you I'm worried about."

Her? "Christian, stay here with Jag. I'm going to show Liam the patio and grass."

"Where Jag will poop?"

She closed her eyes. "You're eating."

"But Jag will have to go potty, Mommy. Don't forget that."

"I won't," she said on a smile, stepping outside, a little unnerved by Liam's serious expression. Whatever he wanted to tell her, he wasn't happy about it.

He closed the door firmly behind them, leaving the two of them alone on the stone patio that was only big enough for a chair, a chaise, and a small table, but fine for her to sip a glass of wine late at night after Christian had gone to bed.

Despite the afternoon sun and flowering bushes that surrounded the area, the space felt very small as Liam joined her.

"I saw a woman outside and didn't like the looks of her."

She drew back. "Was it Nora?"

"I don't know. It could have been, but she was wearing a cap and had blond hair, which might have been a wig and she was pushing a baby stroller that sure looked empty, but I couldn't be positive."

"Oh."

When Andi's shoulders relaxed a little, Liam added, "And appeared to be taking pictures of your house."

"Oh my God." She put her hand over her mouth. "I'm so glad we have Jag."

"As of tonight, you'll have me, too. I'm staying here. I'm sorry, but I have to."

She started to respond, opening her mouth, but nothing came out as she tried to process about ten different reactions to this announcement. Where would he sleep? What would Christian think? And, of course, why was he so damn sorry?

"I think that's a good idea, but all I have is a pullout in my office. You won't be comfortable."

"I'll be fine," he said.

"And I guess it'll help, you know, cement the impression that we're getting married."

Jag barked a few times, and Christian's giggle could be heard through the closed door. "We're going to have to tell him," Liam said.

"We?"

"You don't want to do it alone, do you?"

She puffed out a breath. "I don't want to do it at all."

He flinched a little. "Yeah, I know. Why don't we

spend some time training Jag? We'll go across the street to the square and let Christian get more comfortable with him. And with me. We can tell him later."

"I promised him we'd order pizza for our first school night."

He studied her for a second, the hint of a smile curling his lips.

"What? You expect that I cook every night? That's probably in Nora's formal complaint, too. Not enough home-cooked meals made from scratch."

"That's not why I'm smiling."

"Then why?" she asked.

"Pizza on the first day of school? That's kind of an epic mom move."

The unexpected compliment warmed her. "I better be epic, or I'll lose him."

"Not going to happen, Andi." He put a reassuring hand on her shoulder and guided her back inside, opening the door to another peal of laughter. "And as long as Jag's around, I don't think Christian cares who's staying here."

But she did. She cared a lot. Too much, maybe.

Chapter Nine

"Can I know the secret code word now?" Christian asked the question for the, oh, twentieth time that afternoon and evening, this time as he pulled a gooey piece of pizza from the box.

Did Andi really think this boy was shy? Across the table, Liam glanced at her, noticing how much her expression changed when she studied her son and how her eyes lit up when he made conversation with ease. The kid had certainly been doing that the whole time they'd trained Jag in the square and while they waited for the pizza delivery.

"Not yet. Jag has to know you're the same as me when I'm not around."

"Can we do more leash-training tonight, Liam?"

He considered that, knowing Christian was still struggling with the leash since Christian weighed a little less than fifty pounds and Jag was at least seventy-five pounds of solid muscle. But the dog was tired, and Andi and Liam had something important to tell Christian. "We could, but—"

"Okay." Christian tossed the pizza slice back in the box. "I'm done. Let's train. Jag! *Achtung!*"

They heard Jag jump to attention from his resting place at the bottom of the steps, his nails tapping on the hardwood floor as he came closer.

"You've created a monster," Andi noted.

"Kind of what I do for a living." He put a hand on Christian's narrow shoulder. "He does need to get some rest. So tell him to sit and stay there in the corner, but we worked him pretty hard today. He needs to stay awake all night."

Christian's eyes, as blue as his mother's, widened, and he nodded solemnly. "Patrolling the house is his job."

"Absolutely," Liam agreed. "Every dog has to know what his job is, and that's his."

"Just like yours is to finish your dinner," Andi reminded her son, putting the slice back on his plate.

When Jag came to the table, Christian delivered the commands like a pro, and Jag obediently followed his orders.

"Nice work," Liam said to both of them.

"We're a team." Christian grinned and picked up the pizza slice. "So I should know the secret code word."

Liam chuckled. "You are persistent, I'll give you that."

"What's persist...persis..." He looked at his mother.

"Persistent," she said, enunciating the word. "It means you don't know when to quit."

A little frown formed on his forehead. "I don't like to quit."

"That's a very admirable trait," Liam said. At the child's confused look, he added, "The fact that you don't like to quit is something you should be proud of."

He felt Andi's appreciative gaze on him, but Liam looked down at the cheesy pizza on his plate instead of into her eyes. She had no idea how it affected him when she let her guard down or looked at him like she actually cared for him.

It was like the first rung up the ladder to Misery Slope. He wasn't going to fall.

"So I won't quit asking." A laugh bubbled from Christian. "What's the code word?" He practically screamed the question, a mouthful of pizza threatening to fly.

"Christian," Andi chided with a hand on his arm. "We're at the dinner table. And we eat with our mouths closed. Without talking until there is no food in our mouths."

He looked a little chagrined, but his eyes still sparked with humor, and Liam could tell that softened Andi's heart as her own smile peeked out.

"Maybe Liam could explain *why* we can't know the code word," she suggested. "I'd like to know that myself."

Liam wiped his mouth with a napkin, nodding and taking a sip of water. "Because that word is an order that makes him stop whatever he's doing, no matter what it is. And he will, if you say it. But then, if he doesn't think he was supposed to follow your commands, the code word would make him attack."

"Attack me?" Christian asked fearfully.

He purposely didn't answer so as not to scare the

child. "By the time we're finished with training, and we are close, he will never hurt you or your mom, or anyone you tell him is a friend. But he would hurt someone who *is* trying to hurt you." He leaned a little closer. "Even if that person knows the secret code word."

"Okay." Christian nodded and glanced at Jag as if he couldn't even imagine that dog attacking. But Liam had worn out two bite sleeves training him, and he knew better than anyone what Jag was capable of. "Tell me tomorrow?"

Liam laughed. "Yep, persistent."

Andi shifted in her seat and let out a sigh that Liam knew signaled that it was time. "We do have something we want to tell you tonight, though, honey," she said.

"'Kay. Is it about Jag?" He gave a grin, baring that tooth gap that he'd already demonstrated could hold a straw. "'Cause if it is, I already know."

"You do?" she asked. "I doubt that."

"We're keeping him, right?" He looked from one to the other with expectation in his little face. "He's mine forever, right? He doesn't have to ever leave?"

Andi let out a soft sigh.

"You have to test him out for a while and be sure he's right for you," Liam said quickly.

"He's right for me!" He whipped around to look at Jag. "He's my best friend ever in the whole world."

"Christian," Andi said. "We have to see. He's a very expensive dog that Liam trains for thousands and thousands of dollars."

Liam started to tell her that didn't matter, but instantly read her expression. She needed an out.

"And we could always adopt another dog that needs a home," she added quickly. "They have those at Waterford Farm, too."

"That's where I work," Liam added. "We have lots of dogs."

Christian's whole body looked deflated, making Liam feel bad, so he could only imagine what Andi was going through. Disappointing a kid sucked.

"I don't want another dog." Christian spoke so softly, Liam could barely hear the words. "Jag is my best friend."

For a moment, no one said a word. Liam's instinct was to insist that they keep the dog, ten thousand dollars be damned, but he didn't want to overstep his bounds. He waited for Andi to respond, but her gaze was on Christian, and the light had gone out of her eyes.

"Everyone needs a best friend," she finally said.

Christian nodded, silent.

"Even I need a best friend," she added, giving Liam a quick glance that he had no trouble interpreting. *Here we go.*

"Yeah. 'Kay." Christian started to fidget, clearly ready for dinner and conversation to be over.

"Sometimes people have best friends who live in their house," Andi said.

"Uh huh." Christian looked hard at his mother. "Like *their dog.*"

Oh man, she walked right into that one. Liam smiled and lifted his brows, silently asking her for permission to step in.

"Please," she whispered. "I'm making a mess of it."

Liam leaned forward. "I have an idea," he said, not quite sure where the idea came from, but it was a start. "How about you meet all of the dogs at Waterford to be one hundred percent certain Jag is the one you want to keep forever?"

Christian looked skyward, like even the suggestion that he wouldn't want Jag was lame. "Okay. But he is."

"And while we're there, you can meet my whole family. My dad and my grandmother, my brothers and sisters. We all work there with the dogs."

"Do you live there?" he asked.

"No, I have my own house."

"Do you have your own dog?" Christian asked.

"No, I don't have one of my own. I have many dogs at Waterford Farm. Would you like to meet them all? And my family?"

Giving a little shrug, he nodded, clearly not impressed with meeting the Kilcannon clan or alternate dogs. But Liam plowed on.

"I think you'll like them so much you'll want them to be your family, too."

He heard Andi's slight intake of breath, making him sure he'd blown this, but he didn't take his eyes off Christian. His pulse kicked up as he neared the moment of truth telling.

"Sure." Christian slipped to the side of his chair. "Can I take Jag up to my room for a while?"

"Not yet," Andi said, putting a hand on his arm. "I have something important to tell you."

"What?"

She swallowed and looked at Liam, nothing but fear in her eyes. What a damn shame that she hated this fake marriage so much it literally pained her to tell her son. Oh, he knew she was worried about the short-term impact on him, but if it could be *long*-term…

Stop it, Liam.

"Liam's going to stay here tonight," she finally said, her voice rough, as if that was all the truth telling and long-term she could handle. "For Jag," she added. "Just in case there's a problem."

Christian's eyes narrowed at Liam, the look of a person much older and wiser than his few years. "I can't keep Jag because he's your dog. Isn't that why? Because you won't ever let him go, and that's why I can't have him. You want him at your house because you don't have a dog."

"No, I…no," Liam said, feeling a little lost by the six-year-old logic. "We need to make sure he's the right dog for you, and it is a good idea to have him—and me—stay here."

"Because you won't leave him."

The statement struck Liam as so odd and so full of deep emotion that he reached over and put his hand on Christian's silky blond hair. "I know a lot about dogs," Liam said. "If he's the absolute right dog for you, then you two belong together, and nothing can stop that. He'll be yours forever and you'll be his. That's how it works, I know that."

Christian's face paled a little as he stared at Liam. "You're wrong," he whispered.

"Christian," Andi said. "That's not polite."

He closed his eyes as if polite didn't mean a thing to him, slid off the chair, and snapped his fingers at Jag like he'd been doing it since the dog was born.

Without a word, he walked out of the room and up the stairs.

Liam let out a breath, surprised at how far off the mark that conversation had gone. "I guess I blew that," he said.

Andi shook her head and rested her chin in her palm. "It's everything I feared. The reason I won't get involved. And probably a really, really bad idea."

"What is?" he asked.

"This pretend marriage. Can't you see that his biggest fear is a disappearing act? He doesn't believe in forever any more than I do, and who can blame him? Now I'm going to drag him to a 'wedding' and tell him you're moving in with your beloved dog, and then, wham, we win this and…"

"Operative word, Andi. *Win*."

Her eyes shuttered closed. "I know. I *know*. But maybe there's another way, Liam. A way to show permanence and stability and build a case for my capabilities as a mother without doing this and breaking his heart."

Oh, he understood a broken heart and didn't wish it on little Christian.

"Do you have any ideas?" she asked.

He sure did. Leave out the "annulment" part and make it forever. But that's not what you said to a woman who quaked in fear of that possibility. "I guess we could look at other options," he said quietly.

"Mommy! Mommy!" Christian came tearing into the room with Jag a step or two behind him, barking.

"What?" They both jumped up at the high-pitched exclamation.

"I have an idea!"

They threw a glance at each other, both aware that she'd just asked Liam for an idea, but he had a feeling Christian's wasn't going to help them.

"What is it?" she asked.

"You two should get married!"

They both stared in stunned, shocked silence.

"Then Jag would never leave!" He beamed at them, throwing up two hands like it was so obvious, how did these two clueless adults not see that?

"Married." Andi croaked the word and turned to Liam, her color high. "Imagine that."

Liam had. Every damn day since he met her. "I think that's the best idea I've heard in a long time," he said.

"Yay!" Christian made a wobbly little turn and smacked right into Jag, giving him a huge hug. "It was Jag's idea, really. He never wants to leave."

Off the two of them went, leaving Andi and Liam speechless.

Chapter Ten

Andi rolled over, rustling her sheets again. And again. And *again*. Picking up her phone, she peeked at the time and let out a soft breath. Three thirty a.m. If she'd slept at all since going to bed around eleven, she certainly didn't feel rested.

As soon as she'd start to slip into a slumber, something would wake her. The sound of Jag's footsteps, the knowledge that another person was sleeping in the house, the stab of remembering that someone was trying to take custody of Christian. And, of course, the fact that she'd agreed to marry Liam Kilcannon.

Real or fake, the idea caused a wellspring of emotions she didn't understand. Fear, anxiety, doubt, anger at being forced into this decision, and a bit of wistful sadness at that crappy proposal.

And that other feeling she really didn't relish...desire. Like a hot liquid bubbling in her veins, putting her on edge, making her feel achy and needy and empty.

She pushed back her blanket on a sigh and sat up, blinking into the nighttime blackness. She suffered the occasional bout of sleeplessness, and her answer was always to work. She'd make a cup of tea and take it into her office, settling at the drafting board to sketch a project that had been on her mind.

The balance and focus of the artistic side of her job always soothed her.

But there was no balance or focus tonight. If she went downstairs, who knew how Jag would react? If she went into her office, she'd find Liam Kilcannon asleep on that lumpy old pullout that was probably torturing him. If she even put her feet on the floor right now, he'd probably wake, come up here, and…

She closed her eyes and gave in to the punch of her overactive, underappreciated hormones bubbling beneath the surface of her skin.

Except, the more time she spent with Liam, the more other parts of her body got in on the act. Like her head. And her heart.

Liam was good with Christian, considerate of her feelings, and so protective he'd upended his life to secure hers. Did he even know how much she appreciated that? Maybe she should—

Jag barked, making her startle.

She sat up straighter, listening to a low growl she already recognized as a sound the dog made if a person Liam didn't know got too close.

Without hesitating, she slid out of bed, tiptoeing to her open door to step into the hall and look down the stairs. From the third floor, she could see down to only the landing on the second. Christian's door was closed, but the office was open.

A second later, she saw Liam walk out and head

down to the living room. She followed, silent on the steps, pausing outside Christian's door. She inched it open to see his little blond head on the pillow, his chest rising and falling peacefully.

Saying a silent prayer of thanks, she continued downstairs toward the sound of Jag's low growl, then saw Liam lean close to the dog and whisper, "*Zimmer.*"

He stopped growling immediately. *Zimmer* must be the code word.

She watched Liam move into the shadows of the living room, checking out the front window where Jag stared. She waited for the hitch in her heart, but she wasn't the least bit afraid.

No one was getting past that man and that dog.

"Is someone out there?" she whispered.

"No." He didn't take his gaze from the window, though, and neither did Jag. He put his hand on the dog's head and whispered a word of affection, probably because Andi's arrival hadn't distracted Jag like it often did. "Maybe someone walked by."

"Oh, okay."

He finally turned, keeping his hand on Jag. "You can go back to sleep."

She snorted softly. "Not doing much of that tonight." Coming down the last two steps, she let her eyes adjust to the darkness to note that Liam was shirtless with sleep pants, tousled hair, and bare feet.

Oh Lord. She'd never get a wink of sleep now. "I'm going to make some tea," she said, gesturing to the kitchen. "Want some?"

He didn't answer right away, but she could see him looking at her, his gaze coasting down her own nightclothes, which consisted of a tank top and flannel shorts. "Uh, no. I don't drink tea."

"Water? Soda? A delicious glass of Goodness Grapeness organic juice?"

He smiled. "I should go back to bed."

"You sleeping okay on that thing?" she asked.

He choked out a laugh without answering. That would be a no.

"Oh, Liam, I'm sorry. I should have a proper guest room, but I need the space for when I work at home. The whole room is crowded and uncomfortable." Besides the drafting table, there were the last sealed cartons of Jeff's belongings piled in one corner, a bookshelf laden with textbooks and blueprints, and that aging pullout sofa bed.

"Come on." She waved him to the kitchen. "I have some tea that will honestly make you sleep better."

He watched her walk by and silently followed, his only response a sigh of what sounded like resignation. Because he was saying yes to tea? Or because he wanted to follow her so much he couldn't say no?

Her skin tingled at the thought of him feeling and thinking the same things she was, but then she remembered how easily he'd turned her down when she offered herself to him months ago.

Was it really because he wanted more than one night? Because he had that now.

And she still didn't have what she'd wanted that night: him.

She touched the light over the stove, giving the room a soft, golden light that was just enough to make tea. When Liam sat at the kitchen table, she glanced over. There was also enough light to see each distinctive cut of his muscles, and that bulldog tattoo right above a particularly well-defined bicep. And the fact that he dropped his head into his hands and pulled back his hair on one more noisy exhale.

"Liam," she said softly, making him lift up his head and look at her. "Have I even said thank you? I don't think I have and I'm ashamed of that."

"Don't be. And thanks aren't necessary."

"I don't agree." After putting water in a tea kettle and turning on the stove, she walked over to the table and stood next to him, placing a hand on his shoulder. For some reason, she expected his skin to be cold, but it was warm. Hot, really. And smooth. And so strong, broad, and capable.

"Thank you for doing this for me," she said on a whisper. "You've given up your life, your bed, your dog, and your time."

He gave a slow shrug. "It's the right thing to do."

"Is that why?" She dropped into the chair next to him and studied his face in the dim light, taking in the angles of his jaw, the shadow of whiskers, the slight creases at the eyes of a man very close to forty. "Are you just that good of a guy?"

He laughed softly. "Yeah. That'll do."

"Liam." She took one of his hands, aware of the constant need to touch him but not able to fight it now. "It's huge what you're doing."

"Not as huge as someone trying to take your son."

"But you've moved in here and offered up your best dog, and you're *marrying* me, for God's sake."

"Then getting an annulment," he added, as if that part was so important to him.

That stung enough for her to draw back her hand

and force herself to quit touching him for the sheer pleasure of it. She could express her gratitude without mauling him and making him underscore the annulment part.

"Well, thank you for all that. It's above and beyond."

He angled his head. "I'm a Marine. That's what we do."

"You're a protector. You're the oldest in the family, the leader of your pack, and a man who would do anything to help anyone."

"Not anyone, Andi." The words were low and smooth, in that sexy voice he used to deliver a quiet command to his dog who, of course, obeyed. And they sent a shiver straight up her spine.

She swallowed, holding his gaze, feeling the air crackle between them. Everything in her wanted to lean in and kiss him. Just once. Just to feel his warm lips on hers and soothe the ache that twisted her inside every time he was this close.

"Liam." She moved a centimeter closer, but he stayed still, their eyes locked.

"The tea's ready," he whispered.

"Oh, yeah. Sorry." She pushed up and walked to the stove on unsteady feet, cursing herself as she turned the heat down under the kettle. "And sorry about that room. Maybe I could bring Christian up with me, and you can take his room."

"Don't upset your life. The spare room is fine."

"I've been meaning to reorganize it," she said, brushing some hair off her face. "It ends up being a catchall, like spare rooms are."

"Lots of boxes labeled 'Jeff' in there, too."

She turned, trying to gauge what that tone was. A little bitterness? Jealousy? Sadness that she still had some of his things? "Yeah, I was never sure what to do with it. There's stuff from Europe, many of his designs, his graduate school project, things I thought maybe Christian would want someday. Rather than toss them in storage, I thought he and I would go through them when he's older."

"How do you handle the subject of Jeff with him?" he asked.

She lifted a shoulder. "Honestly but tenderly. I don't want him to forget his father completely. That's why I keep some pictures around."

"And you? Do you want to forget him?"

Sighing, she crossed her arms and considered the question. "He's my son's father."

"Andi, do you think you'd have married him? Stayed with him? Even though, by your own admission, you weren't completely in love?"

Another question that took some time to answer. After a moment, she said, "I don't know. He changed a lot after Europe, as if something unspoken was always eating at him. He disappeared for days on end for work, but never talked about it. He was on edge, almost paranoid at times. But if he'd gone back to being the Jeff I knew in Boston? Possibly, especially if it would have made Christian completely happy. I'm not going to lie. I'd do anything for that boy."

"My mother used to say, 'You're only as happy as your least-happy kid.'"

That made her smile. "Truer words were never spoken, and I only have one. Can't imagine what she went through with six."

"There's a point when sacrificing your own happiness doesn't make sense," he said. "And you would have settled for that." He couldn't hide the disappointment in his voice.

"I know you have some very incredibly romantic notions about fairy-tale marriages, Liam, but that's not always what happens."

"So you'd settle for less?"

She walked across the kitchen to the pantry, looking for the box of tea bags. "I guess that makes me awful," she muttered. "Or stupid. Or maternal." She stared at shelves but didn't see anything but his face and his eyes and the way he just coolly turned her down.

"Or unselfish." His hands landed on her shoulders, surprising her, close enough to feel the heat of his whole body behind her.

Instantly, her pulse thrummed. He had to feel the blood singing through her veins under his fingertips. He had to sense her tension, feel her vibrate with how desperately she wanted to turn around and kiss him.

"I've tried being selfish," she whispered. "And you said no."

He let out the slightest, softest, sexiest grunt, as if he couldn't even think about that night. Then his lips pressed against her hair, his hands still.

Closing her eyes, she leaned back enough for her back to touch his chest.

"This is, without a doubt, the most complicated thing I've ever done," he whispered into her ear. "I don't want to make it worse."

In other words…*he was turning her down again.*

She nodded. "It would be messy."

"It would be amazing."

And she damn near melted. "But?"

He moved one fingertip, sliding it along her collarbone so lightly it could have been air. But it wasn't. It was Liam's blunt-tipped finger, and she wanted it to slide lower, to touch everything, to explore her and thrill her and make her lose control.

"But the last time I let you crack my shell and steal my soul, it damn near ruined me."

She stole his soul? "I didn't know that." The very thought made her breathless.

"I didn't tell you."

"Why not?"

"Because you'd made your choice."

A choice she'd made for Christian, believing down to her very core that she owed her son a life with his biological father and vice versa. Yes, she'd been falling for Liam, but they'd dated for only a month or so. Nothing was rushed, nothing was spoken. They'd just started.

"How did you feel that way...so fast?"

He added a little pressure and slowly turned her around to meet his midnight-dark gaze. "I don't know," he admitted. "But I did. Like, day one fast."

She inhaled softly, suddenly wanting to go back to day one right then and experience it again. She'd liked him—a lot—but she'd been so burned by Jeff's decision to go to Europe and leave her alone, so consumed by being a single mom, so sure that nothing in life was certain, that she simply wasn't open to anything then.

"And you didn't feel the same way," he finished. "I get that."

"I...was on my way, I think." She searched his face, his handsome features and bottomless eyes. How could she not have fallen deeper and faster? She could have stayed with him and not given him up for Jeff. But...Christian. "I held back because I had a child who had ownership of my life, and then his father came back and—"

"I know what happened, Andi. I was there. Lived it. Have the scars to prove I saw the action."

She blinked at him. "Scars?"

"You really had no idea how I felt?"

"You never told me," she repeated, frustration in every word.

"I showed you."

She opened her mouth, then shut it. He *had* shown her. He'd been attentive and considerate, charming and honest. He'd taken her to meet his family and offered to spend time with hers. But she'd held back, so scared to get involved when she had a little boy to raise all by herself.

At least, that was the excuse that felt comfortable. Maybe it was more. Maybe it was deeper.

She narrowed her eyes playfully. "Use your words, I tell my son." She smiled. "You should have used your words, Liam Kilcannon."

"Sometimes words aren't enough," he said, his voice raw with emotion. "Sometimes they can't do the job."

For a long moment, they looked into each other's eyes, silent except for the pumping pulse in her head.

"So now you know how I felt and why I'm doing this," he finally said. "But, trust me, I'm not going to beg again."

Her heart dipped. "Pretty sure I was the one who begged last time."

He glided his thumb into the hollow of her throat, still holding her gaze, heat growing between them. They both breathed at the same rhythm, enough that their chests touched, weakening Andi's knees...and her resolve.

Ever so slightly, she bowed her back, in a silent, barely perceptible invitation.

His response was not imperceptible, and instant. He pulled her even closer, letting their bodies press, angling his head and dipping it so that their lips were barely a centimeter apart.

"You don't have to beg," he said huskily.

She lifted up on her toes to meet his mouth, but they didn't quite touch. A spark could have ignited they were so close, but it wasn't a kiss. Not yet.

His breath warmed her mouth as his fingers slid behind her neck and into her hair as he tilted her head right where he wanted it. She wrapped her arms around him, splaying her fingers over the hot, smooth skin of his waist and stone-cut muscles of his back.

He waited, hesitated, held her there as if she was the most precious thing he'd ever touched, and each second made her heart hammer harder in anticipation.

She ached to kiss him, wanted to smash her mouth on his and taste his lips and suck his tongue. Craving the kiss, she tipped her head, but he still didn't give her what she wanted. He tunneled his fingers deeper into her hair, cupping her head. She could feel him respond, growing harder against her, the sensation stealing her breath and sanity.

His heart slammed against her chest, the steady,

rapid beat of a man losing control as his blood and body took over.

She lifted one more inch and closed the space, making their mouths touch. As if she'd flipped a switch, he gripped her harder, opening his mouth to kiss her so thoroughly, she literally felt the room spin.

His lips were raw authority, taking ownership and the lead. The kiss seared, so much hotter than she'd expected, but tender, too. Loving, even. He moaned softly, the sound coming from his chest...from his heart.

You stole my soul.

The words echoed in her head, as powerful as the kiss, making her reel with what they meant.

She didn't want his soul. She wanted his body and this kiss and the promise of a night that would satisfy her every need. She wanted these hands that slowly threaded through her hair, then slid down her chest and over the thin top she wore. She wanted his help and his support and his patience and concern. She wanted Liam on her own terms.

And that was the most unfair thing she could do.

He whispered her name, lost now, dragging his mouth over her jaw and throat, his breath ragged and his body rock hard.

"Liam." She tried to say they should stop, but the word wouldn't come to her lips. Instead, those silent lips opened and kissed him again, letting his tongue curl around hers, tickling the roof of her mouth and sending sparks to every nerve ending in her body.

His hands roamed her back and hips, teased over her rear end, pressing their bodies even closer with nothing but thin cotton separating them.

Need rolled through her, blinding her, silencing her when she knew...she *knew* like she knew her own name...that this would mean more to him than to her. So much more. Too much more.

You stole my soul.

She didn't even know what to do with this man's soul, and she had to stop this before they were tripping up the stairs and ripping these bits of clothes off.

He eased his hand under her tank top, groaning as he palmed her skin and grazed her breast.

She had to stop. *Say it, Andi.* Just say *stop* and everything would. Just say...

"*Zimmer*," she whispered.

He instantly froze and grunted so softly, like she'd pulled the plug and all the power zinging through him went out. His head was down, his mouth nestled on her neck, his hands still claiming her waist and breast.

"You heard the code word," he said gruffly.

"I can't. Liam, I can't."

Very slowly, he lifted his head to look at her. His eyes were black, fiery hot, and intense. He didn't say a word.

"I don't want to steal your soul again."

He closed his eyes like he'd been shot. "I didn't think that's what we were doing."

"It's where this will take us."

He let out a long, agonizing sigh and carefully removed his hands from under her top, tugging it back into place, his gaze averted. "Ah, yes. The Andi Rivers Relationship Progression chart. Should have checked it first."

"Liam."

"No." His hands on her shoulders, he inched her to

the side. "No talking necessary. This won't happen again."

Without another word, he stepped away, out of the kitchen, up the stairs…gone.

Andi stood stone-still, staring into the soft kitchen light, sexual vibrations still pulsing through her body like electric shockwaves.

At the sound of a footstep, she turned to the doorway to see Jag studying her with that same intense silence she'd seen in his owner. He barked once and put his head down, taking a few steps closer. She reached to pet him, and he dipped a little, accepting affection and offering a little of his own.

Like he totally understood what an enigma Liam Kilcannon was. Closing her fingers over his collar, she nudged him along with her so he followed her up to the third floor and spent the rest of the night on the landing outside her door.

Guarding her from Liam…or making sure she stayed right where she should at night.

Alone.

Chapter Eleven

Just to complicate his already complicated life, Liam had two new K-9 trainees who had arrived from the Baltimore PD. Both dogs were currently with Molly getting a routine check, so he headed into the small vet's office, grabbing coffee in the reception area before wandering back to her examination room.

"Hey, Doc," he said, stepping through the open door. "Came to meet my new students."

"You're going to love these two," Molly said without looking up from the large black and tan Belgian Malinois on the exam table. "This is Fritz, who I can tell right now is going to be a dream to train. Good-hearted, eager, ready to please. And that's his sister Zelda, who's got nothing but attitude."

From the corner where she'd curled up, Zelda looked up without lifting her head, as if she couldn't bear to show too much interest in the new guy. Fritz stood at attention, turning to Liam with his head raised like the eager two-year-old he was.

"Hey, Fritz." He gave the dog's neck a scratch, instantly seeing an intelligence in the deep brown eyes that meant Molly was dead-on about training. His big tail swooshed as he lifted his head and offered more of his neck. "You're a good boy, I can tell."

On the floor, Zelda picked up her head and turned it the other way, making Molly laugh softly. "There's one in every family, right?"

He set his coffee cup away from the action and crouched down to pet Zelda. She definitely got all the beauty in the litter, with a golden coat and black-tipped ears and a long, lean snout designed for sniffing out bad stuff. The whole package made for a dramatic-looking dog, and she appeared to have the diva attitude to go with it, not even flipping her tail once.

He fluttered his fingers under her jaw, knowing it was a tender and responsive spot for this breed.

He got a major dog sigh of disinterest in response.

"Don't worry," Molly said, brushing back one of her wayward dark curls, humor sparking in eyes that hovered between brown and green, exactly the color of Mom's. "She'll be panting after you and doing whatever you ask in a week."

"If only that were true with two-legged creatures," he mused under his breath.

Molly didn't answer right away, her concentration on the stethoscope she had against Fritz's thick chest. Nodding, she flipped the device out of her ears and onto the shoulders of her white vet's coat. "Andi?"

He looked up, still rubbing Zelda's head and neck. "Going right there, are you?"

"If there's one thing I know about you, Liam, it's that you don't make idle conversation. If you say something, it's for a reason. So, spill it to your little sister and see if I can help."

For a moment, he eyed Molly, appreciating so much about this thirty-three-year-old woman who ran two veterinarian offices, raised a daughter alone, and somehow managed to be the sounding board and true friend to anyone in the family who needed one. She was closer than all of her brothers to their father, and as the older of the two Kilcannon girls, Molly had gracefully stepped into their departed mother's shoes and filled a maternal role on holidays and at gatherings.

And weddings.

"There's nothing to help with," he said. "Except this shindig on Saturday."

She laughed, choking a little. "Shindig? It's your wedding."

"It is *not*," he fired back, a little more vehemently than necessary. "It's a favor to a friend and absolutely nothing more, not a bit."

"Me thinks my brother doth protest too much."

He started to argue, but took a big gulp of hot coffee and fried his mouth. He smacked his tongue against the roof of his mouth like it deserved the punishment for being so damn out of control last night.

"Not to mention that you look like hell." Molly squinted at him the way she'd look at a very sick puppy. "You sleep last night?"

"Not much. Jag and I stayed at Andi's."

Both brows shot up. "Oh, so those aren't bags of agony under your eyes."

They sure as hell were. He put the coffee down, crossing his arms and pretending to study the dog on the table, but thinking about all the unanswered questions plaguing him today.

Slowly, he pushed off the counter and shifted his attention to Molly. "Is it Pru that keeps you from getting involved with anyone?" he asked, referencing the now thirteen-year-old Molly was raising alone. Well, as alone as anyone could be in this huge family. She'd never married, and Pru's father, whose identity was the world's most closely guarded secret, was obviously not in the picture.

Molly frowned as she carefully opened Fritz's mouth and examined his teeth. "Having a child makes getting involved with a man pretty thorny, if that's what you're asking."

"But you would, right? If a decent guy came along."

"Decent being the most important word you used," she said, peering at the back molars. "You better wear a thick bite sleeve with this one."

He nodded, appreciating the dog's teeth, but much more interested in what his sister just said. "I'm decent."

She turned to him with a *get real* look. "You are so past decent, you're in the ZIP code of perfection. That's probably why she's terrified."

One of the vet techs walked by, her sneakers squeaking on the tile floor outside the exam room. Liam reached to the door and closed it soundlessly, surprised at how much he really did want to have this conversation with Molly. "She's terrified of this woman taking Christian," he said. "That's the only thing that matters to her."

"Can you blame her?"

"Of course not. But for me, other things matter." He exhaled noisily. "I'm confused."

Molly lifted Fritz's left paw and turned it over to see the pad. "Confused, Fritz?" she whispered. "I think my brother is in *love*."

Dear God, was it that freaking obvious? Wasn't he the king of hiding his feelings?

"Molly. I dated the woman for a month, and she unceremoniously dumped me for an ex. I've seen her a handful of times in the past few years. You can't be serious using that word."

"Oooh, that *word*," she cooed, stroking the other paw before turning it. "I know she affects you unlike any other woman you've dated. Your whole body language changes at the mention of her name. You didn't put up much of a fight when Dad married you off as the first and only solution to her problems." She threw him a saucy smile. "Sounds like love to me."

"Sounds like stupidity to me," he countered. "She says she can't or won't or doesn't want a guy in her life because Christian got messed up when his dad came and went...permanently."

"He *died*," she said. "Not like he had any control over that. Maybe you need to be more specific about what 'a guy in her life' means."

He considered that, watching Molly continue her examination with slender but capable hands that Fritz obviously trusted. He'd been pretty straight about what he meant a few months ago that night in the square.

And she'd been pretty straight about what she wanted. Until...*zimmer*.

"Molly, I don't want..." He couldn't come up with a word that didn't sound ridiculous. "*Just* that. When I'm with Andi, I want more than that. You know, like what Garrett and Shane have with Jessie and Chloe. She knows it and it scares her."

"And yet she is marrying you on Saturday night."

He snorted. "She's making a legal chess move."

A tap on her door stopped the conversation and made Fritz straighten to attention. Yep, a dream dog.

"Molly, you have a minute?" Dad's voice called from outside the door. "Because we need to talk about this wedding on Saturday."

The two siblings shared a look. Molly bit her lip. Liam looked skyward. Hell, even Zelda appeared to raise a mocking eyebrow.

"The groom's in here," Molly called, and the door instantly popped open.

"Why aren't you with Andi?" he demanded.

"And good morning to you, Dad," Molly quipped, blowing a kiss as she zipped around the table to get to Fritz's other side.

"Andi's at work," Liam said.

"You should stay with her."

"She's not alone, and I was going to check on her after I get Fritz and Zelda started on some training. Duane's going to help me, and I'll go into town, visit Jag at her house, and check on Andi."

"Duane's teaching a class on dog behavior, which is what we hired him to do," Dad said. "You know, with all this going on, it may be time for us to look for another K-9 trainer, maybe as backup."

Liam scowled. "We don't need another K-9 trainer."

Dad ran his fingers through his mostly gray hair, his dark brows furrowing. "Where's Christian?"

"At school. Andi met with the principal and his

teacher and explained the situation, so he's being closely watched and no strangers are allowed in without prior approval." He leveled his gaze at his father, keeping his impatience in check in front of the man he loved and respected most in the world. Didn't mean his father wasn't capable of driving every Kilcannon crazy. "We got this, Dad."

"And the wedding plans?"

Now Liam let out an exasperated puff of air. "It isn't a wedding," he said. "It's an act that we will play in front of the people gathered here for two other unrelated relationships."

Dad choked. "Unrelated relationships? Your brothers are *engaged to be married* to wonderful women."

Molly elbowed Liam. "Get Fritz down for me. It's Zelda's turn."

He scooped the dog off the table and gently set him on the floor. "Whatever," Liam said. "All I mean is we don't need to pick songs for a cake-cutting dance or whatever the hell you do at a wedding."

"Oh, you'll find out soon enough what you do," Molly said. "'Cause there are going to be a lot of them around here." She rounded the table and patted Dad's cheek. "Thanks to the Dogfather."

"I didn't do a thing," Dad said. When they both shot him a look, he held up both hands. "A nudge here, a suggestion there. Those love affairs took off on their own. But *yours*..." He looked at Liam, who was trying to get Zelda, but she backed up an inch before relenting.

"Dad. Can it." With a grunt, he hoisted Zelda onto the table, and she held his gaze, assessing him. He stroked her long dark snout and stared into her ebony eyes. "I'll find your soft spot," he whispered to the dog. "You just watch."

She stared for two more seconds, then flicked her tongue at his wrist and instantly put her head down as if to deny she'd ever shown such affection.

Man, he was on a roll with confused and conflicted females.

"Do you have a plan for this event, Molly?" Dad asked, pointedly sending his questions to the person in the room who actually cared about the so-called wedding.

"Darcy and Gramma and I have been talking about it, and I'd love to involve Chloe and Jessie, since we horned in on their engagement party. Of course, Pru is all over this, researching home weddings so that everything is done correctly down to the letter." She smiled. "My little rule follower. But what we need is time with Andi and Liam for everything to go smoothly."

"I'm not helping," Liam said. "I'll show up, say whatever, and do my bit."

Dad whipped around, his blue eyes like gas flames on high. "You will not mess this up, Liam Kilcannon."

"Dad, I—"

"You will take this as seriously as it needs to be taken."

"I am," he shot back, unable to keep calm or quiet anymore. "I take it a hell of a lot more seriously than she does."

"She knows how serious this is," Dad replied.

"I don't think you understand her, Dad. But then,

who does?" He snorted in disdain. "She's the most conflicted, complicated woman I've ever met. She's hot, she's cold, she's ready, she's scared, she's focused, she's lost, she's…she's…she's…" *Not mine.* He closed his eyes, barely swallowing that last thought.

Then he wanted to kick himself for revealing all that crap. What the hell was wrong with him? He'd never hear the end of it from Molly, and all he'd done was put a look of raw hope in Dad's eyes.

"I felt the same way about your mother, and she was all those things, too," Dad said, making Liam think maybe that wasn't hope, but a deep, dear memory.

"But she isn't Mom," he said softly, respecting that his father, of course, still mourned the loss of his wife. "And I'm not you, Dad. And we're not the couple of the century like you two were." And maybe it was time Liam stopped seeking that. Or at least time he stopped seeking that in the form of Andi Rivers.

His life wasn't going to be like his father's, not in that aspect of it anyway, and it was time he accepted that.

He finally looked at Dad, surprised to see a bit of a smug smile. "What?" Liam asked.

"What? I'm happy, is all."

He looked at Molly for an assist. She shrugged and went back to Zelda's teeth, as if she wasn't memorizing every moment of this exchange to share with Pru and Darcy and Gramma at the next Kilcannon coven.

"Well, I'm not," Liam countered. "I'm obviously in way too deep with a woman who has no room for a man in her life, except the six-year-old who is the center of it."

Dad took a slow, deep breath as if he was thinking very, very hard. That was never good.

"Bring her to Wednesday night dinner tomorrow," he said. "And Christian, too."

"Oh, great," Molly chimed in. "We can plan the wedding."

Liam just shut his eyes and stayed quiet. That worked so much better than when he shot his mouth off and told his innermost feelings.

"Molly, send me a text when these two are ready," Liam said, itching for a trip to the cool kennels where the only creatures who could hear him wouldn't know what stupidity was vomiting out of his mouth.

"Oh, we're done here," Molly said. "They passed with flying colors." She took a few steps closer, pressing the stethoscope bell on Liam's chest. "Seems like the only one in this room with heart problems is you."

He glared at her, ignoring Dad, who chuckled as he got Zelda down from the table.

Tilting her head, Molly wouldn't let up. "Yep. Broken and bruised. But there's hope, big brother."

He inched away from her, snapping his fingers to the dogs. "Fritz. Zelda. Let's hit the training pen."

Fritz trotted over, head high, tail swinging, ready for anything and everything. Zelda, on the other hand, took one tentative step, then stared at him like she wasn't sure of anything and everything.

A perfect metaphor for the couple he was now part of, like it or not.

Chapter Twelve

Andi's plan for the day was clear and simple: work. She would review and revise the blueprints Jane Gruen wanted drawn up for the Bitter Bark Bed & Breakfast addition, then start the prelim sketches for Helen and Ben McAfee's guesthouse, and then she had promised her boss that she'd go over a proposal he was doing for a new shopping center in Raleigh.

With this agenda formed in her head and Christian safely ensconced at school, Andi headed toward the luscious scents of the Bitter Bark Bakery, located on the first floor of her two-story office building.

She loved the bright and airy office space she shared with Becca, her assistant, and the intern they currently had from the college, but the primo location did mean she worked with the ever-present scent of temptation in the air. Yes, she could enter her office by way of a small door on the street that led to a narrow staircase, never having to set foot in the bakery. But then she wouldn't get her croissant fix or a chance to chat with Linda May, the owner and her friend.

Plus, today's special was raspberry croissants, and after the sleepless night she had, some sugar was definitely in order.

The bell rang as she stepped inside the sun-washed store, assaulted by a glorious whiff of butter and coffee, along with the chatter of locals and tourists sitting at the dozen or so tables and along quartz countertops that lined the windows.

Andi waved to some people she knew and absently pulled out her phone while she waited behind a man at the counter.

"Hey, Andi," Linda May called from the other side, carefully putting a blueberry muffin into a baker's box. "Heard you got a dog."

Wow, news traveled fast in Bitter Bark. "For the moment. How'd you hear that, anyway?"

"Cathy Burke said she saw you and Christian playing in the square yesterday with a big, bad dog." She grinned, her gray-blue eyes crinkling playfully. "And a German shepherd."

All kinds of news. "Very funny, Linda May."

The man in front of her gave a cursory glance over his shoulder, but Andi looked at her phone, feeling a slow heat rise.

If she was really getting married Saturday night, wouldn't she be telling Linda May? She'd become good friends with the woman and had held her close when her beloved Michael died two years ago. Widowed at sixty, she was another strong, independent woman who ran her own business, and they had much in common.

Wouldn't she invite Linda May to the wedding? A lead weight dropped in Andi's stomach. What was she doing, anyway? Asking drama and trouble into her life, that's what.

Because she was trying to avoid *worse* drama and trouble, she reminded herself.

"Uh, go ahead," the man in front of her said, stepping aside. "I can't decide between chocolate or raspberry."

"Raspberry," Andi said, finally looking up. "No one in their right mind says no to a Linda May Dunlap raspberry croissant. Trust me on this."

He smiled at her, a flirty gleam in dark eyes from a man who was probably in his thirties, with decent features and dressed in a sharp suit. On another day, in another frame of mind, *when she wasn't about to be married*, Andi might have even enjoyed the conversation and then laughed about it with Linda May after he left.

"Raspberry it is, and make it two, Linda May."

"They're filling," Andi warned.

"One's for you."

She blinked at him, taken back. "Oh, no, that's not necessary."

His smile widened, showing straight white teeth. "No one says no to a Linda May Dunlap raspberry croissant," he teased.

"Well, I…" She closed her eyes and chose an easy answer. "Thank you."

She glanced at Linda May, whose neatly drawn brow was raised in amusement and curiosity. How would that expression change when Andi came in here on Monday and casually mentioned she'd married Liam Kilcannon over the weekend? More guilt twisted.

Linda May put the bag on the counter and two empty coffee cups for them to fill from the station on the side. "Coffee's on the house today," she said with a wink. "And there's an empty table by the window."

The comment didn't surprise Andi, considering how long and hard Linda May had lobbied for Andi to start dating after Jeff died. And there was no way to tell her friend, or this stranger, that she was getting married on Saturday without an avalanche of disbelieving questions.

And any one of the people in the bakery right now could have been hired by Nora Scott to watch Andi's every move. So now they'd be able to say she was having coffee with handsome men she met in line five days before she got married and did that make her an unfit mother, so—

The man chuckled softly. "I had no intention of causing a scowl, miss." He angled his head and handed her the pastry wrapped in waxed paper, quite the gentleman. "Thanks for the recommendation."

He stepped away and headed out the door, the bell barely covering Linda May's audible groan.

"What the heck is wrong with you, Andrea Rivers?"

"Nothing, I..." She swallowed, knowing that if the plan was going to work, she had to commit to it. She couldn't let anyone, not even a friend like this, know these unannounced, unexpected nuptials weren't real. Plus, Linda May would start the whisper campaign, and the news would be all over Bitter Bark in no time. So, what better way to test her acting skills than right here and right now?

She leaned over the counter, checking to be sure no

one was waiting behind her. She took a breath and prepared to look a dear friend in the eye and lie. "Um, Linda May. I have to tell you something."

The other woman's eyes brightened. "Oooh, gimme some good gossip, Andi. The grapevine's been dry since the funeral director and spa owner came out in the open with their romance. Whatcha got?"

"I've got...news." A bald-faced lie dreamed up in a moment of insanity. "Big news."

"Tell!"

She stared at Linda May, the words forming in her head but absolutely refusing to come out. Just...no. She didn't have it in her to lie, so couldn't she tell the truth? Which demanded more time than she had during the bakery's breakfast rush. "I'll come down after lunch when you have a break."

"What? After that buildup?" Linda May's eyes flashed in mock humor, but the door dinged with new customers who saved the day. "After that, you better be telling me you're headed down the aisle yourself, woman."

She swayed a little at the accidental prophecy and covered by stepping aside to make room at the counter. "I'll be back at lunch."

Outside, Andi gulped some air and instantly changed her morning agenda. She had to call this off. She wasn't capable of lying.

Turning to the small glass door that led up to her office, she tucked the croissant under her chin so she could open her bag and get the keys.

"Would you like me to hold the door or the pastry?"

She gasped at the sound of a man's voice, only a

little surprised it was the flirty croissant buyer. "Uh, no. Thanks. Buying it was enough." She closed her fingers around the keys, sort of wishing she could have told her lie to Linda May, which would have warned him off. She didn't like the idea of a man lingering outside her office for no good reason.

He could be working for Nora Scott.

She unlocked the door and pulled it, but he held it for her, his arm over her head.

"Thank you," she said, giving him a pointed look. "I'm going to work now."

"I know." He nodded for her to go into the hallway. "I have a meeting with you, Miss Rivers."

Freezing, she frowned and mentally scanned the agenda she'd made. Her calendar had been completely clear this morning. "I don't think so," she said.

"I just made it with Becca, your assistant. I'll walk up with you."

"Who are you?" she demanded, any hint of warmth gone as she refused to walk into this tiny hallway and up these stairs with a stranger who claimed to know her. He could be anyone. He could be *Mr. Nora Scott*, for all she knew.

"My name is Jason Leff, and I represent the estate of Nadine Marie Scott. She's left your son a considerable sum of money in a trust fund, and I am here to deliver the specifics and stipulations for that fund."

Nadine's lawyer? Shane told her this would probably happen next—if Nora was telling the truth about the will. "Oh, wow, yes. I need to talk to you."

"Why don't you go up to your office, chat with your assistant to make sure I'm who I say I am, have your croissant, and I'll come up in ten minutes? Would that make you more comfortable?"

Yes. But was it the right thing to do? His previous words played in her mind. *The specifics and stipulations.* "What are the stipulations?"

"Very simple, really, and they are all spelled out in a document I have. Would you like to see it? Review it before we talk?"

That seemed reasonable. "Yes, please."

He reached into his bag and pulled out a legal-sized packet of paper. "Take a moment and read this, then I can answer any questions you have. All right?"

Despite how considerate he was being, a low-grade anxiety fluttered in her belly, making her fingers shake as she took the document with a hand still holding the wrapped pastry. "That's fine. Thank you. I'll be upstairs."

"Take all the time you like." He pulled the door open for her and let her go inside alone, the door closing behind Andi with a soft thud. Becca would have to buzz him in now.

Feeling safer but still so uncertain, she hustled up the stairs, stopping at the landing to lean against the wall, out of sight from the man downstairs. Unable to control her curiosity, she set everything on the stairs but the envelope, ripping it open to scan a sea of legalese, finally focusing on a list of trust endowment stipulations.

Christian Rivers's name must legally be changed to Christian Scott.

Christian Rivers must reside (with his legal guardian) in the city of Charlottesville, Virginia, at the home of Nadine Scott.

Christian Rivers can never be legally adopted by any father, regardless of the marital status of his legal guardian.

If those stipulations are met, Christian Rivers will receive the amount of six million dollars upon his twenty-first birthday. If not, the money will be donated to the Scott Foundation.

She leaned against the wall, slid to the step, and dropped her head into her hands with a sigh of utter defeat. She didn't know what upset her more, the stipulations or the fact that it said *legal guardian* and not *parent*.

Legal guardian…like the aunt who took custody after proving the mother was unfit.

Rage mixed with fear in her gut, burning. And suddenly, Andi realized she was most definitely capable of lying. In fact, she'd lie, steal, kill, or marry a man for show if she had to, because no one was taking Christian away from her, giving him another name, limiting any opportunities, or donating his inheritance without his approval.

No one, no matter what it cost her.

"I broke the news to Linda May Dunlap today."

Liam took his gaze off Jag and Christian for a moment to make sure he'd heard Andi right. "The baker?" He shook his head. "Our news?"

She gave him a tight smile and nodded, looking around the square for a second, then reached for his hand. "You know any other news?"

"Look, Mommy, I'm gonna throw it!"

Andi turned to witness another pretty sad Frisbee toss, but Liam couldn't take his eyes off her. She actually seemed *into* this. Ever since she'd come home from school with Christian and he'd been waiting in the house with Jag, as they'd planned when she'd given him a spare key today, Andi was different.

A little tense, a little forced, and not exactly the happy woman she usually was around her son, but she was definitely focused on *them*.

First, she very publicly hugged him on the street, then suggested the three of them walk all the way up Bushrod Avenue—holding hands—to get ice cream, and then they'd come to Jag's favorite place in the square to let Christian throw him the Frisbee and practice commands.

And now he learned she'd told a woman notorious for passing news along.

"Try holding it like Liam showed you," she called to Christian, then turned to him, putting her hand above her brows to block the sun and see him better. "Why do you look so surprised? Isn't that the whole idea? Telling people and making it real?"

"*Look* real," he reminded her.

She lifted their joined hands and pressed his knuckles to her lips. "Bushrod Square is crowded," she said softly.

In other words, this was all for an audience. Which he *knew*, of course. But that didn't make the affection any less bittersweet.

"He can't catch it." Christian's whine of disappointment stole their attention, but not enough for Andi to let go of Liam's hand.

"Let's go help him," she suggested, tugging him in

the direction of the child. When he came along, she let go of his hand and slid her whole arm around his waist, gazing up with the look of...well, maybe not love, but the woman sure could act.

What could he do but act with her? She didn't have to know it wasn't an act for him. He slowed them down and wrapped his arm around her, too, pulling her into his side. It felt good and right and sweet to have her there.

"So what did Linda May say?"

"Well, I'm surprised you didn't hear the squeal all the way out at Waterford." She didn't laugh or even smile, but looked a little regretful.

"It's never fun to lie, Andi."

"But a necessary evil. Oh, and I invited her."

"To the...party?"

She sighed as if that invitation had caused agony. Or maybe it was his reluctance to say the word *wedding*. "There wasn't any way I couldn't," she said.

"Show me again, Liam." Christian shoved the Frisbee at Liam, his other hand on Jag's head, where it usually was when they were together.

"I will, but I want you to see something first," he said. "Look at Jag."

He did, meeting the dog's intense gaze. After a second, Christian grinned and gave a goofy little wave. "Hi, Jaggerman." Then his face grew serious. "Oh, I'm probably not supposed to use my 'best friend name' for him or he won't follow orders. I call him Jaggerman. Is that okay?"

Liam laughed, shaking his head. "Christian, you are a natural at this. And you're right about his name when giving orders, but it's okay to call him anything you want during playtime. It's important he knows the difference between play and work. Right now, he's off the clock and having fun. But that's not what I wanted to show you."

Christian waved the Frisbee impatiently. "How to throw this right?"

"Yes, and..." He pointed to Jag. "Where is he looking right now?"

"At me?"

"Yes."

Christian beamed as the realization hit. "He's not distracted! That's good, isn't it, Liam?" He turned his very serious face to Andi. "He has a problem with distractions." Liam could hear his own voice echoed in the statement, including the inflections.

An unexpected jolt of happiness hit him, but maybe that was because Andi laughed and it might have been the first time he'd heard that all afternoon.

"But he's looking at *you*," Liam said. "Not me. That is what we call a breakthrough."

His blue eyes grew with surprise. "Break through what?"

Andi laughed again. "A breakthrough *moment*," she explained. "It means you took something to a new level."

He still looked confused. "Like on Mario Party when you get to the next level?"

"Kind of," Liam said. "You and Jag got to the next level in training. He's looking at you before me."

"Because he's my best friend!" Christian folded over Jag's head, wrapping his arms around the big dog's neck and getting a rare lick of affection.

"I think he is," Liam said.

Christian's head popped up. "Then can you—"

"If you say the secret code word, I'm going to throw this Frisbee so far and you'll have to race Jag to it."

"Secret code word!" he screamed on a boyish chortle, and Liam instantly took the disk, aimed for an open area, and flipped it at exactly the right speed for Jag to bolt after it and snag it in his mouth. Christian ran, too, far behind the dog, sliding on the grass with a squeal of laughter that made Jag go to the child first before returning the Frisbee.

"Damn," Liam whispered under his breath.

"What? Did he do something wrong?"

"No. Jag went to him instead of me."

"Breakthrough?"

He nodded slowly, watching the two of them tussle on the ground, noting that Jag was both playful and protective. He had another kick of a reaction to that, but he couldn't discern what he was feeling.

"I think I'm jealous," he mused.

Andi laughed softly. "Because Jag's got a new master?"

"Yeah." He looked at her, a frown tugging. "I've never felt that when I gave up a dog to a new owner before."

"Jag's special."

"He is, no doubt about it, but..." He watched as Jag let Christian have the Frisbee clutched in his teeth, and Christian jumped up to throw it. "I don't know," he admitted. "This is different."

Christian bent over and commanded "*Gib laut!*" to Jag, who barked in response.

"I'll tell you what's different," Andi said, leaning

her head on Liam's shoulder in a way that felt more real than anything she'd done all day. "That boy."

"Jag's good for him."

"You have no idea, Liam. This is the happiest, the most outgoing, the most joyful I've seen that child since Jeff died."

"Dogs are like that for shy boys," he said. "I swear to God I wouldn't utter full sentences to anyone who didn't have four legs when I was a kid."

"Really?" She inched back, looking up at him. "If I had known that, I would have..." Her voice trailed off as her gaze shifted past him.

"What is—"

"Don't turn," she said harshly, putting her hands on his shoulders. "Don't look. It's a woman with blond hair and one of those old-school prams you mentioned. It might be her. The one you think took a picture of my house. I don't want her to know you noticed her then."

His body tensed, and his eyes gave a quick scan in both directions. He could see Christian and Jag. "Is she close to Christian?"

"Opposite side. She's coming down your left, nowhere near him."

"If she gets too close to him, I'll put Jag on alert. Is it Nora?"

"No, but..." Her body went weak under his hands, and she sighed audibly. "She's still coming closer, down the path by the fence. Nowhere near Christian, but very close to us. Closer. Closer." She looked up at him. "She's coming now. She's almost next to us." She swallowed. "Doesn't seem to notice us, but..." She pressed his shoulders harder. "I'm scared."

"No one is going to hurt him, Andi." He put his hands on her waist to emphasize the truth of that by inching her slightly closer. "Or take him from you. No one is getting near that kid as long as I—and Jag—breathe."

"Oh." Andi leaned into him, lifting her face. "Liam." Before he had a chance to think another thought, her lips were on his, a soft, sweet, almost tentative kiss. "Thank you," she breathed into his mouth. "Thank you."

He heard the stroller rumble by on the walkway next to him. He sneaked a peek, saw a woman who didn't look anything like the one he'd seen yesterday, and she had a green stroller, not a blue one. "Unless Nora has an army of stroller-pushing henchwomen, we're in the clear," he whispered into her mouth, still less than a centimeter from his.

Andi closed her eyes. "But in case she does...." She pressed her mouth into his again, no light kiss this time. She was serious, intentional, and hot. Her lips parted, her arms wrapped around his neck, and she angled her head to give him full access to her sweet mouth.

The only reason he broke away was to check on Christian and Jag, who were currently sitting on the grass, coming as close to "talking" as a dog and a boy could.

"What was that for?" he asked, ever the hopeful idiot dreaming that Andi had just had her own "breakthrough." "She was past us when you kissed me."

"I know. But I see Nellie the librarian over there talking to Ned Chandler from the *Bitter Bark Banner*."

"So it was for show?"

She sighed, long and slow. "I have to tell you something."

He waited, silent.

"Nadine Scott's probate attorney came to my office today," she finally said. "This is real, Liam. There is a will, and it is complicated, and this is real."

He nodded, cupping her face to make her feel safe. "Don't worry," he said softly. "I won't let anything happen to you or Christian. I swear."

"Thank you." She inched back, giving him a look he couldn't interpret and wasn't sure he wanted to. "And thank you for Jag and...everything."

"You've thanked me enough, Andi." Any more thanking and he'd be taking that one-way ticket back down the Andi Rivers Slippery Slope to Misery again.

She blinked at the comment as if she hadn't been expecting it. "Yeah, well, now you know why we have to convince *everyone* this is real."

Everyone but him. "Okay, then. Another kiss? A few more and Ned'll put us on the front page of the *Banner* tomorrow."

She laughed softly. "That would expedite things."

Yeah, like the terminal heartache he was going to suffer when this thing was over.

Chapter Thirteen

iam's words—*you've thanked me enough*—echoed in Andi's head for twenty-four hours. During that time, she kept as much distance as she could, managed to stay alone in her own bed all night, and all day, she finished revisions on the B&B expansion design and took the blueprints over to Jane Gruen for approval. On Tuesday, she cancelled her class at the college, but it was only a review for the final. She'd have to go next Tuesday.

Still, there'd been no sign of lawyers, stroller walkers, or Nora Scott, who seemed to have disappeared. Shane said Andi would likely be served with a summons of some kind from Nora, but that hadn't happened yet.

Tonight, she felt safe, driving to Waterford Farm for a midweek family dinner.

She stole a glance at Liam, his hands somehow looking even stronger and more masculine wrapped around the tan leather steering wheel of his big Ford F-250. He'd been true to his word about never leaving her house. He'd somehow gotten clothes in the guest room/office and changed into khakis and a green polo shirt that fit snugly on his shoulders and showed off his biceps.

When he'd come out to the kitchen, Christian took one look at him, signaled for Jag to come, then the two of them disappeared. Christian returned ten minutes later, having ditched his denim shorts and a Superman T-shirt for his dress-up khakis and a baby blue polo shirt.

Andi didn't comment on the wardrobe change, but she couldn't help thinking about it.

It was happening. Christian was getting attached to Jag *and* Liam. And there was nothing Andi could do about that as long as the Nora Scott threat loomed. The threat that had been complicated by stipulations that Andi had pointedly decided not to tell Liam.

He had enough reasons to help her, and she would talk the legalities over with the lawyer Shane had arranged for her to meet tomorrow. No need to add anything to the weight on Liam's broad shoulders. The future was her problem; he was doing enough to help her in the present.

What she needed to be doing was keeping things easy and light and warm, especially with Christian occupied with Jag and quiet and happy in the backseat of Liam's truck.

"So, Wednesday night dinner is a Kilcannon family tradition, right?" she asked as they turned onto the last road on the way to the massive homestead where he and his siblings had grown up and now worked, with the exception of the youngest brother, Aidan, who was overseas in the military.

"Whoever is in town usually shows up. It's like Sunday dinner, without the drinking."

"I don't remember much drinking at the Sunday dinner you took me to," she said.

He answered with a silent shrug.

"Sorry, didn't get that one," she teased.

"My mother had died less than a year before that," he said. "It took us a while to get the festive back on Sundays."

"Oh." She nodded sympathetically. "Of course. I sometimes forget because your dad seems like such a happy man."

"He's mostly content," he said. "Has a full life, a good business, a lot of family."

"But not happy?" she guessed, reading a little more into the subtext of his words. "I know you said they had a great marriage."

"Went way past great," he said. "Ideal, really."

She heard a note of wistfulness that didn't really surprise her, but made her wonder if it was caused by grieving for his mother or remembering his parents' happy marriage. "Lucky."

"No luck involved," he said simply. "They found each other, knew they were meant to be together forever, and made the most of every minute."

"That's romantic," she mused.

"That's life," he countered.

She tipped her head, frowning. "Not for everyone, Liam."

"I know." He didn't elaborate, but something told her there was a lot of emotion layered into those two words. It wasn't the time to ask and, in fact, might never be. Especially now with the gated entrance to Waterford Farm in sight and a night full of the Kilcannon family swirling about and making decisions for her.

No, she corrected herself. *Helping her keep her son.* Which was all that mattered. Not Liam's distance, not his subtext and indecipherable emotions, not the fact that she'd *thanked him enough.* Just Christian.

"You're going to meet a lot of dogs today," she said, turning around to look at her son, who was sitting with his arm around Jag. The dog sat erect, at attention, and didn't seem to mind the little fingers that somehow made their way into his ears.

"S'okay. I like dogs."

"You'll also meet a lot of people," Liam added.

"Oh, well. I don't like people."

Liam choked a laugh and held a fist over his shoulder for Christian to give him a knuckle tap. "I feel ya, kid."

"Why don't you like people, Liam?" Christian asked with that sweet guilelessness that only a six-year-old could pull off.

"They want to talk. Not big on talking."

Christian's jaw dropped like he'd found his kindred spirit. "Me neither. Do I have to talk to people tonight?"

"Not if you don't want to," Liam said.

"Well, you have to be polite," Andi added.

"How polite?"

They both laughed, but Andi gave him a warning look. "Be polite to everyone you meet."

He squirmed. "Do I have to shake people's hands?"

Liam glanced at Christian in his rearview mirror as he pulled into the long drive that led back to the house and canine training facility. "All you have to do is say hello, thank my dad for dinner, be sure to listen to Gramma Finnie, but her Irish accent is thick and she can be hard to understand. Oh, don't let Shane make you laugh so hard you spit your food out. All that and you're golden."

"But no, you know, long talking with people?"

"Only to the dogs."

"And you," he added, smiling at Liam.

Oh boy. *Oh boy oh boy oh little precious boy*. This male-bonding thing was definitely happening again.

Andi shifted in her seat and fought the urge to tell Liam to stop, but what was she going to say? Stop being so nice to my son? Stop making him like you? Stop making him comfortable and filling a void and being exactly what he needs?

Hadn't he said he wouldn't do those things when he laid out his *guidelines*?

"Look at those dogs!" Christian shot forward so hard his seat belt pulled taut as they turned into the circular drive between the house and the training pen. "What are they doing all lined up like that?"

"Oh, it's graduation for our latest obedience training class," Liam said.

"I graduated from kindergarten last year!" he announced.

"Then you'll love this, Christian," Liam said. "It's one of the highlights of being at Waterford. Shane'll let you give out the diploma-shaped dog bones if we get over there fast enough." He parked the truck and popped open the door, climbing out to help Christian down from the high step.

For a moment, Andi didn't move, a little stunned by all the emotional land mines that littered this landscape. Doggie graduation. Waterford highlights. Family fun.

But Liam grinned at her as if they should bask in the moment of Christian's joy.

"Can I take him to the training area?" Liam asked, obviously sensing her hesitation.

"Yeah, of course." She flipped off her seat belt and her silly concerns. "Let's do that."

"Not you."

She blinked at him, not following.

He pointed over her shoulder toward the house. "Uh, I think the women's welcoming committee is waiting for you for a different kind of event."

She turned to look at the back porch of the huge pale yellow clapboard house with rich green shutters and multiple chimneys. As she'd had the first time she'd seen the home, Andi felt a visceral reaction to the sight of such a grand North Carolina Southern beauty that touched her architect's soul. She never failed to appreciate the asymmetry of the house, which somehow broke a lot of rules but always reminded Andi of a beautiful older woman with just enough flaws to be unique and enough wrinkles to be real.

But she didn't take note of the cantilevered transoms or the wraparound porch today. All she saw were three, four, five—no, *six*—women ranging in age from thirteen to eighty-six, each one holding a champagne flute.

Slowly, she opened the truck door to get a better look.

"Let's go, Andi Rivers," Chloe called, lifting her glass in a mock toast.

"Where are we going?"

Molly took a few steps down, a wide smile

169

beaming, chocolate curls bouncing with each move. "We're planning your wedding, girl."

Andi swallowed, then glanced over her shoulder at Liam, who was taking it all in with, of course, a scowl of utter disapproval or disgust or *dis-something* that revealed how he really felt about this charade. No amusement, no secret pleasure, certainly no happiness.

"We are?" she asked, her voice sounding unsure.

"Dress, music, flowers, attendants, you name it," Molly said, getting closer. "We thought we'd break some bubbly and make a party out of it."

Darcy came, too, in a half run with her blond mane flying and a white ball of puppy fur at her heels. "It's going to be a blast, Andi!" she promised.

A blast.

Kind of like hitting another emotional land mine.

Liam had to stuff disappointment away and focus on Christian. There wasn't time to wallow in the thud of sadness that Andi was going through the motions of planning a wedding without one molecule of whatever it was a bride should feel.

Instead, he urged Christian along, sensing the boy's inner battle between wanting to explode into a run and get in with those dogs and fearing that so many strange people turned and looked at him.

Liam knew what shy felt like. He knew the frustration of not knowing what to say and not wanting to say it even if he did. He knew the burning desire to fade into the background and observe rather than be the center of attention.

With one hand on Christian's shoulder, he led the child to the training area, letting him clutch Jag's leash like a lifeline.

"What grade are they graduating from?" he asked Liam.

"It's not a grade as much as a program. These dogs and their owners come and stay for two weeks to learn advanced obedience training. Some of the people might be trying to become professional dog trainers. Some just want really good dogs." And a vacation at Waterford, but he didn't add that.

They stepped inside the pen, and immediately, Christian tugged Jag to the back, leaning against the fence.

"You can get closer," Liam said gently. "Shane will let you help him hand out diploma treats."

He shook his head solemnly. "I want to watch."

Man, he understood that. Well enough that he'd never push Christian to do what he didn't want to do. Liam knew that life, family, and the love of a few good dogs rounded out those introvert edges eventually, but at six? Let him be shy.

"I know this young man." Dad's voice came from behind them, just as Shane was announcing a border collie named Bonnie who'd won Best Fetcher.

As Dad reached them, Christian turned slowly, looking up at Liam's tall father.

"Welcome to Waterford, Christian," Dad said, tousling the boy's hair. "I hear you and Jag are best friends."

"Yeah. I mean, yes, sir."

Dad smiled at the added title. "He can stay next to you at dinner, I promise. Would you like that?"

"Really?" Christian lit up, not realizing he'd already fallen under the Dogfather's spell. "I'd love that. Right, Jag?"

Jag nudged Dad with his nose, proving that neither man nor beast was immune to the older man's charms.

"You want to stay out here for a few minutes while I take Liam into the house?" Dad asked Christian.

"I think I should stick around with him, Dad," Liam said quickly, putting a hand on Christian's shoulder. "Until he gets used to things. Or bring him in with us if you want to talk."

"I do need to talk to you, Liam," Dad said. "It's important, but—"

"I'm used to things." Christian looked up at Liam, all blue-eyed sincerity. "I have Jag. We can stay and watch. I won't move, I promise."

Liam considered that, knowing the kid needed a little freedom and that he couldn't have been safer if he'd been locked in a tower. "Okay," Liam agreed, but signaled Garrett from across the pen. "If you need anything, you ask my brother Garrett."

"I have Jag," he repeated.

"Jag won't take you to the bathroom if you need to go." Liam leaned down. "But you can take him."

Christian giggled a little, and when Garrett came over and took a handoff, Liam went with his dad to talk business.

"I know I've been out of pocket," Liam said as they crossed the grass and headed to the house, already sensing what this was about. "You don't need to go off hunting for another K-9 trainer, Dad. I was able to work with Fritz and Zelda."

"This isn't about Fritz and Zelda," his father said

when they stepped into the kitchen, immediately getting a whiff of something delicious.

Crystal, the housekeeper who'd worked for the family for at least the last ten years, turned from the sink to give him a warm greeting. "Hello, Liam," she called, waving a wooden spoon. "Made your favorite pot roast tonight."

"I smell it, Crystal, thank you."

"Big night tonight, right?"

He glanced at her. Was it? "Wednesday night dinner?" She didn't live in the house and didn't usually cook dinners during the week since Dad, Darcy, and Gramma were the only actual residents here and they could fend for dinners. But Crystal always cooked on Wednesday nights when the Kilcannons who didn't live here anymore came to eat, so this didn't seem like that big a deal, right?

"Weddings and engagements and little children at the table," she said in a singsong voice, her bottle-green eyes sparkling and white-haired head bobbing side to side.

"Uh, yeah." He threw a look at Dad, who seemed impatient to get back to his office at the opposite side of the house.

Liam followed, and on the way, they passed Dad's setter, Rusty, who was curled under the dining room table as if he was staking out his place before they all sat down to eat. But Dad turned at the wide staircase and headed up to the second floor, and instantly, Rusty got up and followed as if he sniffed something more important going on.

Which it very well might be.

"So, what's up, Dad?" Liam couldn't remember

the last time he'd been upstairs in this house. He'd long ago given up his childhood bedroom as a guest room, and with his own house situated between here and town, he had no other reason to visit the sprawling second-story where all the Kilcannons had slept as kids.

"Come into my room." Dad walked down the hall to the double doors at the end, heading into a master suite his parents had added above the family room a short time after Liam had joined the Marines. He honestly couldn't remember being in this room more than five times in his life.

He knew that it had been his parents' sanctuary and off-limits without an invitation. After Mom died, he doubted anyone went in here except Crystal to clean.

"Come on in," Dad said, gesturing Liam farther into a room that was surprisingly cozy and comforting. Liam braced himself for something that might hit a memory nerve, like the soft powdery smell he associated with his mother, or a picture capturing a moment of happiness.

He doubted the room had changed much in the way of décor since she died, but it somehow now had a distinctly masculine feel to it. Across from a king-size four-poster was a wood-burning fireplace and a small seating area around a coffee table. The newspaper was folded on that table, and Dad's slippers were under a chair. It was a lived-in room, relaxed, and still someone's sanctuary.

Rusty jumped up on the sofa and got into a spot Liam suspected he'd long ago claimed as his, and Dad gestured for Liam to take the chair.

But he didn't, shaking his head. "What is going

174

on?" he asked, anxious to get back to Christian and not at all interested in some discussion about a new trainer because he needed backup. He didn't need—

"I want to give you something. In private."

Curious, Liam stayed silent, spinning through possibilities as his father walked to a mahogany-toned dresser and opened the top drawer. He reached in and took something out that was so small, Liam couldn't tell what it was.

"Sit down, Son," his father said with that slight edge of authority Liam knew so well. "You're going to want to for this."

This time, he followed the order, barely perching on the edge of a chair and glancing at Rusty as if maybe he knew the mystery to be solved. Dad turned around slowly, his gaze on whatever was in his hand. When he looked up at Liam, his eyes were misted over.

"Dad." He started to stand, but his father held out a hand to stop him.

"I gave this a lot of thought," he said slowly. "I think, of all the kids, she'd want you to have this. I thought maybe Molly, but no, this is right. Especially since you're getting married in this house, just like we did, when we were expecting you."

And then he knew exactly what Dad was holding.

Taking a few steps closer, Dad finally sat down next to Rusty and held out his hand, palm up, showing Liam the simple diamond ring.

But Liam didn't need to look at it. He'd seen it a thousand times on his mother's long, lean fingers—a square diamond set in gold, a humble engagement ring that rested next to a wedding band that he knew she'd worn to the grave. Dad had kept this ring, though, one that was perfect for a woman who put everyone else before herself.

Liam swallowed, knowing full well where this train was headed and wanting like hell to jump the tracks. But nearly forty years as Daniel Kilcannon's firstborn son taught Liam to not say a word until his father said his piece. Then he'd tell him how wrong this idea was.

"When I gave this to your mother, we were half the age you are now, Son. And you were already growing in her belly." He looked down at the ring, taking it between his thumb and index finger. "And, good Lord, were we terrified, kind of like you are now."

He wasn't terrified at all. Except about the end. Still, Liam didn't argue.

"I was headed to vet school, she was in college, and you were..." He chuckled softly. "Well, that was before we discovered that all I had to do was walk past Annie's underwear drawer and she'd get pregnant." He thought for a moment as the smile faded, then looked up. "What I'm trying to say is our marriage wasn't planned, either."

This isn't a marriage. But he stared at Dad, silent.

"And it took place right at the bottom of those big stairs, like yours will. Surrounded by people who might doubt it will last, but hope for the best."

That did it. "C'mon, Dad," Liam interjected gruffly. "This isn't ever going to be the marriage yours and Mom's was, okay? I'm not taking that ring. I'm not giving it to Andi, and we're not going to sit here and pretend what we're doing is anything other than a way to protect Christian and help Andi." He pushed up. "End of—"

"Sit down."

Of course, he did. Slowly, and only because his father deserved utter and total respect, not because he was going to participate in this *sham*.

"I know you don't think this marriage has a snowball's chance of being real."

"That's where you'd be wrong," Liam said.

His father started to respond as if Liam hadn't spoken, then stopped. "I would?" The hope in his voice was just this side of heartbreaking.

"If it were up to me, it would be," Liam said simply. "I would have married her three years ago, or at least tried to get us to that point."

It was Dad's turn to stare, then nod slowly. "I suspected that."

"Considering this is me we're talking about, it's surprising to know I did a pretty crappy job of hiding my feelings. Usually my strong suit."

"You don't hide your feelings, Liam. I could read them from the day you were born. You don't vomit them out and expect the world to care. Big difference."

He shrugged. "Yeah, well, maybe I should have told her when I had the chance, but it's too late now. She's dead set against this, wants Christian to be the only focus of her life, and would like us to be as *superficial* as possible."

"Exactly like your mother."

Liam snorted. "Dad, nothing about this relationship, if I can even call it that, is like you and Mom. How can I make you understand that? Believe me, I wish it was. All I've ever wanted when it comes to women was to replicate that. You set the bar so damn high, no one can reach it, despite your meddling and pushing."

He hinted at a smile. "The whole family's meddling and pushing on this one."

"You know what I mean."

"Son, listen to me." He leaned forward, planted his elbows on his knees, and pinned his blue gaze on Liam. "Your mother did not want to marry me."

Liam almost laughed, the statement was so ridiculous.

"She, too, was dead set against it and only agreed to walk down those stairs because we conceived you and it was 1977 and marriage was the only viable option in our world. Like Andi with Christian, you were the focus of your mother's life, even before you were born. Like Andi, she knew marrying me was a way to protect her child. And if by 'superficial,' you mean she'd like to keep it physical and not emotional?" He angled his head. "Another similarity. In fact, I'm pretty sure Mom was in it for the sex at first."

Liam's jaw unhinged.

"Every time the soundtrack to *Saturday Night Fever* played, well…" He laughed. "You might have been conceived to the Bee Gees."

Liam dropped his head in his hands, not sure whether to laugh or cry at a revelation he could have lived his whole life without knowing.

"Liam. Look at me."

When he did, his father stood up, walked to him, then crouched to get eye to eye, much like Liam did with Christian when he really wanted to make a point. He held out the ring, offering it to Liam.

"I gave this to her a few days before we were married, one night on the back porch of this house. She got teary and told me that this wasn't the way she'd always dreamed of getting married. Pregnant, poor, having to move in with Gramma and Grandpa, and her parents wouldn't even come because they were so mad at her."

Liam searched his dad's face, familiar with the story, but seeing it in a completely different light. "What changed her mind?" he asked.

"Time. Love. Patience. Some inside jokes and plenty of time in bed together. By the time you came along, we were *us*. Daniel and Annie. Mom and Dad. The thing…"

"The thing I've always wanted." Liam's admission came out rough. "But I never told anyone, especially not Andi, because wanting that seems…"

"Weak?" Dad suggested.

He nodded slowly. "Exactly. Aren't we men supposed to be, I don't know, above that kind of longing?"

"Well, that's where you'd be wrong, Son. Wanting that, building that, making a love that lasts a lifetime takes the strongest man you can possibly be. There's nothing weak about that kind of man or that kind of marriage. Nothing at all."

Liam's chest ached with a pressure he didn't understand, like someone was squeezing his heart and trying to get out every drop of whatever was in it. He looked down at the ring, a tiny little thing without any of the glitz or glamour of the ones his brothers had given their fiancées.

But this ring had resided for thirty-six years on the finger of a woman who understood the power of love and family. A woman who might not have wanted it at first, but wore it like it was the Hope Diamond.

And, in a way, it was.

"I guess she should have a ring if people are going to believe this."

Dad's mouth curled up in a wry smile. "That's one reason to take it."

Liam looked at him. "And maybe it will fit so well, she'll keep it."

"That's another."

Liam closed his eyes, took the ring, and stood, slipping it into his pocket.

"I thought you might give it to her at dinner, in front of everyone," Dad said as he pushed himself up.

"Oh, really? You thought wrong. I'll do it my way." He put a hand on his father's shoulder, always amazed at how sturdy and strong he was. Inside and out. "Thanks, Dad."

"Hey, thank *you* for not accusing me of being the Dogfather by pulling strings and trying to make you do things because I think they're best for you."

Liam smiled. "Oh, you are. It's just that sometimes you're right."

At least, he hoped so.

Chapter Fourteen

Andi looked from one beautiful face to the next, that feeling of being pulled into the vortex of a rogue wave of Kilcannons threatening again. But it was different this evening, up here on the third floor that was probably designed as an attic but had been revamped into a small suite for Gramma Finnie.

The ceilings were low, not that it mattered for the tiny woman. The décor was vintage chic with a distinctively genuine feel to it. The windows were covered with lace, the hardwood floors with braided rugs and a few dog beds. The only thing that wasn't classic grandmother's cottage was the corner desk that held an open laptop, a hand-painted sign that said, *Life is short, blog unconditionally,* and a framed newspaper article with the headline Local Grandmother Writes One of North Carolina's Top Ten Blogs.

But there was no chance to ask Gramma Finnie about her writing, because the entourage had taken Andi into a sitting room, planted her in the middle of a settee as old as the woman who owned it, put champagne in her hand, and circled her.

So no, this wasn't the tsunami she'd first felt in this house. This was more like a lifeboat of ladies determined to keep her afloat.

The youngest one, Molly's daughter, Prudence, sat right down on the floor at Andi's feet and opened a large notebook. "I'm in charge of the customs and requirements, and my research tells me that old, new, borrowed, and blue is the most important of all, followed by the throwing of the bouquet."

Andi stared at her, not even sure how to respond to that, except that the social niceties of a wedding were the last thing on her mind.

"Don't worry about Pru knowing the truth," Molly said quickly, obviously misreading Andi's expression. "She's a hundred percent trustworthy, and we need her to keep us on the straight and narrow."

Pru's grin revealed impressive orthodontic hardware with neon green bands to hold it all together. "That's kind of my role in this family, so I gave each of your team a job. Aunt Darcy is in charge of the décor and setup, including music, so you can work with her to decide where and when you want to walk in and what song should play."

"Song?"

"Whatever song is yours and Liam's."

Andi angled her head. "We don't have a song."

"We'll get you one." Darcy's eyes, that deep Kilcannon blue that so many of them got from their father, glinting playfully. "I have a whole list of possibilities, like *I've Had the Time of My Life*."

"Gross," Pru murmured.

"Okay, maybe something more modern, like John Legend's *All of Me*."

Gramma Finnie choked. "This is Liam, Darcy."

"Seriously," Molly chimed in.

"Okay, we'll go with *Who Let the Dogs Out*," Darcy exclaimed, cracking them all up.

Pru swiped her hand through the air, gesturing for quiet. "You two can work it out after we get through the assignments. Moving on. Jessie is in charge of getting the right officiate. She's already talking to Pastor Blake from Southside Presbyterian for her wedding to Garrett, so if you go nonsecular, she'll help you."

"Nonsecular?" Andi whispered, having given exactly zero thought to the actual ceremony, religious or not.

"Oh, I know, lass," Gramma Finnie said on a sigh, patting her hand. "It's shocking to think about anything but a Catholic wedding in this family, but sadly, our church has such rules. A priest can't marry you outside a church, and our faith requires marriage classes." She leaned in. "And there is the issue of the eventual annulment, which we Catholics do try to avoid handing out like communion wafers."

Andi gave a weak smile to Chloe. "Couldn't your aunt do it?" Mayor Blanche Wilkins would be so much less...holy.

"I can ask her," Chloe said.

"Of course, it's up to you, lass," Finnie said, her soft Irish lilt more like music than words. "And since Father John will be here, maybe he'll whisper a wee prayer over you."

"A wee one," she said softly as Pru cleared her throat and powered on.

"Next up is the wedding party. If all of us got

involved, it would be overwhelming, so we think one attendant, and Chloe volunteered to be maid of honor."

Andi blinked at her friend. "That makes sense since I'm going to be yours."

"Yes!" Chloe leaned over to take her other hand. "Actually, by the time Shane and I get married in the spring, you'll be matron of honor, which has a horribly archaic ring to it."

Next spring? This marriage would be annulled, and she might very well be living in Charlottesville with Christian...unless she lost him to a legal guardian. The thought was sobering, so she lifted her glass in a toast. "You are the perfect choice, Chloe." And took a deep slug of champagne.

"Then come the vows," Pru said.

"And I'll be writing those." Gramma gave her hand a solid squeeze.

"Expect Irish proverbs," Molly joked. "A lot of them."

Gramma lifted a narrow shoulder draped in a bright pink cardigan. "Some, yes. But I can make it more modern for you, if you like. I've already asked my Twitter followers to send me their favorite wedding vows and have so many of ideas."

"Twitter? That'll keep them short," Andi said on a dry laugh, trying to wrap her head around the fact that her wedding vows would be written by an octogenarian social media maven who got her script from the Internet.

"And last—"

"But most important," Molly interjected.

"The wedding dress."

"Oh no." Andi shook her head, rooting around for a grip on reality since these lovely ladies had lost it. "I'm not wearing a wedding dress. I'm not wearing white. I'm not..." She took a breath and exhaled slowly. "Getting married."

"You're not?"

"You changed your mind?"

"What about Christian?"

"Does Liam know?"

"What happened?"

Okay, now it *was* a tidal wave. She set her champagne flute down and held up both hands, closing her eyes to gather her wits. "I am still going through with a marriage for the sake of establishing that my life is stable and Christian is secure. I do believe it's the best way to fend off Nora Scott before we even have to have any courtroom drama. But, guys..." She looked from one to the next. "Thank you so much for all this planning and worry and...and sisterly love. But it isn't a wedding. Not like you want."

"Not like *you* want," Gramma Finnie said softly. "But it isn't for you, it's for Christian. And if you don't at least put on a show that has some semblance of a real wedding, no one will buy it. People will talk. Talk will get to Nora. You'll lose your child."

Andi opened her mouth to argue, then shut it again, looking directly into the old woman's eyes.

"All we're trying to do is help in that regard, lass," she added. "We do things the Kilcannon way, which might be a bit much for some, but—"

"No, no, you're right," Andi said, guilt squeezing her chest. "I'm being completely ungrateful. You're so right."

"And you're so scared." Gramma Finnie wrapped both her parchment-soft hands around one of Andi's, lifting their joined hands between them. "But that's why you have a big family to take care of the details. All you need to do is show up, say 'I do'—or whatever I write for you, and I promise it won't be too mushy—and make sure every single person in the room and in town believes in this marriage."

"Except...Liam."

Gramma Finnie raised a brow, then glanced at Molly. Who looked at Darcy. Who bit her lip and fought a smile. Pru busied herself with the notebook.

Andi looked from one to the other, frowning at the weird response. "Trust me, the whole thing is distasteful to him."

Chloe tipped her head and gave her a *get real* look.

"It is, Chloe," she insisted. "You know that."

"What I know is that Shane calls you Liam's kryptonite."

Andi stared at her, letting that sink in. "His..."

"I don't get it," Pru said. "Kryptonite paralyzes Superman."

"Kryptonite is his weakness," Molly supplied, giving Andi a smile. "We all have one."

Andi tried to respond, but nothing came out. Molly clapped, breaking the awkward moment. "So, have you given any thought to the dress?"

"No," Andi admitted. "I suppose I have something in my closet. I have a pretty yellow sundress I wore to a wedding last year, or maybe a cool linen pantsuit."

"*Pantsuit*?" Gramma Finnie barked the question as if Andi had suggested wearing a burlap sack.

"We can go shopping," Molly said. "We have two days."

Shopping for a wedding dress? "I don't..." Andi shook her head. "I'll just wear something I have."

"It has to be at least a little wedding-ish," Pru said. "Or no one's going to believe you."

"People will ask why the rush," Darcy said. "And assumptions will be made."

"I don't care as long as they believe it's real," Andi replied.

Chloe leaned forward. "Then you better *look* real."

Andi nodded, knowing they were all right. "Okay, well, obviously I can't get a wedding dress, so I guess I can try and find something that is appropriate for a fast wedding at someone's house that will be a surprise to almost everyone in attendance."

"Well, that wouldn't be a first here at Waterford Farm," Gramma Finnie said, raising a meaningful brow. "And Liam was at that wedding, too, in a sense."

"When Mom and Dad got married," Darcy explained, reading Andi's confused look. "It was super shotgun, and Liam was born six months later."

"It was not 'super shotgun,'" Gramma Finnie fired back. "It was lovely. I put the whole thing together with a week's notice since they were so scared to tell me until I figured it out on my own. Annie's parents wouldn't even come, so we..." She gave a wistful sigh. "We made it nice."

Andi tried to imagine Daniel Kilcannon and his pregnant wife getting married downstairs in this house, scared twenty-year-olds, uncertain about the future.

"They had the best marriage," Darcy said with a crack in her voice.

Molly smiled and leaned closer to Andi. "We put her dress in Gramma Finnie's bedroom on the off chance you might want to think about wearing it," she whispered. "Do you want to see it?"

Andi looked into Molly's sweet hazel eyes, holding her gaze as she searched her heart for a truthful answer. Talk about an emotional land mine—the dress worn by their dearly beloved mother, coming down the same steps for a second time, once again part of an unconventional marriage.

"It'll be a little big on you," Molly said. "But Pru can sew."

Pru got up on her knees, joining them. "I brought my pins and sewing kit."

"Of course you did." Andi's heart slid around in her chest, hitting her ribs so hard it might have cracked a few. "Okay, then," she said softly, looking from one dear woman to the next and finally landing on Gramma Finnie's blue eyes. "It would be an honor to wear Annie's dress."

"Well, wait," the old woman said, pushing herself up. "You haven't seen it yet."

"It's kind of seventies," Darcy warned.

"But I can take the shoulder pads out," Pru said, getting up when Molly did, both of them pulling Andi with them.

"And I hope those hideous ruffles come off the sleeves," Darcy added.

"Yes, but you have to keep the blue ribbon," Pru told her as they all swept Andi into the next room. "Then the dress meets three requirements—old, borrowed, and blue."

"All you need is something new," Jessie said as

they headed into Gramma Finnie's bedroom en masse.

But right then, everything was new. This family, this warmth, this giddy excitement over a marriage that shouldn't be happening. It was all new, and Andi finally decided to quit fighting it and ride the Kilcannon tidal wave, hoping she didn't drown.

Chapter Fifteen

Christian fell asleep so quickly after they left Waterford Farm at nine that night, that Liam looked into the rearview mirror three times to check on him before they hit the main road. Jag draped himself along the backseat of Liam's truck, his head on Christian's lap.

"Pretty sure Jag belongs to him now," he said, softly enough to make sure he didn't wake Christian.

"Might be time to teach him the secret code word."

"Shhh." He put his hand on her arm, as much for the warm contact than to quiet her. "You want him to wake up and start demanding to know it?"

She laughed. "What are you waiting for?"

"The right time." He turned onto the main highway that led to town. "Everything has to be done at the right time."

Everything. Like giving her his mother's ring.

It shouldn't matter so much, Liam told himself for the twentieth time since he'd accepted the diamond ring from his father. All through dinner, he thought about what would be the right time, and while he did, each moment slipped into the next. There was a lot of laughter, teasing, talk, and even a few quiet moments, but not *the* moment.

Not that it was a real proposal—he'd already handled that with about as much flare as a wet match. Not that it was a real engagement ring—she'd certainly give it back, and Dad could give it to Molly as a keepsake, which made a hell of a lot more sense. And not that it was a real relationship that would end up with them all over each other in celebration of the moment—he'd already decided never to try that move again.

But the night wore on, and the ring in his pocket got heavier and heavier.

He heard Andi sigh and glanced to his right, catching her eyes slowly close as she dropped her head back.

"Tired?"

"Overwhelmed."

He laughed. "My family can do that to the strongest of guests."

"I wasn't a guest." She picked her head up and turned to him. "Neither was Christian. It was amazing, really, how comfortable they made me feel. How much a part of the…" Her voice drifted off. "You have a great family, Liam."

"I know I do." He pulled up behind a slower car on the two-lane highway, automatically checking for oncoming traffic so he could pass, then remembered Christian and laid off the accelerator. "Must seem different from yours, huh?"

She laughed. "My family are like people from a different planet compared to yours. Don't get me wrong, I love my parents, but…"

"But they don't even know what you're going through right now, do they?"

She gave a little moan as if she just remembered that fact. "No, they don't. I don't bring them into my day-to-day life. Not because of any bad feelings, but we're not designed that way. They've always treated me like an equal, not a kid. I mean, they love Christian and only want the best for him, but I don't lean on them, if you know what I mean."

"There's leaning and there's sharing. Don't you think you should give them a heads-up that you're getting married on Saturday?"

"I'm not really getting married on Saturday, Liam."

He flinched. When the hell would he stop walking into that same trap? "No chance some investigator that Nora hires would talk to them and find out they have no idea their daughter is getting married?"

"Oh, I never thought of that," she admitted. "I'll call them tomorrow after I talk to the lawyer Shane has coming to town."

"Do you want me to go with you to that meeting?"

"Oh, that would be…" She caught herself. "Not necessary."

He heard it. Heard the desire to say yes, then the instant backing away. As if she would do anything to keep herself from getting any closer to him. Refusing to be gutted by that, he closed his damn mouth and drove the rest of the way home in silence.

If the quiet bothered her, she didn't say, but he noticed her staring out the window into the blackness of night all the way back to town and around the square until they reached her house, pulled up, and saw the woman sitting on her stairs.

"Oh my God," she whispered, grabbing his arm. "It's her, Liam. It's Nora Scott."

Jag was up before Liam took his next breath, instantly sensing the tension in the car. Christian stayed sound asleep.

"What do we do?" Andi asked, a low-grade panic in her voice. "I don't want her to talk to Christian. I don't want her to scare him or for him to say anything."

In less than a second, Liam flipped through all the options and came up with a plan, parking directly in front of the stairs. "Jag stays in the car with Christian. You and I get out and talk to her, get rid of her, then you go inside, and I'll bring Jag and carry Christian in."

"I don't want to talk to her."

"You should," he said. "You're with me, your fiancé, and you are living your normal life taking full care of your son and being a loving, caring mother who spent the evening with a big, happy family. Show her what she's up against, Andi."

"Yes, okay." She nodded a few times as if getting used to the idea. "You're right."

She grabbed her door and started to open it, but he found her other hand in the dark and held her back. "Hang on, hang on."

She looked at him, a mix of terror and determination darkening her eyes as her gaze darted from him to the steps less than twenty feet away where the woman stayed seated, staring into the truck. "I want to get this over with."

And so did he. "Here." He shifted in his seat, reaching into his pocket, and pulled out the ring, glancing at the woman on the stairs who was pushing up to a stand.

"What?"

"Some hardware to support your case." Keeping her hand low so Nora couldn't see, he slipped the ring on her left hand effortlessly. "It was my mom's."

Andi gasped as she realized what he was doing. "Your mother's ring?"

"Shhh." He put his hand behind her head and pulled her closer. "She's watching."

Inches from him, close enough that he could hear her quick pants as her breath tightened with anxiety. "Liam, I'm scared of her."

"Don't be. I won't let her hurt you, and I won't let her get near Christian."

Jag barked and stared at the woman, adding his low, menacing growl.

"Neither will he," she said on a nervous laugh.

Liam turned to the dog. "*Achtung*!" Jag's ears perked even higher and his dark eyes darted from side to side, ready to do what he was trained to do. "You wait here," he said to Andi. "I'll come around and get your door."

She nodded and he got out, eyeing the woman silently as she stood bathed in the truck's headlights he'd purposely left on. He slowly walked in front of his truck, then opened Andi's door, but kept his gaze on Jag. He knew something was up, and Liam was certain they'd gotten to the point where Jag would do serious damage to anyone who even remotely threatened Christian.

With one arm around Andi and his free hand on the truck door handle, they turned in perfect unison and faced the visitor.

"Can we help you?" Liam asked.

She took one step closer, her gaze moving back and forth. "I want to talk to Christian," she said. "He's my nephew."

"He's asleep," Liam said.

"You can't keep him from meeting me," she said harshly, directing the statement to Andi.

"You can meet him," Andi said. "When he's not asleep, when it's daytime and perfectly safe, and when—"

"You think I would hurt him?"

"We don't know what you would do," Liam answered. "But now is not the time. Andi's going inside, and you're leaving."

The woman took a step closer, and Jag barked, his noisy warning easy to hear even through the closed windows of the truck.

"You saw the lawyer?" Nora asked.

Andi stiffened, but didn't answer.

"You know the stipulations on that will?" Nora demanded.

"I do," Andi said. "They're none of your business."

"They're all my business," she shot back. "You don't want to agree to any of that, Andi."

Agree to what? Liam frowned, not recalling any "stipulations" but certainly not wanting this conversation to go on one minute longer than necessary.

"You don't want to move to Charlottesville," Nora said, taking another step.

Charlottesville? What was she talking about? "You get one inch closer to her and you're going to meet our dog," Liam said.

She sniffed in a gasp, her eyes widening. "Who *are* you?"

195

"He's the man I'm about to marry," Andi said, getting a quick flicker of disbelief in the woman's dark eyes. Andi lifted her left hand. "On Saturday."

Even in the washed-out light from the Ford's headlights, Liam could see blood drain from Nora Scott's sharply angled cheekbones. "How convenient," she muttered. "Last week, you weren't—"

Liam clicked the door handle, making Jag bark.

"You wouldn't," the woman said.

He stared at her, silence so much more effective than a warning.

She took a few slow breaths, then shifted her attention back to Andi. "You don't have to do this," she said. "You don't have to agree to anything, change his name, or accept her requirements. Just sign the trust over to me, the rightful heir, and I'll leave you alone. Just settle this now, Andi."

Liam opened the door one inch, and Jag stuck his snout in the opening, his full weight pushing hard, but Liam resisted. His growl was enough to make Nora back away and shoot him a vile look.

This time, Andi took a step forward. "Here's my settlement: Get the hell away from my son, my house, and my life."

Nora snorted softly. "So you want the money more than you want your kid?"

"I don't care about money. Just leave me alone!"

"Do as she asks or I let this dog free," Liam ground out.

"You wouldn't."

Probably not, he agreed silently, since she hadn't threatened physical harm. But Jag's very presence should be enough to scare her off.

After a moment of a silent stand-off, Nora pivoted and darted down the street into the shadows.

"Get your keys out," Liam ordered Andi, who instantly pulled them from a clip on the side of her purse. "Go in the house, close the door but don't lock it."

She followed that order, and only then did Liam open the back door. Jag bolted with pent-up protective energy, barking loudly until Liam commanded him to stay. Then he noticed that Christian's eyes were open, but the child was too sleepy to really understand what was going on.

He reached over to unlatch Christian's seat belt. "Climb out and let me carry you into the house."

He scrambled across the seat without argument, wrapping his arms and legs around Liam. Scooping him up, Liam ordered Jag to follow and got all three of them up the stairs and into the house in a matter of seconds, without Christian having any sense that anything was wrong.

Inside, he transferred Christian into Andi's arms, who took him and pressed his head against her shoulder, looking up at Liam.

"She's gone?" she mouthed.

"Let me turn the truck's lights off." Back outside, he saw no sign of a woman who he really didn't think was a physical threat, but couldn't be sure. After locking up the truck, he went back inside, where Andi hadn't moved.

"He's asleep again," she said softly.

"Good. Let's get him to bed. Jag's on duty now." In fact, he was already charging into the kitchen, sniffing, growling, barking at the back door, then trotting around the first floor, trying to lope off all the frustration of not being able to respond in a tense situation.

Liam took Christian from her and scooted his small frame higher so he had a shoulder for his head. Then, Andi led the way up the stairs and pulled the covers back on his bed for Liam to lay him down.

"Guess we skip brushing teeth tonight," she mused.

"Extenuating circumstances."

"He didn't know anything was going on."

"Then we succeeded." Liam stepped back and let Andi tuck her son in, exhaling out a breath as all sense of impending danger disappeared.

She leaned over to kiss the sleeping boy, her hair falling and covering her face. "Good night, my little love. You're home and safe and mine."

The words squeezed his heart and made Liam more certain than ever that whatever his role was in keeping Christian home and safe and with Andi, he'd do it. No matter how much it hurt.

She stood then and turned, surprising Liam as she slid her arms around his waist and pulled him hard into her. "I don't know what I'd do without you," she muttered, pressing her face into his shoulder. "Thank you."

"You don't have to—"

"Shut up," she said, her voice rough. "Don't tell me that anymore." She lifted her head to meet his gaze. "I want to thank you. I want to..." She stood on her toes and slid her hands up to cup his jaw and hold his face. "Christian's asleep."

And he knew exactly what that meant. "Our very own secret code words," he murmured.

"Yeah."

He wrapped his arms around her and guided her out to the dark hallway, closing the door behind them. Then he leaned her up against the wall, lowered his head, and quit fighting what he wanted more than his next breath.

Maybe it was the roller coaster of adrenaline she'd just ridden. Or the way Liam had taken over and protected them so effortlessly. Damn, maybe it was the fact that he'd slid his mother's engagement ring on her finger in a dark car, showing a willingness to go to any length to help her.

Andi would find a list of rationales for this kiss, but the truth would never change.

She *wanted* him. And she was so damn tired of not having him.

Complicated and messy as sex might be, she didn't care about anything but the sweet taste of Liam's mouth and the tease of his tongue and the touch of his hands getting more and more familiar with her body.

Heat coursed through her, making her nerve endings sing and her hips rock against the hard ridge of a very aroused man. It was flat-out *glorious*.

She moaned as sensations sparked in her body, and they broke the kiss but not full-body contact. He had her firmly against the wall as his hands moved from her waist and hips over her breasts, and his lips left a trail of kisses over her throat and under her jaw.

"Liam." She tunneled her fingers into his silky

dark hair, gripping his head to press his mouth even harder against her skin.

He answered with a groan that came from deep inside his chest, the sound of resignation and desire and maybe a plea for no talking, only kissing.

Taking control of her mouth again, he plunged his tongue against hers, sliding his hands under her arms to raise them and pin her helplessly against the wall as he kissed her and let their hips roll against each other, building the heat to a frenzy.

"This isn't going to stop," she managed to say when getting her breath.

"Not unless you want it to." He found a sweet spot on her neck, driving her crazy as he flicked his tongue and suckled lightly. "I can stop anytime."

"I can't," she admitted.

He stilled for a second, very slowly lifting his head to look at her. "Can't or won't?"

She didn't know how to answer. "I don't want to stop." She pressed a palm against his jaw, feeling the brush of whiskers and a pounding pulse. "I know I should, but I'm not strong enough. I want to sleep with you." She mouthed the plea, only air and desperation instead of voice. "I want to have sex with you."

"And you're afraid I want to make love."

"Isn't it just semantics?"

His eyes closed a little as his body moved like it had a will of its own, rocking against her, hard and mighty. "I don't care what you call it, Andi. Make the rules. Set the boundaries. Give it whatever name you want, but..." He used his whole body to press her against the wall. "Let me have you."

"Yes," she whispered. "Yes."

It was all he needed. In one easy move, he inched back, bent over, and scooped her in his arms, stealing her breath. Holding her as if she weighed no more than a cloud, he marched up to the next level, turned into her darkened bedroom, and walked her to the bed. There, he laid her down carefully, the only sounds their unsteady, rough breaths.

And somewhere downstairs, the soft padding feet of a protective dog.

She blinked as her eyes adjusted to the muted stream of light that spilled in from the hall, enough to find his face and see his expression as he leaned over her.

"What'd you decide to call it?" he asked softly.

"Why do you need to know?"

"Because it will tell me how you want to undress. Fast and desperate or slow and sweet."

Oh, she wanted slow and sweet. She wanted achingly slow and insanely sweet. She wanted the undressing to take as long as humanly possible and wanted to allow him to touch and explore every inch of her before he entered her.

But then it would mean too much to him. And her.

"Fast and desperate." She yanked at his shirt, pulling it up his back like she couldn't stand for it to be on for one more second.

He obliged, pulling it off and tossing it to the floor.

"And these." With shaking fingers, she unbuttoned his fly and unzipped his khakis, dying to get her hands on him.

He helped in that regard, too, he got out of his clothes in a smooth move that left him in nothing but boxer briefs on her bed.

"My turn," he said, brushing her hair off her face and spreading it on the pillow under her head. "And I want slow and sweet."

Her heart folded in half as he reached for the bottom of her short cotton top. Very, very slowly, he drew it up, taking his time to reveal her body inch by inch.

"I thought you'd want fast."

"You thought wrong. I've waited too damn long to rush things."

Liam's kryptonite.

Chloe's words floated in Andi's head as she closed her eyes and gave in to his measured moves. He took off her top and laid it to the side of the bed. He grazed his fingers over the rise of her breasts, following the lace outline of her bra, for what seemed like a good long minute. A *very* good long minute.

With each passing second, her heart rate ratcheted higher and her breathing became more labored, and her poor lower half turned to a pool of liquid. Finally, he unhooked her bra and drew the straps slowly down her arms, his fingers caressing her skin as the bra came off.

His breath hitched as he looked at her bare breasts, and he let out a soft grunt when his lips took his first kiss.

She was immediately lost, moving and moaning and clutching and cooing as his mouth traveled south.

With more maddeningly deliberate hands, he took off her linen slacks and passed what seemed like an hour slipping her panties lower and lower and finally, finally touching her most private place with more reverence than anything she'd ever felt in her life.

"You're killing me," she murmured when she wanted to scream for more.

"I'm loving you," he corrected, kissing her mouth before she could argue and taking her whole body to a place where she didn't care at all what they called this, she just wanted more.

She could hear the low rumble from his chest as he—

He shot straight up, ripping his mouth from hers.

"What?" she asked.

He quieted her with a quick shake of his head, and then she could hear that it was Jag's low, angry, threatening growl that rumbled from the first floor. Liam narrowed his eyes, his whole body frozen as he listened, and suddenly, Jag barked. Loud, sharp, furious. And pawed at something.

"The back door?" Liam muttered, rolling away from her in one move, wearing nothing but his boxer briefs. "Stay here."

With that, he charged downstairs, the sound of his footsteps on the stairs drowned out by a wild frenzy of barking that would wake the dead. Certainly Christian. Without letting herself think about what was just interrupted, Andi jumped out of the bed, her son her only concern. She grabbed a robe hanging over a chair from that morning's shower and wrapped it around a body still vibrating with need.

But her pulse was kicking for a completely different reason as she listened to Jag's bark change in a way that made her guess Liam had him on the back patio. Why? Standing on the second-floor landing, she closed her eyes to listen, but Christian's door popped open and he stepped out.

"What's wrong with Jag, Mommy?"

Instantly, she circled him in a hug and stepped him back into his room. "I don't know. Liam is checking on why he's barking."

"He misses me at night," Christian said, wiping his eyes. "But he has to work."

He sure was working now. Her heart still thumping, she led Christian back to bed. Was Nora trying to break in?

"Time to get back to sleep, honey," Andi said, trying to stay calm and cool and not let Christian sense any tension.

"I can't sleep without Jag."

"Of course you can," she assured him, noticing that the barking had slowed, but not stopped. "You know he's doing his important job at night, making sure we're safe."

"Why wouldn't we be safe?" His voice cracked, along with Andi's heart.

"We're completely safe."

"We might die." The pitch rose to a precry she recognized so well.

Andi folded her arms around him, rubbing his back, sliding him under the covers.

"I'm scared to die, Mommy."

"Christian, you're not going to die. You're going to sleep."

"Daddy died." The words came out on a sob. "I'm scared to sleep because I might die."

"Oh, honey." She lay down next to him, holding his little body, transported back to the many, many nights she'd slept in here with a tiny boy sobbing and scared. "Don't even think that."

Jag's barking had settled to a few sharp noises followed by a growl, then the low timbre of Liam's voice issuing commands. Andi rolled to her left to listen, but Christian's hand seized her arm.

"Don't leave, Mommy. Don't leave me."

"I won't, baby," she promised, easing right back next to him. "I'll be right here until you fall asleep."

"But I'll wake up. Those scary dreams will wake me up."

"And I'll be here. I promise." She heard Liam's footsteps coming up the stairs, so she kissed Christian's head. "Let me talk to Liam and tell him I'm sleeping here with you tonight."

"Promise? Promise you'll be here, Mommy?"

"I give you my word." With one more kiss, she slipped off the bed and into the hall to meet Liam's concerned look with a questioning one of her own.

"Something on the patio spooked him." He whispered softly so Christian wouldn't hear.

Her eyes widened. "Nora?"

He shrugged. "It's secure, and he's on full alert. Did Christian wake up?"

"Yeah and…" She swallowed, tightening the robe a bit. "He needs me tonight."

Liam's eyes flickered, but the reaction was gone in a split second. "Of course he does. Stay here, and I'll get…" He gestured to the robe. "I know what you sleep in," he finished.

Grateful, she let out a sad sigh. "Sorry."

"No. Are you kidding? It's not…" He shook his head. "He needs you. Number-one priority."

She gave him a silent nod of gratitude, stepping back into the darkened bedroom.

"Is Jag okay, Mommy?" Christian asked.

"He's fine. He heard a car or something, nothing to worry about." She sat down on the side of the bed, aching for a different solution but knowing this was the only one.

This was why she'd made her private vow in the first place: no man before Christian.

"Andi." Liam tapped lightly on the doorframe, but didn't step into the room.

"Hang on," she whispered to Christian, going out into the hall.

"Here." He handed her a tiny bundle that she recognized as her sleep shorts and a tank top. He was dressed again, too, in light sweat pants and a T-shirt. "I'm going to sleep downstairs in the living room," he added. "Just…because."

She sighed and put a hand on his chest, not surprised to feel his heart still pumping like hers. "Guess I'm not destined to thank you for all this." She added a weak smile, but got none in return.

"That's not what we were doing," he said softly.

"I know, it's just that…" She looked down at her hands, suddenly remembering the ring he'd slid on her finger in the car. "You're a good man, Liam Kilcannon."

He gave a dry laugh, as if being good hadn't gotten him where he wanted to go. "Take care of Christian, and we'll talk in the morning."

She nodded and leaned against the wall, watching him go downstairs and into the shadows.

Chapter Sixteen

At the first hint of dawn, Liam got up from the living room sofa and took Jag out to the patio, curious to see how he'd act in the daylight. He'd been worked up as hell last night, desperate to get outside. When Liam had let him on the back patio, the dog launched himself to the wall, up on his hind legs, barking as if someone had just climbed that wall and barely escaped the dog's wrath.

This morning, Jag sniffed outside like a drug-hunting hound, walking the perimeter of the small, grassy area, focused on one corner where the wall and house met, digging, barking, rooting for whatever his powerful scent glands had picked up. Then he'd peed like he was literally pissed off at not finding what he wanted.

Nothing looked unusual to Liam, and the lock on the back door wasn't scratched like someone had tried to pick it. Had Nora come back?

Liam walked across the dew-damp grass to look at the six-foot wall again. The side facing the street had no foliage, which would make it really tough to scale.

From the inside, it would take some doing, using

the vines for footholds, but getting out would be easier than getting in. If someone breached the patio, Jag would go nuts.

The latch clicked on the back door, making him turn and Jag cease his sniffing. Andi stepped outside, her hair still unbrushed and tousled, the same bathrobe she'd had on last night tied tightly around her waist, and the same question in eyes dimmed by sleep-deprived shadows.

"What are you doing out here?" she asked.

"Checking it out in daylight. Trying to figure out what had him worked up last night."

She looked at Jag, who'd resumed his furious digging. "He's still worked up."

"He smells something."

"Oh." She stepped closer, inhaling and letting it out on a sigh, absently reaching for Jag, who stopped digging to nuzzle his nose against her leg. Who could blame him? "Do you think Nora tried to get in?"

"I don't know how unless she had a ladder. Could have been anything, you know. An animal would make him crazy, too. A possum or a rabbit. Maybe not this crazy, but…" He shrugged and looked at the dog, because Andi was so damn beautiful it hurt his eyes to stare too long.

She lifted her hand, though, getting his attention, then turned it so the morning sun caught the light of the ring he'd given her last night.

"We haven't discussed this yet," she said.

"We were busy."

A soft flush darkened her creamy complexion. "Was this your idea?"

"Uh, this might shock you. The Dogfather."

She almost smiled, but that whisper of disappointment was in her eyes again. "Of course. I should have known."

"He wanted me to give it to you at dinner last night."

"Why didn't you?"

He shrugged. "Bone-deep hatred of being the center of attention and handing my brothers reasons to mock me."

She gave a dry laugh and stepped barefoot onto the damp grass, not answering him.

"Be careful where you walk, Andi," he warned. "You might step in…"

"Kryptonite."

Under any other circumstances, he would have laughed. Except he knew exactly why she said it. "I might have to kill Shane."

She made her way to the wall, placing her hands on it, standing on her tiptoes but too short to look over it. The move showed him how difficult it would be for a woman her size to scale this wall.

"Am I your kryptonite?"

Behind her, he placed one hand on her shoulder, slowly turning her around. "Yes, Andi Rivers." His voice came out husky as he lightly touched her bottom lip with the pad of his thumb. "You are my weakness."

She closed her eyes.

"You don't like that."

When she looked at him again, she searched his face, eye to eye, her brows drawn as if trying to find something she couldn't. "Liam, you're almost forty. Why haven't you ever married? And if you say because of me, I'll know you're lying. We dated for one month, and it was great, yes, but hasn't there ever been anyone else?"

He swallowed hard. "My standards are high."

"As they should be."

"No, mine are ridiculous. I've met terrific women, yes. I've been involved and had relationships over the years, but they all fizzled out because…" Oh hell. What did he have to lose? "I think the world of my dad, as you know. And we laugh about him trying to get us all married, one by one. But, Andi, I have always wanted to be exactly like him."

She waited, listening intently while he gathered his thoughts.

"He's a lot of things, you know," he finally continued. "A great father, a gifted vet, a good citizen. But first and foremost, he was Annie Kilcannon's husband. He took that job to heart, lived it every day they were married, and shared something with her that I don't think ten percent of the world's population manages to find."

He took a breath, the long speech so foreign to a man who despised talking, especially about feelings. But it was important she know that he took love and marriage so seriously.

"I refuse to settle for less than that." He stroked the column of her neck with two thumbs, lost in her eyes as he made the admission. "You are the first woman I've ever met that makes me think that kind of life is possible for mere mortals and not just my parents."

"Oh…Liam." Her eyes misted, and she came closer. "That's a lot of pressure for one single mother."

"Don't feel pressured, Andi. Be honored. And honest. Could you ever feel the same?"

"You know how skeptical I am about being so certain. Things change."

"Like where you're going to live?" At her frown, he added, "Nora said something about living in Charlottesville last night."

"There are stipulations in the will that say I'd have to change Christian's last name to Scott, he'd have to be raised in the family home in Charlottesville, and he couldn't be adopted by anyone I marry."

He made a face as the ridiculous reality of those *stipulations* hit him. "What the hell?"

"I'm talking to the lawyer this morning," she said quickly. "I'll get some kind of clarification."

"Would you follow those in order to secure the trust?" he asked.

She studied him, thinking. "You heard me last night, Liam. I'm not going to 'settle' and accept anything. I'm going to fight this with everything I have."

"And now you have me."

She smiled. "Pretty good weapon, I'd say."

He lowered his head an inch, moving in for a kiss he'd wanted since he left her last night, but Jag barked and the kitchen door popped open at the same time.

"Mommy! *There* you are!"

They both whipped around at the sight of Christian in his pj's, looking a little terrified that he hadn't been able to find her. Instantly, the moment was lost as Andi swooped into mom mode and Liam would have to wait again.

After all these years, what was another few hours or days?

Andi walked slowly to her office later that morning, and not only because her body was wiped out from sleeping next to a restless six-year-old instead of a relentless forty-year-old.

She'd done the right thing, no doubt about it. But with Liam's admission echoing in her head, along with his question—*Could you ever feel the same?*—she had to take a good long look at her life, and at him. And what she saw scared her.

Not because she wanted to cling to her oath of independence and focus exclusively on Christian…but because she'd spent a long sleepless night questioning the wisdom of that decision.

And then he hit her with: *You are the first woman I've ever met that makes me think that kind of life is possible for mere mortals.*

Longing twisted in her chest, squeezing the air out of her as she opened the door to the stairs that led to her office above the bakery. She could taste that "kind of life" as clearly as she could taste Linda May's butter-laden croissants just by the whiff of deliciousness in the air. She could imagine the pleasure and security of it, the laughter and love, the big wonderful family, and…

Then something would change. Because that's what *always* happened to Andi. She'd get close to bliss, and life would throw her a change so big and unexpected that everything she hoped to have would melt away.

And did she forget that Christian's six-million-dollar inheritance came with strings? Not only might she lose him, but if he was going to get that money—which belonged to him—she'd have to move. And he'd never have a proper father, which hadn't bothered her these past few years when she clung to solitude, but after seeing him with Liam?

Yeah, the idea that the door to someone adopting Christian was closed and locked *definitely* bothered her.

She pushed open the wooden door to Bruce Williams Architects satellite office to find Becca, her assistant, rolling up a blueprint at her desk. She flattened Andi with an accusatory look.

"You didn't warn me he was gorgeous."

Andi inched back. Had Liam come here after all?

"The lawyer!" Becca said on a soft whisper, pointing to the conference room adjacent to Andi's office. She picked up a business card, fanned herself, then looked at it. "Nicholas Stillman, attorney at law."

"He's not supposed to be here until eleven," Andi said, unconcerned with his good looks but thinking about stipulations she didn't want to follow.

"He knows he's early, but said he'd wait for you. He had some other business to take care of, so I let him use the conference room. Is that okay? Which client needs a lawyer, anyway?"

Becca was a trusted assistant and should be in the know about the situation, but Andi hadn't even had time to tell her. She'd told only Linda May, but Becca should also be informed that her boss was getting married on Saturday night.

Guilt squeezed, along with a little sadness.

"It's a personal matter. I'll talk to him now."

"Brace yourself, he's hot."

"Oh…okay." He could look like Frankenstein's monster as long as he was able to help her get Nora Scott to go away. And do something about the stipulations of a will that could very well put her in the situation of having to decide between millions for her son or a lifetime of love for herself.

With dread like a lead ball in her stomach, she headed into the conference room and, of course, Becca let the blueprint unravel and hustled ahead of her. "Let me do the introductions."

Moments later, after Becca left the room, Andi sat across from the attorney, who was good-looking if you liked piercing gray-blue eyes and wavy blond hair. But all Andi cared about was Nick Stillman's assessment of the documents covering the small mahogany table in her conference room.

Before she told him about the stipulations, she decided to wait to hear what he said about custody.

"Does she have a case?" Andi asked bluntly, not willing to dance around the question any longer.

He let out a slow sigh. "Not a good one," he finally said. "It is not impossible to take a child from his parent, but the law sits firmly on your side."

She almost melted with relief.

"There are many steps to the process, and she appears to have completed a few of them," he added, yanking her back out of that pool of relief. "She's clearly done her homework on the family and juvenile codes in the state of North Carolina." He flipped a paper. "She's listed the state's requirements for a custody hearing and the type of evidence required to prove you are an unfit mother."

Andi winced at the words, only then realizing how much her heart was pounding. She didn't trust her voice or the burn behind her eyelids, so she nodded and let him continue.

"She has to gather more evidence than she has in this document." He fingered another paper. "The court will require video or audio files, some solid proof that you've in some way abused your son, or have a possible criminal record, which you don't, but please keep your nose clean. And a strong and unbiased—"

"Nick," she said, leaning forward. "Whatever she has is made up. Christian is my whole world. The only thing she has is that I'm single and I went out to a bar twice in the last three months."

He nodded. "I'm sorry, Andi. I'm going all lawyer on you with worst-case. You aren't going to lose this one, especially if what you mentioned on the phone holds true. You're marrying Liam Kilcannon on Saturday?"

She stared at him. "That's the plan."

"So you'll march into that courtroom with the power of one of this county's most-beloved families behind you. As long as she can't prove it's not a legitimate marriage and that the court-ordered evaluation of Christian shows that he is comfortable with the family, then—"

"*What* court-ordered evaluation?"

"The one she's petitioned to have." He slid a paper toward her. "I did a quick search of the county courts this morning and found this."

She barely looked at the official order in front of

her, those tears really threatening now. How could she put Christian through that kind of torture? Sitting in front of a child psychologist, answering questions, and wanting to roll into a ball and hide?

Then she remembered the paperwork Nick Stillman hadn't seen yet. Reaching into the soft-sided laptop bag she took to and from work, she pulled out the documents the other lawyer, Jason Leff, had handed her a few days ago.

"He represents the Scott family trust," she explained as she handed them over. "This says the money willed to Christian comes with some stipulations."

Frowning, he took the papers and scanned them while Andi dropped her chin in her hands and shifted her gaze out the window. What a mess. What a big, hot mess.

What was worse—putting Christian through an ordeal at six or denying him a massive inheritance that could change his life at twenty-one? He wouldn't care now, but what about when he was an adult? Would he accuse her of being selfish if she didn't fight for his inheritance or meet the stipulations?

"This is invalid," Nick said simply.

"What?"

"A stipulation placed on a last will and testament is only valid if both parties agree to it, and Christian certainly hasn't agreed and neither have you, nor has Christian's father. So, this will never hold up in court."

She blinked at him as her whole body started to vibrate a little, shocking her with how much she wanted that to be right and real. "Are you sure?"

"I mean they can try to put limitations like this on a will," he said. "And the other lawyer will attempt to get it through, but it won't fly. I'm one hundred percent certain of this law because I've argued it before."

"Is anything one hundred percent certain?" Because it wasn't in her life.

"This is. Placing bizarre clauses and preconditions in wills is the stuff of fiction, I assure you. A stipulation like this requires full agreement, with witnesses, from both parties. I have a file full of case law that will convince any judge in any court."

"Court." It was coming to that. "Nora Scott wants me to sign this trust over to her, and then she'll go away." Because she wanted to *scare* Andi.

He eyed her. "You have that option, but…"

"But would she really go away?" Andi mused.

Nick lifted a shoulder, unsure. "But do you want to do that, Andi? It'd be safe, and I agree it would keep you, and possibly your son, from having to walk into a court of law, but if this money is his, why not fight for it?"

"Because I could lose him."

He shook his head. "I sincerely doubt it. I don't know this woman, but my guess is that she's banking on how good a mother you are to get away with scaring you into signing the trust over to her."

Exactly what Andi thought.

"Of course, you can offer her a financial settlement, a portion of Christian's trust, which you'd probably have to come up with in cash now."

"Like a million dollars?"

"At least."

She almost laughed. "What do you recommend?"

"Fight her. All the way. Brace yourself, and your little boy, and let it go to a hearing. A decent judge won't put a kid through the courtroom if his end can be handled in conference or chambers. You won't lose and you'll be done with her permanently. Settling for less is like letting her blackmail you, and she might come back for more. A court order is much more secure, and I think you're positioned to win. Honestly, I hate that this sounds sexist, but it's going to ultimately help you in court to have a husband like Liam."

A husband like Liam.

She braced her hands on the table as the words made her lightheaded with longing and power and *certainty*.

"Of course, you don't have to go as far as a marriage to prove yourself a fit mother," he added, misinterpreting her expression. "Single mothers win custody battles all the time. The vast majority of the time, I might add."

"Then I don't *have* to marry Liam."

"If you want to, by all means, it will help the case, but it isn't absolutely crucial. You should only do it if you want to." He added a smile that showed off dimples that would probably make Becca swoon. "You know, for the usual reasons one gets married."

Reasons like...falling in love with a man who wouldn't settle for less. "Okay," she said softly. "Thank you."

He leaned forward, all business. "So what will it be, Andi? Fight or settle?"

There really was no decision. "Take her to the

mat," she said simply, standing up with a strength she hadn't even known she had.

Nick grinned. "Music to an attorney's ears. I'll have the response drafted this morning."

Feeling more optimistic than she had in days, Andi walked him out to hand him over to a very attentive Becca.

While the two of them chatted in the reception area, Andi went into her office, closed the door, and walked to the window with a surreal feeling of floating on air with each footstep. Leaning against the cool pane, she looked out at Bushrod Square, her eyes blurring as she stared at the thick summer foliage and brightly colored flower beds.

She glanced at her left hand, at the modest diamond ring that represented so much to him. She didn't *have* to marry Liam on Saturday night.

"But I want to marry him," she whispered, the words so airy and soft they fogged the glass in front of her.

It would help her case, but she recognized that thought as the rationalization it was the minute it hit her brain. The truth was she was falling hard for him. Falling for that strong and steady and loving man who offered her everything she needed and didn't even know she wanted.

And they'd made the plans. Pulling the rug out now would disappoint people more than anything…and delay the inevitable.

She put her hand over her mouth as she accepted that new truth.

But what about Christian? Was it selfish to risk Christian loving and losing a father figure again?

Only if she thought she'd *lose* Liam, and deep inside, down to her very soul, she knew she could count on him forever. She might not be able to say *I love you* now, but she was well on her way. The only things holding her back were fear and uncertainty.

Maybe it was time to let go of both.

"Hey, Andi?" Becca tapped on her door and gave it a nudge, coming in. "Hottie lawyer is gone, but..." She frowned. "Are you okay?"

"Yeah, why?" She touched her cheeks, which felt warm.

"You're all bright and...like you're lit up from the inside."

Which was exactly how she felt. "Mr. Stillman had really good news."

"Yeah? Well, Mr. Stillman asked me on a date, so that's even better news."

Andi gave a tiny hoot. "Well. Go you."

Becca laughed and held out a yellow slip. "You didn't hear the phone. I was flirting my heart out with my future husband, so Molly Kilcannon left a message to call her."

"Oh, really? Did she say what it was about?"

"She said..." Becca frowned at the paper. "A fitting this afternoon? Does that sound right? Or did she say sitting?"

"Fitting. For a dress. A...wedding dress."

Becca's jaw unhinged a bit. "So Linda May isn't blowing smoke? The rumors are true?"

Were they? Was she getting married on Saturday night? She didn't have to, but...she wanted to. For all kinds of reasons.

"Yes," Andi said, surprised at how vehement the

one syllable came out. "It's true. I'm marrying him Saturday at Waterford Farm in a surprise ceremony for friends and family during his brothers' double engagement party."

"Oh my God." Becca opened her arms and threw them around Andi. "I've always known you two were meant for each other!"

"You have?"

"Oh yes! Ever since you dated him years ago, I thought you were perfect. I'm so happy for you, Andi!" She squeezed harder. "Take the day off, please. Go get Christian out of school early. Get fitted for your dress and don't come back here until you've had a honeymoon. Oh, and I'll be there!"

Andi leaned back, reeling. "On a honeymoon?"

"At the wedding. That's the date Nicholas Stillman just asked me to go on—to Shane's engagement party." She yanked her closer. "Throw that bouquet at me, woman!"

Andi laughed, her heart so full of joy and expectation and hope and *certainty*, she would promise anyone anything right then.

What better time to go see Liam?

Chapter Seventeen

A breakthrough with this girl was so close, Liam could taste it. Or maybe that was the sweat rolling down his face under the helmet. The weight and warmth of the bite-training suit was like hot iron on his shoulders and arms, but he couldn't give up on Zelda now. He took off his helmet for air and tossed it, wearing only the suit for the next pass.

This would be the one, he thought. He'd finally gotten through her wall of doggie coolness with tactile stimulation he'd perfected when he learned and used biosensor dog training in the Marines.

But then, he thought he'd gotten through Andi's wall with a somewhat *different* tactile stimulation, only to hit a different wall.

Could you ever feel the same?

She'd never answered, but they *had* been interrupted.

Huffing out a breath of frustration that had rocked him all morning long, Liam eyed Shane across the wide field, noting that his brother looked more sick of this exercise than Zelda was.

"One more time?" he hollered to Shane, who stood holding Zelda's collar as Liam lumbered across the field, blinking sweat out of his eyes. "I really think she'll do it this time."

"She better, or I'm coming over there and biting you myself," Shane fired back, waiting until Liam got in place. "Ready?"

Liam waved his arm just as something caught his eye on the side of the classroom building. Blond hair bouncing, a familiar dog running, and the happy squeal of a boy he instantly recognized. But there was no time to process the fact that Andi, Christian, and Jag were on their way to the field as Zelda took off at full speed, headed straight for Liam, who had the tasty treat she wanted. But she had to attack his arm to get it.

As she reached him, he held the treat high in the air, ordering her to bite. She did, getting a nip chunk of the sleeve but falling off with Liam's first swing. That didn't earn her a treat, and she knew it.

Frustrated and angry, she leaped again, biting down a second time on the sleeve with a vicious growl and pulling left and right.

Perfect.

"Liam!" Christian's frantic voice carried over the field and pulled Liam's attention. "Say the code word! Use the word!"

Liam looked across the field and that one second of hesitation made Zelda pounce again to prove she earned the damn treat. She slammed two hundred pounds of jaw pressure into the woven padding and gave a vicious fight while Liam worked the snarling, furious dog to the ground.

"Use the word!"

Zelda ignored the panic in Christian's voice, but not Jag, who could be heard in a barking frenzy as he saw something he shouldn't: Liam getting attacked. That was compounded by Christian's fear, sending Jag over the edge with the need to respond.

Liam dropped the treat, and instantly, Zelda let go, but Jag was still freaked out, barking and snapping and jumping at the fence. Fully distracted, he stood on his hind legs and slammed the chain link, then turned and lost all control, throwing all his weight against Christian, who fell backward.

"*Zimmer!*" Liam yelled, running as fast as he could in the damn fifty-pound suit. "*Zimmer!* Jag, *Zimmer!*"

The barking stopped, and Jag froze over Christian, looking from him to Liam, not sure of where he should focus as Andi reached the two of them. She dropped to Christian's side with a soft shriek of horror.

"*Zimmer!*" Liam called one more time, more out of frustration because Jag was stone-still now. The dog backed up, sat down, and stared at Christian as if he, too, was horrified at his own behavior.

"*Zimmer,*" Christian muttered, still horizontal but pushing up on his elbows on the grass that had surely softened his fall.

"Are you okay?" Andi asked, putting her hand on her son's face.

"Yeah, I'm fine." He stared at Liam, who would have vaulted the fence if not for the bite suit, so he held the chain link instead, scanning Christian for any sign of an injury. "Is that it, Liam?" Christian demanded. "Is that the secret word?"

Liam let out an exhale of pure relief, aware that Zelda came trotting over to check out the scene. She barked once at Jag, who didn't move or even glance at her, far too chastised to communicate with the new arrival.

"Yes," Liam finally said. "*Zimmer* stops him from doing anything."

Including taking his agitation out on someone he should protect.

Christian sat all the way up, pale but smiling. "Jag told me we'd get it out of you."

Liam wanted to laugh, but his heart was slamming his chest too hard. "I should have told you sooner. What are you guys doing here?"

Andi looked up at him. "Is it okay? Were we not supposed to bring Jag here?"

"No, it's fine," he assured her. "Better if he doesn't see me getting eaten by the new girl, but he's fine." He glanced at Jag, who hadn't budged, abject self-hatred in his eyes. "Hang on a second."

By this time, Shane came over with a leash for Zelda, but his attention was on Christian, too. "You okay, bud?" he asked.

Christian nodded. "Jag just got scared, is all."

Shane threw a look at Liam. "Kid's a natural. You should have them do a little makeup playtime."

Liam unzipped the wretched suit, spreading it wide to let air on his chest. He pushed it off his shoulders and shook out of it, realizing that both Andi and Christian were staring at him. Maybe for two different reasons.

Liam glanced at the T-shirt he often wore under bite suits, reading the words upside down.

Dogs (Because People Suck)

Christian giggled. "Mommy says suck isn't always a nice word."

"Shane gave this to me last Christmas," he said, throwing a look at his brother. "He's not always a nice guy."

Shane laughed. "That captures you in a shirt, big man."

Stepping out of the suit completely, he glanced at Andi, who was still catching her breath after the run, but her attention was definitely off her son and on him. She stared at the sweaty shirt, let her gaze drop lower over his thousand-year-old khaki shorts, and her expression suddenly looked very much like it had in bed last night. Hungry. Hot. Ready to pick up where dogs and kids and noises in the night had stopped them.

Hell, one more minute of a look like that and the dogs would smell the pheromones in the air.

"Not all people suck," she said softly, finally meeting his gaze. The heat melted into something less sexual but no less powerful. "Sorry if our timing was bad. We wanted to surprise you."

"I'm glad," he said simply. "Shane, can you take Zelda and my suit back to the kennels? I want to help Christian and Jag smooth things out."

"Sure thing." He gave Christian a wink as he put a leash on Zelda. "You were good and calm," he said. "Jag's lucky to have a master like you."

"I'm his master?" Christian asked, pushing himself up to a stand.

"You know the code word now," Liam said. "That makes you the boss."

His little face lit up to a thousand watts.

Carrying the suit, Liam walked with Shane and Zelda to the gate about fifty feet away. As they reached it, he handed Shane the suit and put a hand on his brother's shoulder. "Thanks, man."

Shane shot him a look. "I'll tell you one thing, big bro. That woman is not *acting*."

He snorted. "Lust ain't love."

"You sound like one of Gramma Finnie's blog posts."

Liam grunted.

"What the hell?" Shane asked. "Normally, even you would laugh at that."

He stole one quick glance to where Andi and Christian were talking, noticing Jag had still not moved. He had to get Christian and that dog together, fast. "'Cause nothing's normal," he mumbled.

"Want my advice?" Shane asked.

"Not particularly."

"Try and remember she's not a dog."

He gave his brother the dirtiest look he could muster. "Shut the hell up, Shane."

"I mean it. You can't *biosensor* her into loving you. She's a woman, not a female. There's a big difference."

"I don't even know what you're talking about." Not to mention that three or four months ago, cocky Shane would have been doling out the polar-opposite advice, but Chloe sure had changed him.

"You got to get to their heart, Brother. Not just their body."

"What the hell do you think I've been trying to do with her since day one?"

227

Shane looked past him, back to Andi. "Well, in my kind of professional opinion, you've succeeded. Now close the deal."

"I am. On Saturday night."

Shane grinned. "Make it real."

Liam closed his eyes. That was all he wanted in the world. "Thanks for the brilliant advice," he said, layering some sarcasm in there.

"Oh, I know you think you have this all figured out, but trust me, sometimes we gotta be hit with a two-by-four."

"A two-by-four?" Liam nodded. "You're a freaking genius, Shane."

"I know."

Rolling his eyes, Liam hustled back to Andi and Christian.

"Is Jag okay?" Christian asked as Liam approached. "He's not moving."

"He's a little traumatized because he scared you, and he knows that was wrong." Liam put his hand on Christian's shoulder and reached for Andi's. "Here's what we need to do now. We take Jag to a place where he's never had anything but good memories. It's his play place. I've never trained him there, but only took him for fun and love."

Christian nodded, all serious as they took a few steps toward the dog. "Then what, Liam?"

"Then you are going to play with him, hug him, pet him, throw tennis balls to him, and every single instruction, every word, is going to come from you, not me. You'll establish the bond and show him that you not only forgive him, you love him completely. And he'll love you back so hard you won't believe it."

"Wow." Christian's jaw dropped as he looked from Liam to Andi to Jag and back to Liam. "Will that really work?"

"Guaranteed," Liam promised him, nudging him closer. "You take over from here. You know everything about him now. Even the secret code word. Stay here alone with him and pet him while your mom and I get the Jeep."

"Where are we going, Liam?" Christian asked.

"Somewhere special." Special to Liam, anyway.

"Where is it?" he demanded, proving the dog hadn't knocked the *relentless* out of him.

"My place."

"Your house?"

"My…" He glanced at Andi, who was looking at him intently. "My favorite place in the world."

Her eyes flickered with interest—in him and his favorite place. He could only hope she loved it like he did.

It had taken only a few minutes to reach Liam's destination, but it might as well have taken a few hours, the expansive setting seemed so far away from the house and outbuildings of Waterford Farm. They'd traveled over a rutted dirt road, through some thick woods, past a mud-filled gulley that Liam swore was the best part of a long trail built for mudding, and along a creek. Finally, it became impossible to drive anymore, even for an off-road vehicle like the Jeep.

When Liam stopped and they all climbed out and

gazed up the good-sized hill, Jag barked for the first time since they'd left the training field.

"You take him from here, Christian," Liam said. "Up to the top of the hill. There's a wooden bench under a big oak tree. Lift the lid and you'll find a treasure trove of dog toys. Jag will show you."

Both Christian and Jag took off, running up the hill at full speed, but Andi held back, still trying to take in this piece of paradise she'd never seen before.

"Where are we, exactly?" she asked.

"We're at the northeast border of Waterford's one hundred acres. Gramma Finnie calls this Mount Leinster, after one of her favorite places in southeast Ireland, near where she was born. She says this reminds her of those hills, and she used to bring her son Liam here when he was a little boy."

Andi slowed her step, taking in this family history. "There's another Liam in the family?"

"Not anymore. He died young. He was my father's older brother, and the baby Gramma Finnie and Grandpa Seamus had with them when they moved here from Ireland."

"Waterford," she said slowly. "So Waterford is named after that Waterford? The place famous for the crystal?"

"The very same. My Grandpa Seamus's family business was glassblowing, and he'd inherited it in the early 1950s when Waterford Crystal came roaring back to life to rebuild their dying brand. They offered Grandpa a ton of money for his business, and he and Gramma Finnie had just had their first baby. So they took the money and moved to America, settling in Bitter Bark because, as the story goes, their dog howled when he heard the name."

She chuckled at that. "You never told me all of that."

"Can't believe Gramma Finnie hasn't told you yet. It's her favorite story." He took her hand and led her toward the sound of Jag barking and Christian laughing. "Give her a shot of Jameson's and you'll get the long version."

She laughed, thinking of the little old woman throwing back whiskey. "So, is this the highest point of Waterford Farm?"

"There's a place on our mudding trail we call the lookout, and it might be higher, but it's not, in my opinion, quite as pretty."

"It is stunning, Liam." They climbed higher, and with each step, the view was more incredible. There were groupings of trees and acres of verdant grass, with creamy patches of Queen Anne's lace fluttering in the breeze.

"It's mine."

She stopped walking. "Excuse me?"

"When Dad came up with the idea that we all leave our lives and jobs and return to Bitter Bark to run the canine training facility, he thought he had to sweeten the deal by giving us each ten acres and keeping forty for himself."

Her jaw loosened, and a few unexpected chills rose on her arms. "You own this land?"

He nodded. "Don't know what I'll do with it, but Gramma picked this parcel for me, on account of my namesake, Uncle Liam. I like to come here, though, to think and chill. It's my own personal sanctuary."

They almost reached the crest of the hill, the sun warm enough to have Andi's neck feel damp under her hair. There, she could turn a three-sixty and drink in the endless scenery that literally hurt her heart, it was so beautiful.

"Can you build on it?"

"I can do anything I want, but I haven't given it much thought. None of us have, actually, and we all have spectacular pieces of land. Dad's dream was a Kilcannon compound, I'm sure, all peppered with happily married couples he matched up." He gave an easy laugh. "He's transparent as hell, isn't he?"

"He's wonderful, and so is this. What a house you could build here, Liam. I mean, I'm sure you're happy where you are."

"My little split-level that was built the same year I was born? It's just a house, not a…" He cleared his throat as if he'd realized he'd gone too far.

"Not a home?" she suggested.

"Yeah."

"Well, this could be." She narrowed her eyes as she turned, imagining the best location on the site for a house. In the distance, Jag ran after a ball with Christian, and instantly, she could see that as a huge backyard, perfect for kids and dogs and…

She swallowed as an unexpected pang of longing hit. "There's lots of potential," she said quickly.

He walked her under a massive oak, lowering the lid of a weathered, wooden box to make a seat for them. "I keep the dog toys in here," he said, brushing some dirt and leaves off the top. "But I like to sit here and look."

She nodded. "This would be the front porch, then."

"You think?" A smile tugged. "That would be… Maybe you can give me some ideas some time?"

"Sure."

"I'll pay for your time."

Because it would, of course, be a business arrangement. She tamped down the twist of disappointment. "After what you've done for me? You can have some plans on the house."

"Literally."

She laughed at the pun. "*For* the house and *on* the house."

She gazed out at the vista, which seemed to be nothing but miles and miles of undulating green hills under blue skies. "This is absolutely glorious."

"Oh, you should see it in the fall. About the third week in October? It's nothing but red and gold and…heaven."

"I'd like to see that," she admitted. "Think I will?"

He looked at her, quiet for a long moment. "I don't know," he said softly. "I guess it depends."

Holding his gaze, she had to ask the question. "On what?"

On us, she waited for him to respond. "On how fast the wheels of justice turn."

"Of course." She turned and focused on Christian for a moment, where her focus should *always* be. "And speaking of those wheels of justice, I need to tell you about the meeting with my lawyer this morning."

"Oh, yeah. We were so busy with Jag, I forgot to ask you. How'd that go?"

She sighed, wishing they could talk more about houses and history and not legal wrangling and wheels of justice. "I'm fighting everything," she said. "The stupid, illegal stipulations, her claims that I'm unfit, any possibility of anyone, anywhere raising Christian other than me. Here, in Bitter Bark, where I want to be."

The speech finished, she turned to him, waiting for a response.

Typical Liam, he nodded silently. After an interminable minute, he said, "Then we have an important errand to run tomorrow morning."

She lifted her brows in question.

"A marriage license. We can get one at the town hall and double-check to be sure that Mayor Wilkins will be at the house on Saturday."

For reasons she'd never understand, her heart flipped around a bit at the idea of actually getting that marriage license. Even though it was part of her fight against Nora Scott. "Okay, then we're really doing this? We're getting married."

"For better or worse."

She smiled. "Very funny."

"And, if you don't mind, I've gone ahead and booked the night at the Bitter Bark Bed & Breakfast."

Her eyes widened. "For optics?"

His mouth kicked up in a half smile. "Yeah. For optics." He slid his arm around her and pulled her a little closer. "Come on, let's make this official and teach Christian the secret doggie massage that will make Jag love him and only him forever."

"There is such a thing?"

He laughed as they walked toward the spot where Christian and Jag lay together, spent. "Guess you'll have to wait for our wedding night to find out."

Chapter Eighteen

hen the double engagement party at Waterford Farm was in full swing, Andi's entourage of Kilcannon women—including Kilcannon women-to-be Chloe and Jessie—whisked her upstairs. Pru had worked her magic and managed to transform Gramma Finnie's private third-floor suite into a bride's dressing room.

She'd made a special chair for Andi to sit in so Darcy could touch up her makeup and do her hair. She'd spread the newly tailored wedding dress on the four-poster bed and even situated an old cheval-style mirror so Andi could get a good look at herself.

There, with the champagne flowing and the music and laughter from downstairs floating up, Andi gave in to the festivities, making the event somehow feel much more real than it had a week ago when Daniel Kilcannon dreamed up the idea.

Pru stood to the side with a clipboard and checklist, taking her wedding-planning role as seriously as she took everything in her young life.

Molly laughed and gave her daughter an eye roll as she and Andi stepped into the bedroom. "My perfect daughter," she mused. "Her motto is 'do it right, or don't do it at all.' I don't know where she came from."

But she did know, Andi thought. She'd asked Liam once about Pru's father, and all he said was that it was Molly's secret that she refused to share. No one knew, not even Dad, and Molly and Daniel Kilcannon were extremely close.

"She's an amazing kid," Andi said. "As one single mom to another, I applaud your great work."

Molly laughed. "Single can be a benefit. No pesky husband around to tell me what I'm doing wrong."

Andi slipped off the sandals she'd worn with the short black cocktail dress for the "engagement party" portion of her evening, giving Molly a teasing elbow jab. "Maybe not the thing to say to a single mom about to say her wedding vows."

"Yikes, Pru says my inability to coordinate my mouth and brain always gets me in trouble. But...this is going to be annulled, right?"

Angling her head, Andi managed a playfully stern look. "Another thing you don't say to someone taking their vows."

"It was a legit question," Molly said, gently lifting the white dress spread over the bed and sliding her fingers over the pale blue ribbon Pru had artfully managed to work into a more contemporary look. "*Are* you going to get an annulment?"

Andi opened her mouth, but nothing came out, because she really didn't know the answer. The last two days—and nights—with Liam had been just this side of magical. Every kiss, every laugh, every touch, every conversation felt like slipping under a warm and comfy blanket that she never wanted to leave. They'd slept in separate rooms…barely.

It had been a week, but she'd known Liam for years, and he hadn't changed from the solid, steady man she'd met outside this very house three years ago.

Yes, they had a long way to go to get to something that she could be certain would last—if there even was such a thing. But Liam seemed to think there was, and when she woke up this morning knowing it was her "wedding day," she'd felt as close to committed as a woman who'd been planning this moment for months.

"I don't know anymore," she finally admitted. "Liam is the definition of certain, a concept I've never really embraced."

"Nothing is certain," Molly said softly. "But Liam isn't going to change. He was born a great guy and he'll die a great guy. I'd just like to be sure he doesn't die alone."

"I'm sure he won't," Andi said, eyeing Molly closely. "Have you ever known a guy that great?"

Molly gave a sad smile. "I thought I did. But he disappeared. Without a…trace." She emphasized the last word as if it mattered, somehow. As if she'd tried to follow a trail that led nowhere. But then her smile lifted. "Left me the best gift in the world, though."

"I understand that."

Her eyes welling, Molly blinked and quickly turned Andi around. "Let me get your zipper and get you in that wedding dress. Pru, can you come in here?" she called into the next room. "We need the shoes. And where's Gramma? She wants to document this all with pictures." She leaned into Andi's ear. "You'll be the subject of tomorrow's blog, but that's okay, right?"

Andi looked over her shoulder. "Of course. And if you ever want to talk, Molly, you'll never find a more sympathetic ear. It might be hard to share your feelings with Pru, but God knows I understand why a woman makes a decision to walk the path and do this job alone."

"Thank you." Molly surprised her by kissing Andi's cheek. "You're going to make a great sister."

The conversation ended as Pru and Gramma came in, followed by Darcy, Chloe, and Jessie, kicking up the noise and excitement level. Andi felt a little like Cinderella surrounded by chirping birds as they helped her into a simple but elegant tea-length white dress that Pru had transformed from seventies to spectacular.

Jessie helped put her hair in a soft updo, and Darcy touched up her blush and mascara and added some tiny roses from the bushes outside the back porch for her hair. It was like having a little piece of Waterford on her.

"What song did you pick?" Andi asked as Darcy worked in the last rose.

Darcy gave a meaningful look to Gramma. "I ended up asking my dad for an idea."

"Dr. K picked the song?" Andi asked.

"Well, I helped things along, so you can blame me," Gramma said.

Everyone laughed, but Andi studied Gramma Finnie and definitely saw a serious expression on her old face.

"Daniel and I sat out on the patio last night, lass," she said, as if that explained anything.

"Never good," Molly joked.

"Especially when someone opens the Jameson's," Darcy added. "And I'm going to fully admit I did three shots, so that's why I agreed to this."

"Agreed to what?" Andi asked.

"The song we picked…" Gramma Finnie averted her eyes, looking down to pluck at a silver thread in tonight's sparkly party cardigan. "Is, um, from an old movie."

One more look between Darcy and Gramma Finnie and all of the rest of the women grew very quiet. Like they knew something Andi didn't.

"What old movie?" Andi asked.

"Oh, you know." Gramma Finnie was suddenly very interested in her cell phone. "I can never get this flash to work right."

Pru gently took the phone to help. "I've got it, Gram."

"Is no one going to tell me until I actually walk down the stairs?"

Molly cleared her throat. "Just a wild guess, but is the song by any chance from *Saturday Night Fever*, Gram?"

"Yes, that's the movie. The slow song. You know…"

"*How Deep Is Your Love?*" Molly, Jessie, and Chloe asked in perfect unison, their voices rising a bit.

Andi frowned, definitely not getting something. "The Bee Gees?" she asked. "I know that song. It's really…" She looked from one to the other, getting various degrees of *oh boy* to *oh no she didn't* to *wow, that's a shocker*.

"It was Daniel and Annie's song," Gramma Finnie

finally said. "I thought it would make a nice title for tomorrow's wedding blog."

All gazes shifted to Andi as if they were ready for her to put up a fight. That this was too much—the house, the dress, the song. Too much like they were trying to replicate the greatest love story the family had known.

And maybe, a few days ago, a week, she would have balked at the idea. But now?

"I think that's a beautiful song," Andi said. "Won't be a dry eye in the place."

She turned to Gramma Finnie, whose blue eyes were definitely not dry. "God love ya, lass."

"Gramma?" Andi asked in a teasing voice. "Did you use their vows, too?"

"Oh please." She waved her hand. "They sounded like a couple of hippies promising sunsets and moonrises. I went straight-up traditional, because, well, I think that suits Liam."

"I think so, too," Andi agreed, relieved not to be repeating Annie and Daniel's vows.

"Left out the 'promise to obey' part on account of it being the twenty-first century, and Pru wouldn't let me put it in there."

They all laughed. "Good call, Pru," Molly said.

"But they're real vows, lass," Gramma Finnie insisted. "I want to give you two a fightin' chance."

She inched back and put her hands on Gramma Finnie's crinkly cheeks. "I think we have one."

Gramma blinked a tear from behind her bifocals. "Oh, Annie would have loved you, sweet lass."

"I hope so, since I borrowed her dress, usurped her wedding locale, and snagged her firstborn son."

"Then let's get this wedding under way with an Irish toast!" Gramma snagged a flute of champagne from the dresser and held it high. "Say it with me, Kilcannon lassies."

The others stepped forward and formed a little circle around Andi.

"May God bless you and keep you," Gramma started. "May you see your children's children." She circled an arm around Pru on the last word. "May you be…"

"Poor in misfortune and rich in blessings," Pru and Molly added together, smiling at each other.

"And may you know nothing but happiness from this day forward!" They all said it in unison, followed by a high-pitched cheer while Gramma Finnie gulped the champagne.

Nothing but happiness from this day forward? Was there such a thing? Andi doubted it, but she clung to the words as she headed to the top of the stairs to marry Liam Kilcannon.

"Ladies and gentlemen, can I have your attention?" Dad dinged on his glass a few times, his voice booming over the crowd of about a hundred milling about the downstairs and patio of the house.

All the guests, which included the extended family of the Mahoney cousins, Waterford staff, town locals, and good friends, slowly made their way to the center hall where Dad stood with Liam next to him. And next to Liam was Christian, who'd been informed over dinner last night about what was happening at the party.

He hadn't seemed fazed, even a few minutes ago when Liam gave him the two simple gold bands and asked him to be in charge of them for the wedding.

Christian had had only one single question about this ceremony: Could Jag be there?

Andi and Liam had agreed to that without a second's hesitation.

"The announcements, toasts, and celebrations are not quite done," Dad announced, getting a rumbling response from the crowd as they started to pile into the dining room, family room, and main living area all the way back to the kitchen.

Questions hummed, and a few people joked. Shane and Garrett broke off their conversations with Declan and Connor Mahoney to work their way over. Liam welcomed his brothers to the inner circle.

"Sure wish Aidan was here," Garrett said, referring to the one Kilcannon currently somewhere in the Middle East kicking ass and taking names.

"Me, too," Liam admitted, a little surprised at how much his heart was hammering, considering this was not even supposed to be a real wedding.

Molly and Pru were at the top of the curved stairs on the upper landing, locking arms with Gramma. They escorted the little old lady down the wide stairs, with a sweet touch of extra formality. Behind them, Jessie and Darcy came down, joining them in the center hallway.

Jessie nestled close to Garrett, and Liam heard her whisper, "I can't wait for our turn."

And Garrett looked as lost and in love as Liam felt. Except Garrett's love was real. And this was…real enough.

Maybe it was the final drop down the Andi Rivers Slippery Slope, but something told Liam that contentment, not misery, was at the end of this ride.

"We have a very special treat for our guests tonight," Dad said, quieting the crowd once everyone was downstairs except Chloe and Andi. "It's not merely an engagement party for my two middle sons. Tonight is the wedding of my oldest."

A gasp, cheer, and a lot of loud hoots rose from the crowd as Mayor Wilkins made her way through to the front, holding what Liam instantly recognized as the family Bible.

Would Liam's and Andi's names be added into that? For a second, he almost couldn't breathe at the sheer permanence of the possibility.

But then a note of music played from one of the speakers, then another, high pitched and familiar. A song he'd seen his parents dance to a hundred times. Well, thirty-six times. After every anniversary dinner, which they insisted on sharing with the kids, his parents would dance to this old Bee Gees song.

The words were embedded in Liam's memory, the distinctive voice starting the ballad.

I know your eyes in the morning sun...

He felt his father's hand on his shoulder, and when he turned, Liam fully expected to see tears in the older man's eyes. But he was smiling and nodding toward the top of the stairs, where Chloe, wearing a pale blue dress that accented her dark hair and dark eyes, started her way down.

She clutched a tiny bouquet of flowers and held Shane's eyes all the way down the stairs.

Mayor Wilkins, Chloe's aunt and the woman who

brought her to Bitter Bark, gave a little whimper of pride and joy.

"What the hell did I do to deserve her?" Shane muttered. Liam threw his brother a look and notched his brow in silent agreement.

The song hit the chorus, and a few of the guests started to hum along softly, but they all stopped when Andi came to the top of the stairs.

Her hair was up with flowers in it, and she wore a white dress that...oh man. Was that Mom's? Liam blinked at it, noting it wasn't exactly as he remembered it in pictures, but yes, it had the same lace with little holes and a blue ribbon.

Liam wanted to look at his dad, but he couldn't take his gaze from the most beautiful woman he'd ever seen. And she couldn't take hers from his.

"Look at Mommy," Christian whispered in awe. "She's so pretty."

No kidding. Liam pressed his hand on the little boy's shoulder, using the small child for a little bit of stability since right then he seemed to have lost his.

This had started as a favor. Moved into a fantasy. And now, this very moment, this wedding and this woman and this possibility at a lifetime of happiness became the focus of his whole world.

Everything faded into the background like it had that night a few months ago when he'd seen her in the bar. The music, the people, the colors, the sounds.

She reached the bottom of the steps, and Liam stepped forward without thinking if it was right or not, but knowing if he didn't take her hands and hold her, he wouldn't be able to take another breath.

They looked at each other without saying a word,

then he guided her toward the group under the chandelier and stood in front of Mayor Wilkins.

"Dearly beloved, we are gathered here tonight to celebrate the union of Liam Daniel Kilcannon and Andrea Leigh Rivers in the state of matrimony."

Good God, he felt tears burn behind his eyes. Fighting them, Liam looked straight ahead, trying to focus on the mayor and not get knocked over by the words.

She opened the Bible to a page marked by a single index card. "I'm informed this Scripture has been read at every wedding in the Kilcannon family for many generations. And so it will be tonight, too." She cleared her throat and looked down at the Bible. "'For this reason a man will leave his father and mother and be united to his wife, and the two will become one flesh.'"

Liam swallowed hard. When he'd agreed to this, he honestly hadn't known it would be like *this*. This powerful and meaningful. He'd known it would be a wedding, but these *words*.

Finally, he stole a look at Andi, who gazed up at him. Her eyes were full of warmth and affection and *certainty*.

The thing she never thought she could have. He would give it to her. He would be her for-sure, dependable, certain man as long as she would have him.

"Is there a ring bearer?" Mayor Wilkins asked.

"Right here!" Christian stepped forward in his little suit and tie, Jag right beside him. He held out his hand and smiled up at Andi, his eyes so like hers. "I've got them, Mommy."

"Give them to Mayor Wilkins, honey," she instructed softly.

After that exchange took place, Christian stayed right next to her, with Jag. A few people chuckled at the unorthodox grouping, but not Liam. How many times had his mother whispered to him, once he was old enough to understand why, that he'd been at their wedding?

This seemed right.

Mayor Wilkins handed Liam the smaller of the two rings and reached for Andi's hand, joining them.

"Repeat after me. With this ring, I, Liam Kilcannon, take you, Andrea Rivers."

"With this ring..." The words came out husky and low. "I, Liam Kilcannon." He paused, lost in the sweet cornflower blue eyes and the hope he could see there. "Take you, Andrea Rivers."

"To have and to hold..."

He repeated every word Blanche Wilkins said, the weight of each promise growing heavier and more honest until he whispered the last ones...till death do us part.

Not annulment, not divorce, not the end of a charade.

He slid the ring on her finger, nestling it next to the engagement diamond that now looked so familiar and right on her hand, he'd forgotten what it looked like on his mother's. Exhaling now that his part was done, he listened to her say the same words, with the same shaky voice and the same trembling hand when she put the ring on him.

"I now pronounce you husband and wife."

Liam didn't wait to be told what to do next. He

pulled Andi into him, lowered his head, and kissed her with every ounce of love he had. He heard the cheer, felt her shiver in his arms, and tasted the sweet return of everything he felt.

When they broke the kiss, it didn't surprise him a bit that they both had tears in their eyes.

Chapter Nineteen

"I've been here before," Andi whispered as Liam turned the key to the top-floor suite of the Bitter Bark Bed & Breakfast.

"You've been to the honeymoon suite? Not exactly what your man wants to hear right now, Andi."

"My man." She chuckled and leaned into him, a whiff of the roses in her hair teasing him as they had since the first time they'd danced a few hours ago.

He was her man. For now, for tonight. Nothing could change that or steal Liam's strong belief that he was the happiest man alive.

"I was in this room a few weeks ago when I did the first design pass on the addition Jane commissioned." Andi stepped inside when he held open the door, gasping softly. "But it didn't look like this, Liam."

She paused in the small entry that led to a large room dominated by a fireplace and a four-poster bed. As he'd requested, candles flickered from every surface, and champagne chilled in a bucket at the sitting area, along with chocolate-covered strawberries that Molly and Darcy assured him a woman would want on her wedding night.

"You did this?" she asked.

"Jane Gruen did the dirty work, but I, you know…I asked for it."

She looked up at him, a sly smile pulling at her lips. "Damn, Liam Kilcannon. You are a die-hard romantic."

He studied her face, brushing a stray hair from her cheek, which felt so delicate under his big hands. "I wanted it to be special."

"It is," she whispered. "For one thing, no child and no dogs."

"You're not worried about Christian, are you? Because he couldn't be safer at Waterford."

"Not a bit," she assured him. "And he was so tired he'll sleep the night for sure."

They'd left him conked out in the guest bed in Liam's old room with Jag next to him. The party had dwindled, but the house was still full, since Shane, Chloe, Jessie, Garrett, Molly, and Pru were all crashing there, along with a few family friends.

But Liam couldn't wait to leave and bring Andi here.

After a moment, she slipped away from him, dropping onto a fancy sofa that faced the fireplace. "You know, the day I did that walk-through with Jane, if someone had told me I'd be here in this suite three weeks later as a guest with…my *husband*?" Her voice rose in disbelief. "I would have bet everything I ever had or will have that they were wrong. I would have been so sure." She shook her head. "Life constantly surprises me."

He came over to sit next to her. "And sometimes those surprises are good."

She held his gaze. "This one is," she said simply, reaching up to pull one of the flowers out of her hair and giving him a sly, sweet, sexy smile. "And I'll take the champagne now."

He popped the cork and poured while watching her take one clip after another out of her hair, setting each on the coffee table, along with the tiny roses. When she finished, she shook her head and let the wheat-toned strands fall over her shoulders, the shiny mane glinting in the candlelight.

"You're staring," she said softly.

"You're so beautiful," he whispered, holding a glass out to her. "Like the day I met you at Waterford. It was your hair I saw first and noticed it matched your little boy's."

"And what did you think?"

"I thought..." He took a moment to dig into his memory for the real truth of his first thought. "Well, I thought, shoot, a kid. Someone beat me to her."

She took the champagne he offered. "But you came over to talk to us anyway."

"Christian liked the dog I had."

She angled her head and lifted her glass. "Here's to Christian liking dogs that bring us together."

The glasses dinged, and Liam took a sip, not usually a fan of the sweet bubbly flavor, but this drink was perfect.

"Would you like to know my first thought when you came over with your big dog that day we met?"

"I don't know, do I?"

She bit her lip and leaned back. "It was sex. Just plain and simple lust. I wanted you."

He raised both his eyebrows, not expecting that.

"The first time I saw you, I thought...that man belongs in my bed."

He pointed over her shoulder. "It's ten feet away."

Sipping her champagne, she didn't answer.

"Unless you changed your mind," he added.

"I have."

He almost choked on the drink, setting it on the table. "Oookay."

"Because that was all I wanted that afternoon. And, again, a few months ago when I saw you at Bushrod's."

He nodded slowly. "I remember you were, uh, focused."

"Now I want more."

Taking a slow breath, he felt his pulse quicken. "More," he repeated. "How much more?"

"I don't know." She sipped slowly, her gaze on his over the rim of the champagne flute. "But for the first time in my life, I'm willing to find out."

"The first time?"

"I didn't love Jeff, Liam," she said softly. "We liked each other a lot when we were in school, and when we worked together, I was intrigued by him, but then he left. When he came back, he was different, and the only real connection we had was Christian. None of that is love."

"And yet you hang on to all his stuff."

She searched his face, gnawing on her lower lip. "I told you..." She shook her head. "Yeah, I guess I'm hanging on to it. Never said goodbye, never had closure, never even got to see his grave." She looked down for a moment, then up at him. "I'll put it in storage. Would that make you feel better?"

"What would make me feel better is not talking about him on our wedding night."

She smiled. "Our wedding night. Can you believe it?"

"Yeah." He stroked her cheek, curling a strand of hair over his finger. "You were worth the wait," he admitted softly.

"A week? Hardly a wait."

"Andi." Did she really think that this week was the extent of his feelings for her? "I would have waited until Christian grew up and went to college."

She inhaled softly as if the words stunned her. "Liam. Really?"

Sliding his hand down her arm, he turned her to face him. "You see, you have issues with certainty, but I don't. I was certain about you pretty much from the day I met you. I knew we were meant for each other."

"But what if I hadn't come around?"

"You still haven't come around," he said on a soft laugh.

She looked for a long time right into his eyes. "I'm on my way," she whispered. "I'm just not sure where we're going."

"No problem." He took her glass and put it on the table next to his, then stood and took her hand. "I know exactly where we're going."

She came up to him, reaching both arms around his neck. "I have to ask you a question, Liam."

"Anything."

"Anything, really? You mean that? Because this is a tough one."

"You can ask me anything, Andi, and I will answer one hundred percent honestly."

She swallowed and looked into his eyes. "Do you love me?"

He looked at her, a little stunned by the question. And speechless. She really didn't know?

He sighed in response, making her frown slightly, as if that little bit of an answer surprised or saddened her. How could he possibly answer that?

Silently, he glided his hand up her arm, over her shoulder, and around her neck. Pulling her closer, he kissed her lips lightly, then peppered more kisses over her jaw and down her throat.

She responded instantly, her chest rising and falling under every touch and every kiss, moaning in anticipation as he walked her back to the great big bed. He turned her around and slowly unzipped her dress, the single sexy sound punctuating his unspoken feelings.

Letting the lace rustle to the floor, he took a few seconds to admire her body and choice of a heart-wrecking white lace bra and a sliver of silk that barely covered exactly where he wanted to be.

Blood coursed through him as he eased her back onto the bed and loosened his tie, then unbuttoned his shirt. When he shook it off, she reached for him, grabbing his hand, pulling him down, kissing him with the pent-up need they both felt.

He still hadn't said a word, undressing in the same silence, except for a soft groan of delight as they started to explore each other.

Do you love me?

The echo of her question played in his brain like the refrain of a song he couldn't stop humming. He let the words roll around his head and heart as his fingers and lips found their way to her breasts, rocking and rolling when he eased himself on top of her.

He still didn't say a word, not even her name, not a single endearment as her legs curled around him and her hands dragged over his body and down his abs. Every move was made in complete silence except for the swish of sheets, the caress of skin, the tear of the condom wrapper as he opened it.

He didn't utter a single sound as he positioned himself over her and locked his gaze with hers, easing back before he entered her in one long, slow, perfect move. They both gasped when he filled her, though, and he fought the overwhelming need to move faster and harder and deeper.

He let her get used to him, watched her turn her head from side to side as pleasure took control, and finally held her gaze as they found the rhythm of this union.

The beat matched the thumping of his pulse and the short, shallow breaths they both fought for. His lower half twisted in a knot that had to be unraveled, but each second only made the ecstasy deeper and stronger. He watched her unfurl first, gritting his teeth, squinting at the sweat that trickled into his eyes, grinding harder until he lost the fight and let go, completely and totally satisfied.

Do you love me?

He slowly relaxed his whole body and pressed his cheek against hers to whisper one word in her ear. The only word. The truth.

"Yes."

Chapter Twenty

A ndi still hadn't come down off her cloud by Monday afternoon, which was Labor Day, and meant no work or school. Liam had to go to Waterford to work with Zelda and Fritz for a while, then promised to be back for a little barbecue they'd planned. The minute he left, Andi made a decision.

It was time to let go of Jeff, the past, the fears, and the uncertainty. For the time being, Liam would be living here, which was fine. Wonderful, in fact. Of course, he'd sleep in her bed, as he had last night and would again tonight. She wanted to purge Jeff's stuff without Liam, but with Christian. She wanted to do everything in her power to make sure that Christian knew Jeff would always be his father, but feel free to move on.

Christian, however, was not as interested in the dusty boxes spread out in the office as he was in the toy toolbox Gramma Finnie had found for him in some secret space in her third-floor suite. It was old enough to have belonged to Liam or his brothers, containing small but very real and functioning tools, like a hammer with a metal head and pliers that actually worked.

No wonder he was bored by old, dusty boxes.

With Jag resting in the doorway, Christian unpacked his little tools, hammered and screwed everything he could find, and could not have been more bored by the process of going through Daddy's belongings.

She'd done this once, after she learned of his death and accepted the fact that his family didn't want contact with her or Christian, so obviously they didn't want Jeff's things. She'd given his clothes to Goodwill, and stored the rest of his things in a few cartons. And there were some packages he'd shipped from Europe and had never opened that had been tucked in the back of the spare-room closet since the month he'd come back.

It was time to go through those, too, she thought, pulling out a box with a shipping label from Trier, Germany. She knew why she hadn't examined these particular items when Jeff died, and now she could admit it to herself.

He'd gutted her when he'd gone to Europe to take the transfer they had both applied for and gotten together. She'd cried for the loss of her baby's father and for the loss of her dreams of studying under some European masters.

She and Jeff were both building an expertise in the restoration of medieval landmarks, an arcane but wonderfully challenging area of architecture that would have surely led to the academic career she'd once thought she craved.

All that was lost when Christian was conceived.

"I can fix that!" he muttered from the corner, taking his hammer to a row of paper clips he'd taken from her desk to tap them on the rug. "I'm a carpenter now."

She smiled at him, looking at the sun making his blond hair glisten, listening to his little-boy voice, and admiring every angle of his face and the way his childish body moved.

No, nothing was lost when Christian was conceived, she reminded herself. Everything was gained.

Turning back to the package, she found a pair of scissors to slice the tape.

She hadn't even known he'd gone to Trier, she thought as she pulled it open, a little pang of jealousy tweaking. No doubt to work on the cathedral there. She'd written a paper on the massive church her last year of school, for a class in Roman-influenced design, a few facts slipping from her memory banks.

The Cathedral of Saint Peter, as it was known, was the oldest in Germany. They had something big there, as she recalled, that drew tourists in droves. Tons of art, too, all housed in a magnificent twelfth-century Romanesque structure that could have been a fortress as easily as a church.

Her paper had debunked the veracity of most of the relics they claimed to have, except a seamless robe that Christian tourists believed to have been worn by Jesus. There were other important pieces in the church, too, but they hadn't been stored in her memory banks.

Some answers came as she peeked in the box and spied some tourism brochures from the cathedral, along with some rough sketches she recognized as Jeff's distinct drawing style that must have been for a restoration project. Oh, how she'd have loved to have worked on that.

"Let's put all the screws in this part, Jag."

She looked up from the papers to gaze at Christian again. Instead, she worked on *that*. And that was better.

Deeper in the container was yet another wrapped package, covered with plain brown paper and no shipping label. She turned it over and opened the wrapping, taking it off as if opening a gift.

As the last piece came off, she let out a soft gasp of disbelief.

"What is it, Mommy?"

She blinked at the box, which was about ten inches square at the bottom but topped by a tall angular lid with four sides. Automatically lifting her hands as if she knew she shouldn't be touching it, the possibility of what this was hit hard.

A reliquary?

No, that wasn't possible. Although it certainly looked like an ancient container that was used to house beloved and blessed relics in ancient churches all over Europe, this had to be a knock-off Jeff had purchased at the gift shop.

Mother of pearl stones lined the top with gold embossing on an intricate carving. The box was wooden, but heavy, as if it had iron inside. And it sure felt...real.

Was this from the Cathedral of Trier? She dug deeper into those dormant memories again, coming up with nothing that looked quite like this. But she couldn't be sure.

"That's pretty, Mommy." Christian had come closer, intrigued by the box. "Open it."

She shook her head, instinctively knowing its value. "I need to figure out what it is first."

And a reliquary missing from the Cathedral of Trier would be on the Internet. She pushed up to go get her laptop, which she'd left with her bag in the entryway. "Be right back, Christian. Don't touch that."

"Not even with my hammer?" he teased.

"Not funny." She shot him a look from the doorway, where Jag was instantly up and focused as one of his charges was on the move. She signaled for him to stay, which he did, as she trotted down the stairs and remembered she'd left her dang laptop at the office because she was getting married this weekend and didn't dream she'd do any work.

She could do a quick Google search on her phone, and she still might have a textbook from her Roman architecture class on the shelves in the living room. Perusing a row of titles, she dug around her memory for what that book had looked like, but had no recollection.

She pulled out one massive tome on the churches in the Constantine era, checking the index for a mention of Trier, but it hadn't been included. Her phone was up in the office, so she could search online at least. And maybe the Vestal Valley College library would have some books on Trier. The collection was small, but this church was well known and included in many different classes on art history, world religions, and architecture. She might find something tomorrow before her class started.

"Mommy? Where did you go?"

"Coming!" She'd look on her phone and check the school library tomorrow.

Back in her office, she noticed that Christian had

lost interest in her find, having returned his attention to the row of paper clips and tools. So she picked up the box very carefully and set it on a high shelf, and then grabbed her phone to open up a search on the relics of the Cathedral of Trier.

"Mommy, I'm bored."

Of course he was. "Honey, look I've found some pictures of churches your daddy worked on," she said. "Do you want to see? He was a very talented architect, and he helped rebuild these—"

"Can we take Jag to the square?"

She bit back a sigh, tapping her phone when an image of the cathedral came up, and dozens of relics, the pictures too small on this screen to really study. "Later. This is important, Christian. I want you to know who your father was."

"I do know. Jefferson John Scott." He stuffed his last tool into the metal box Gramma Finnie had given him. "I want to go to the square. With Jag."

"After you look at these things and I get them ready for storage."

His shoulders dropped in disappointment. "Mommy, please. You're on your phone."

"But I…" Oh, why push him? He was too young to care about Jeff's work, but maybe he'd have an interest later in life. She'd go to the college early tomorrow and put in a few good hours of research on this box. "All right. It's too nice to sit in here today anyway." She pushed up and ruffled his blond hair. "Let's go, schmoe."

He grinned, all bright and happy again. "Let's go, schmoe!" he fired back, on his feet, holding his little toolbox, snapping for Jag.

As Jag and Christian bounded down the stairs, Andi turned and took one last look at the box she'd discovered, sitting on a shelf over her drafting table, questions plaguing her.

Why would he have that? Why would he not show it to her? How could she tell Christian about him when there was so much about Jeff Scott she actually didn't know?

Downstairs, Jag's barking rose to a crescendo, stealing her attention.

"Liam is here!" Christian called out, the excitement in his voice at this news impossible to ignore.

So why was she trying so hard to tell him about Jeff when a new man—a good, real, alive man who truly cared about them—made Christian so happy? A man who, judging by the way her heart soared as she hurried down to the front door, made her happy, too?

"What are you doing back so early?" she asked as she opened the door, stepping aside so Jag could greet him and Christian could jump up and down and show him the toolbox.

"Hey, I recognize that!" Liam lifted it into the air. "That's my toolbox."

"It's mine!" Christian yelled. "Gramma Finnie gave it to me."

Liam held it out, too far for Christian to reach. "I bet you a million dollars there's an Amazing Spider-Man sticker on the bottom with his left hand missing three fingers."

Christian's jaw dropped, proving he'd already looked at the bottom. Liam turned the box and, sure enough, there was a slightly defaced Spider-Man sticker, circa early eighties. "But you can have it,"

Liam said, handing him the box. "Hammer in good health, boyo."

"I want to fix the pirate ship now!"

"With that?" Liam shot Andi a look of amused incredulity.

"Yes," Christian replied. "I have everything we need right here, but Mommy won't let me go up to the top alone." He raised the toolbox in victory. "But now we can bang that board down so I can go to the very top of the pirate ship. Will you help me?"

Liam didn't hesitate, reaching down and scooping Christian up in his big arms, practically throwing him over his shoulder. Christian let out a high-pitched squeal, and Jag barked to get in on the action.

"I will help you do anything you want," Liam promised, scooting him higher and getting the expected shriek in response. "As long as this beautiful woman…" He reached his free hand to take Andi's. "Comes along for the ride."

Andi smiled at him, almost unable to handle the swell of joy in her heart, the boxes and the past and the task upstairs forgotten.

"Anywhere," she whispered.

Then the three of them headed over to the square…just like a family.

The next afternoon, Darcy stuck her head in Liam's office, pulling him from some paperwork. "Yeah, what's up, Darce?"

"There's a detective from Virginia in the reception area asking to see you. With his dog."

"I don't have any appointments," he said, checking the clock on his desk. He had less than forty minutes to get Christian from after-school care and bring him to Waterford, like he'd promised Andi. He had Jag here at Waterford because Andi was going straight from work to her Vestal Valley classroom early for her Tuesday night class. "Is he a drop-in looking for K-9 training?"

She shrugged and glanced at a card in her hand. "Detective Paul Batista, Charlottesville PD."

Liam was up instantly. "He came in person?" Liam had talked to Paul briefly last week, asking for anything he had on the Scott family that might help Andi's case and planned to follow up in a day or two. "Of course I want to see him. And he has Hawk with him?"

His schedule momentarily forgotten, Liam rounded his desk and thanked his sister, heading out to the front of the small office building. "Paul!" He greeted the short, stocky man with a combo handshake and hug, getting one in return.

"How are you, Liam?" the other man asked, his dark eyes gleaming and warm smile in place.

"Fantastic," he said, meaning it for the first time in years. "And how's this hound of yours?"

Hawk stood at perfect attention, a glorious Malinois with nothing but heart. Liam had trained Paul and Hawk about two years ago, and the men shared an instant friendship and bond over the dog. That bond was why Liam had felt so comfortable digging around for information on a family in Paul's community, but he'd never expected an in-person response.

"I thought you'd call if you had anything to tell me," Liam said after he gave Hawk some affection and a treat.

"I had a few days off and really wanted to come and see Waterford again. Training Hawk here was so great. And..." He lifted his brow. "We might be in the market for another dog for the department. Any good trainees for possible sale?"

"Fritz," he said instantly. "I do have a good dog for you. I don't have a ton of time today, but—"

Paul waved it off. "I'm in town for a few days, but I really wanted to talk in person about the subject you mentioned." He lifted his brows to indicate he wanted confidentiality, despite the empty reception area.

"Come on back." Liam gestured toward his office. "You want to bring Hawk or let him chill in the training area?"

"He never leaves me," Paul said on a laugh. "Just like you trained him."

"Good boy." Liam gave the dog a scratch and took them back to his small office, offering coffee, which Paul turned down.

"So, what's up with this Scott family?" Liam asked as he sat at his desk and Paul settled in the lone guest chair.

"Nothing on the family, Liam. Nadine and Jefferson Senior are both deceased. Their house, which is huge, sits empty, and the sister, Nora? No idea where she is."

Liam knew where she was, or at least where she'd been lately. But he just looked at Paul, sensing there was more to the story.

"It's this Jeff Scott, the son, who has the interesting background."

Liam inched back in surprise. "He's dead."

Paul nodded slowly. "And that case remains open."

"What case? He drove off an icy road in the mountains two years ago."

"And a witness saw another car cause the accident, but that other car has never been found."

"Hit-and-run?" Liam guessed. Paul gave his head a grim shake, and Liam exhaled. "He was murdered?"

"No one knows, but it hasn't yet been ruled an accident. His body burned so badly forensics was damn near impossible, though he was ID'd by next of kin. I talked to the sheriff in Wytheville, where the accident happened, and they're still looking for a navy blue Chevy pickup that someone saw at the scene, but that someone..." He pulled out a small notebook. "Joseph Higgins, was shot and killed, with no leads in his death."

A cold sweat tingled at Liam's neck. "So someone killed Jeff and then killed a witness?" He could barely say the words as he tried to imagine how Andi would take this news. Not well. "Any suspects? Motive?"

"Some of both," Paul said, flipping through his book. "Which brings me to Interpol."

"Interpol?" He leaned over the desk. "Why the hell would European law enforcement be involved?"

"Because Mr. Scott was suspected of being involved with some pretty shady characters over there, possibly involved with the sale of antiquities on the black market. They were close to bringing down one German art theft ring in particular, but it split up and went underground three years ago. Jeff Scott had disappeared off the face of the continent and stayed off the radar until he was killed two years ago."

Disappeared and reappeared in Bitter Bark, North Carolina, claiming to want to be a father again, using his ex for a safe place to hide.

Bile and fury rose in Liam's throat when he thought about the scum being anywhere near Andi and Christian.

"Is that art crime investigation still open?" Liam asked.

"Definitely. They arrested a few people and I can tell you those individuals had some not-so-nice things to say about Jeff Scott. He might have tried to cheat the wrong people out of money, which could mean someone from that ring closed on Scott, found him, and..." Paul lifted a shoulder. "Got rid of him."

"So you think that's who might have killed him? People who were involved with art crimes in Germany?"

"That would be my guess. So, now I'm helping on this open case and you have information. Can I interview you on the record and the woman you said he was involved with?"

Liam swallowed. "I married that woman on Saturday."

"Oh." Dark eyebrows rose. "Well, congratulations." He didn't sound entirely enthusiastic, but Liam ignored it.

"Why wouldn't the authorities have already talked to her?" Liam asked. "She has no idea that Jeff's death wasn't an accident or that he was involved in art crimes."

"Are you sure?"

"Absolutely," he said without hesitation. "Jeff's the father of her six-year-old son. But this will all be news to her."

"And she'll be news to them. No one in Interpol and, my guess would be the thieves either, know that this woman exists or that Scott had a kid. So now the authorities will very much want to talk to her."

Liam nodded. "I'm sure she'll help." After she came to terms with this mind-blowing news. "As I mentioned, his family is trying to get custody of her son, who's inherited a trust fund worth six million dollars."

Paul's eyes flickered, the way a really good law enforcement officer silently said, *Oh, is that so?* without giving away too much. "Well, I assume since you know her well enough to marry her that you would know if she'd been party to—"

"Party to?" Liam's voice tightened. "She's not party to anything."

"How long have you known her, Liam?"

"Three years."

He frowned, the math not adding up. "So you must have known the dead guy."

"I met him in passing, yeah. I was seeing her before he came back from Europe."

"And again, after he died." Paul's statement was direct enough to put Liam on edge.

"We've only been together...briefly." Liam shifted in his seat. "Kind of had a, well, surprise wedding on Saturday."

Paul tried, and failed, to hide his amusement. "Can't say I've ever heard of a surprise wedding."

Son of a bitch. "Paul, it started as me helping her

out. With this custody battle, she was under the microscope for her mothering, which, by the way, is flawless, so we thought if we got married, it would…" His voice faded as Paul's expression shifted from amused to, well, not amused.

"So she married you to fend off a custody battle?"

He made it sound so heartless and cold when it was anything but. Liam looked away to gather his thoughts, but his gaze landed on the clock. Damn. He was going to be late to pick up Christian.

"Paul, I gotta go. But I really do want to talk to you, and I know Andi will, too. Tomorrow?"

Paul nodded slowly, clearly not thrilled with that, but too good of a friend to go bad cop on him.

"How well do you know her, Liam?" he asked as he quietly closed his notebook.

Intimately. Completely. Inside and out. At least…for the last week. "Well enough to know she is completely in the dark and will help you in any way possible. Well enough to know that learning her ex might have been murdered will upset her so much, I'd like to break it to her gently."

Paul nodded slowly, getting up. "Oh, and one last thing."

Good God, what now? "Yeah?"

"Have you ever seen anything that looks like this in her house? Or your house? Wherever she lives since you, uh, got married."

Liam ignored the subtle dig and looked at a small pencil and watercolor sketch of a brown and gold box with a strange triangular top. "No, I…"

Wait a second. He'd seen it that morning. He'd gone into her office where he'd left some shirts hanging in the closet and noticed the bizarre-looking box on a shelf above her drafting table, certain he'd never seen it before.

"Yes?" Paul urged, obviously sensing his hesitation.

"I'm not sure," he said, clinging to the fact that he really wasn't sure. It might have been the same box...or not. "What is it?"

"Priceless," Paul answered. "It has never been photographed and may or may not actually exist. But one of the suspects who's been arrested in Germany claims he was with Scott when this was found during some restoration construction, and then the box and Jeff Scott disappeared days later."

"Maybe he worked out a deal with this ring of thieves."

"Or maybe he didn't. Which might be why he dropped off the face of the earth." Paul added a wry smile. "Literally."

Liam's heart kicked harder, but he wasn't willing to say a thing until he talked to Andi, who, he had no doubt, hadn't known about Jeff's troubles. "Well, I gotta go get Christian."

"Her kid?" Paul asked.

Irritation he'd never expected to feel toward this man skittered up his spine when it was obvious he thought Andi was somehow involved. "My stepson," he answered, ushering Paul out before he could ask another question.

He got Jag, piled him into the truck, and broke a few speed limits on the way to Christian's school.

But he didn't call Andi. Telling her this was something that had to be done in person.

Chapter Twenty-One

The third-floor library at Vestal Valley College was devoid of both people and the answers Andi had been looking for since her first Google search revealed nothing quite like the box she'd found.

Tucked into a corner study carrel, Andi dropped her head into her hands, staring at the image in the textbook and the picture she'd taken that morning of the box. They did not match. Maybe created by the same artist or at the same general time in history, but none of the reliquaries from that cathedral matched the one she had at home.

Surely that was a replica or poor man's attempt at a reliquary, worth nothing.

But if it wasn't? Several of these types of boxes had been stolen, found, and replaced over the last ten years—at least that's what she was getting out of German articles she'd read, relying on a questionable online translation. There were rumors of missing reliquaries that had been hidden behind stones in the church, lost for centuries, but nothing definite and nothing that looked like what Jeff had hidden away.

Still, the possibility that the reliquary might be real had started to torment her, the feeling deepening with the hours of research she'd done. If that was a real box meant to hold a holy relic, then she had to get it back to its rightful owner, even though she'd opened it that morning when she took pictures and found nothing inside but a nest of empty velvet.

The tiny desk was covered with books she'd pulled from the architecture section, printouts she'd made about the Cathedral of Trier, and a few dozen articles that confirmed what she'd learned way back when she'd done that paper on the famous church.

Trier had had multiple reliquaries over the centuries, holding a range of items the church claimed as holy relics. Pieces of the apostles' clothing, a holy nail from the cross, a thorn from the crown, a ring believed to have belonged to Saint Peter. Some had been debunked and proven by testing to be fake, as she'd written about in her graduate-school paper. Others had been moved to other churches, and some had been hidden somewhere in the bowels of the cathedral.

Some had been stolen and were now in the collections of people who had the money to pay for such treasures and hide them from the world.

She heard footsteps out in the stacks, reminding her that she still had a class to teach in an hour. She couldn't waste time. Something had to be here.

Flipping open another textbook with pictures from Trier, she turned the pages slowly, scanning words and images for a clue.

"Where's the nail, Andi?"

She shot up in shock at the man's voice behind her,

but was instantly pinned by two powerful arms that held her shoulders. In front of her face, he smacked the reliquary onto her desk, hard enough to make the top wobble. "Where's the damn nail that was inside here?"

For a moment, a long, impossible, insane moment, she simply couldn't breathe. Her head almost exploded with a mix of shock and fear and the sense that everything was wrong. The world had tilted. The sky had fallen. The bottom of life dropped out from under her.

Jefferson John Scott was alive and holding her to a chair from behind.

"Jeff?" she croaked the word.

"Where did you put the nail, Andi?"

"I didn't...I don't...you're *alive*?"

His breath was warm, coming down on top of her head. She wanted to move, to drop her head back and look up or spin the chair around and face him, but it would be like looking at a ghost.

"I'm sure as hell not dead."

She closed her eyes and tried to process anything that made sense, but nothing did.

"I...thought you were."

"That's what we wanted," he said gruffly. "That's why Nora and I went to great lengths to make it appear that I died. So the people who wanted that nail, and me, would not follow the trail to you. You can thank me for that."

Thank him? She'd *mourned* him. And so had Christian. "How could you?" she managed to ask.

"I had no choice. They would have found me sooner rather than later. Where's the nail, Andi? I know for a damn fact that you hadn't touched that box until yesterday, so you haven't had time to get it to anyone who can verify its authenticity."

She tried to shake her head, but he bracketed her with thick biceps. He'd never been muscular, but there was no mistaking his voice. Or his hands. This was Jeff.

"How do you know that?"

"Because I've been in and out of the house twenty-five times in the past two years, always making sure you hadn't touched it."

She sucked in a shocked breath, horror ricocheting through her. "*What*? You've been in my house?"

"I had to make sure you didn't do anything with it. But then a few weeks ago, I decided it was finally time to move it from its safe place. But that day you came home early."

The day she'd found the back door open and nothing missing. "You were there?"

"I hid in the front hall closet until you went into the kitchen. You really should change your back lock, too."

When only a dead man had a key?

"While you were fussing about that, I walked right out the front door."

A lock she had changed after she found it open. She shuddered under him.

"Then you went and got that damn dog, and I had to wait for a time when it wasn't there."

"Wednesday night," she muttered.

She felt him nod. "Nora tried to keep you outside as long as she could, since it was the first time that damn *hund* wasn't in the house." The use of the

German word for dog sent another shiver through her, as if he shouldn't know any words that Jag could understand. "I got stuck on the damn patio when you got home but managed to climb the wall, which made Rin Tin Tin bark like a blood hound."

That was *him* on the patio making Jag crazy that night. Jeff. On her patio. While she almost made love to Liam. She literally couldn't breathe.

"Then I couldn't get back in there until today, when, lo and behold, I found this on the shelf." He slapped a hand on the reliquary. "Empty. Back to my original question. Where is the nail, Andi?"

"It was empty."

"It was in there." He squeezed her neck with those thick muscles, a feeling of desperation transferring from him to her and back. "The *holy* nail. The nail from the cross. The nail that is worth a lot of money to some very rich people. The nail I risked my life to get out of Europe. *Someone* must have taken the nail."

Christian. Her stomach tightened as she remembered Liam coming down from the playground structure, laughing about the "nail" Christian had produced from his tool kit.

It must have been a thousand years old, he'd joked. *Or two thousand.*

"So, you give me that nail and I'll give you Christian."

A white light popped behind her eyes, blinding her with fury and fear. "What?" she demanded, almost managing to get up from the chair, propelled by the sheer force of her reaction to his words. "You have him?"

"He's fine. Nora has him."

That did it. A surge of wild, hot emotion burst through her whole body, making her writhe and push and free herself from him. She spun halfway around before he grabbed her arms and took control of her again.

"You *took* him?" She blinked at him, too wild with horror to drink in the changes in a man she'd lived with and shared a child with.

He was bigger. There were probably twenty or thirty pounds of sheer muscle on this man who used to lift textbooks, not weights. His once-short chestnut brown hair had grown long, wavy. His face was beefier, covered with unshaven whiskers, but his eyes were the same. A memorable and distinct green that used to look at her with humor but were now dark with…desperation.

For a dead man, Jeff Scott was damn desperate. And desperate men did very, very bad things.

"Where the hell is the nail?" he demanded.

In a playground structure in Bushrod Square.

Those scary green eyes narrowed at her. "Andi?"

"Why…the will? The custody? Why?"

He sniffed out a dry laugh. "My mother left him money, which is actually laughable but I guess she had more of a soft spot for that kid than I thought."

"And you want it?"

"I need it," he fired back. "And so does my sister, it's part of our…ransom."

Ransom? "What are you talking about?"

He shook his head. "Now they want the nail *and* money not to kill me. And we are the rightful heirs to the Scott money. 'Course, I never dreamed you'd marry some local yokel dog catcher and put up a legal fight. I figured you'd buckle under the first threat of taking Christian and sign the trust over to her. But the money's only half of it. I *have* to have the nail, Andi."

But all she heard was Nora…Christian…ransom…and nothing made sense. "She has Christian now?" That was impossible. Liam had to have him. Liam was picking him up. *He had to be with Liam.*

But Jeff nodded. "And, Andi, she'll take him far, far away. She'll keep him hidden. We're very good at that, my sister and me. And it could be a long time before you see him again, and if those German bastards want me dead, they won't hesitate to kill my son, too."

"Christian," she whispered, barely audible over the sound of her heart breaking.

"So get me the damn nail, Andi."

She could very probably find it on top of the play structure, but if he believed that only Christian could find it, then he'd have to produce Christian. Andi had to take the chance to get to him. "I don't know, but Christian does."

He glared at her. "Get real, Andi."

"He does. He mentioned a nail to me that he had at the square, in the playground." Her voice was remarkably calm, considering her heart rate was anything but. "He must have taken it from the box. He's the only person who knows, so you give him back to me, and I'll get you that nail."

He searched her face. "You lie to me and you'll never see him again. You understand, Andi? I'm fighting for my life here."

And she was fighting for her son. "I understand."

As she stood to leave with him, Andi eyed the man

she'd been sure was dead for two years. Once again, absolutely nothing in life was *certain*.

Except that she'd do anything, including kill or be killed, to protect her son.

Liam stared at the young woman at the front desk of the Sweet Peas Day Care center adjacent to the elementary school as if she'd spoken an absolute lie.

"*No*," he insisted. "He has to be here. Christian Rivers. No one has permission to pick him up but his mother or me. Check the list."

Her gaze darted from him to Jag, who sat at perfect attention, but still managed to look pretty damn threatening. "I did check the list, and his father's name has been on it for years, and he picked him up a few hours ago."

Someone had had Christian for *hours*? Liam's stomach turned. "Do you mean to tell me you released that child to a stranger?"

There was no way Andi would use an after-school care that was less than one hundred percent secure.

"His *father*," she corrected, tapping on a computer keyboard. "He had a photo ID, and his name matched the one on file. Jefferson John Scott, approved since Christian started coming here four years ago." She turned the screen to him to underscore her point, showing a face Liam recognized from his pictures around Andi's house.

"He's dead."

She lifted both brows. "Looked pretty alive to me."

"It was *someone else*."

"Someone else who Christian called Daddy and ran to him, jumped into his arms, and kicked his legs with excitement?"

Every vein in his body turned to ice. "That's impossible."

"Should I get the day care worker who was here with me and also witnessed it?"

Liam shook his head, backing away, trying to make sense of something that made zero sense.

His body burned so badly forensics was impossible, though he was ID'd by next of kin.

Paul Batista's words hit him in a gut that was already on fire. Was it possible? Jeff Scott had faked his own death? Had help from his sister?

But why come back now and take Christian?

Because Andi wasn't giving up the trust fund. And Andi had that box Paul Batista was asking about.

"Do you want me to get the other teacher?" the young woman asked, her edge of sarcasm dulled, probably because there wasn't any blood left in Liam's face.

"No...no." He backed away, trying to think this through. He had to call Andi. And he had to find Christian. Jogging back to his truck, he pulled out his phone and dialed Andi again, swearing softly when he got her voice mail.

Then he made another call but had to leave a message with Paul Batista, giving him Andi's address and asking him to meet Liam there as soon as possible.

Andi's house. Would Jeff go there with Christian? It was on the way to Vestal Valley College, so Liam headed there first, almost unable to concentrate on driving as he put the pieces together and came up with one pretty screwed-up puzzle.

At her brownstone, things looked quiet and normal. No strangers rolling buggies, not many people around at all. Using his key, Liam let Jag inside first, and instantly, the dog went crazy. He barked ferociously and started sniffing the ground, going back to the kitchen door, which was locked, then following a scent with a determined focus Liam had rarely seen.

Barking, he headed straight upstairs, and Liam followed, bracing for an intruder and ready to give Jag the order to attack.

But the second floor was quiet. Christian's door was open, his room exactly as he'd left it. Jag headed straight for Andi's office, growling low and menacing and mad almost immediately. Liam followed the sound as it kicked up to a frantic bark, finding Jag sniffing the floor and drafting table and—

The box was gone.

For a second, Liam stared at the empty spot on the shelf, digging around his memory of that very morning when he'd walked in here and seen it. He'd left the house with Andi, and she hadn't had it. He was certain. She'd worn a bright red dress with heels to work and decided to switch her handbag on the way out. The bag she carried was far too small to hold that box.

Had Andi come back home to get the box? Or had someone else been in this house since then? Someone *with a key* to the back door.

Jeff Scott was alive. If that theory was right, he couldn't waste another second here. He had to get to Andi and figure out where Christian was. Grabbing

Jag's collar and ordering him out, he ran back down the stairs, formulating a plan as he got outside and locked the door behind him.

He'd call the police on the way to the community college and start a search for Christian. He'd get his brothers, too. Turning to where he'd parked, he froze as his gaze fell on something red in the square. A red dress...

He blinked at the two people who walked briskly along the path, headed for the playground area, as one more seismic shock rocked his world.

It was Andi in that red dress and heels, walking with a man who had a secure arm around her, leaning close to her. He looked huskier than he remembered Jeff Scott being, but Liam knew the walk, the posture, the tilt of the guy's head. He wouldn't forget the man who stole the woman Liam loved.

What the hell was she doing with him?

Unable to stop himself, Liam walked closer, to the end of the street, gauging traffic as he crossed, a sickening sensation of déjà vu rising up in him.

"Daddy! Daddy!" The words smacked him from across the street, and he saw a familiar little six-year-old breaking away from a dark-haired woman—Nora?—and running toward Andi.

Andi seemed to stumble a little as the man holding her let go and extended his arms to capture one happy little boy in his arms.

How was this even possible? What the wretched hell was going on?

Andi slowed her step and held back, watching Jeff spin Christian in a circle, making Jag let out a sharp bark.

Liam tugged hard at his leash, but Andi turned at the sound. She looked right at him, too far away for Liam to read her expression. But he could interpret her rigid posture of flat-out fear.

Still holding Christian, Jeff reached back and snagged Andi's arm, pulling her closer, his face away from Liam.

She threw one more look over her shoulder at Liam, and in that instant, he knew the only way to protect her was to let Jag tear into a man Christian was hugging with all his might. Not only would Christian hate Jag and Liam, the sight could scar the child for the rest of his life.

Chapter Twenty-Two

elp me, Liam. Help me.

Andi could only hope Liam recognized her silent plea and didn't assume the worst. Did he trust her? Would he come to help her or walk away, believing that history was repeating itself no matter how impossible—and wrong—that belief would be?

Still holding Christian, who was bubbling with joy over the return of his father, Jeff got a solid grip on Andi's arm and brought her along without following her gaze, thank God. He'd surely have recognized Liam and Jag.

While they walked to the playground, Andi tried to slow the spinning of her head and make sense of what Jeff had told her on the drive over here. And the fact that she'd had no idea that Jeff was so motivated by greed, but it was clear from his story that that was the source of his downfall.

Jeff had reconnected with his sister when she'd gone to visit him in Europe, and true to her ability to find the worst types of people, she'd soon connected with a ring of "art dealers" who dealt exclusively in stolen treasures.

Soon after, Jeff learned there was a way to make a lot more money in architecture than by drafting blueprints. A piece of art here, a holy treasure there…the underground market for such things turned out to be quite lucrative.

Then, a small team with Jeff unearthed a reliquary that had been hidden in the bowels of the Cathedral of Trier for centuries with a nail inside. Could have been a nail from the building, but could have been a nail from a crucifixion, since Trier already had another nail like it. Jeff knew that possibility made it worth a dizzying sum and made a quiet deal with the witnesses, paying them handsomely to "forget" it ever existed.

He could have taken it to the "dealers" that Nora knew, but Jeff wanted this one for himself, with only Nora in on the take.

That was his first greedy mistake. One of the "witnesses" was part of the same circle of thieves, and suddenly, Jeff was on their deadly radar. That's when he picked up and moved off the continent and returned to a small town where he could hide out for a while and keep the nail off the market for five or six years until any interest in it or rumors about it died down.

Still, he worried they'd find him. So faking his death was Nora's idea, and it worked beautifully until his mother died and Jeff made his second greedy mistake. He and his sister were so infuriated by their mother's inexplicable decision to leave Christian a small fortune that they felt justified in going to Charlottesville, with Jeff disguised as her husband, to meet the attorneys and fight for Nora's rights.

But the Germans suspected Jeff wasn't really dead,

and they knew his mother had passed away, so they had a spy watching Nadine's lawyer's office. Jeff walked right into their trap.

Now, they wanted the nail *and* five million dollars. The only way to keep them from killing him was to give them both…and disappear again.

Which, as he hugged Christian and did the whole "returning dad" thing, Andi knew would mean she would once again have to pick up the pieces of Christian's broken heart. But with a man this desperate? She'd take a broken heart over something worse.

Far-off in the square, Andi could see Nora watching them. The woman could have a gun for all Andi knew. And any one of these people passing by could be these so-called evildoers who would kill for this nail that Andi, remembering that graduate school research paper, doubted was real anyway. But now wasn't the time to fight that battle.

She didn't dare do or say a thing that would put Jeff on alert. As long as he believed she would help him, he wouldn't hurt Christian or her. He'd ordered her to act normal, not touch her phone, and stay with him while Christian took him to the nail, so that was exactly what she did.

"Mom says you found a nail here," Jeff said, scooting him from one arm to the other with ease. "Can you take me to it?"

"Yes!" He squirmed to be let down but Jeff held him tight. "It's at the very top of the pirate ship!" He turned to point to the play area where two children, both a little younger than Christian, played at the foot of the slide.

Were they safe? Andi's heart rate, already impossibly high, kicked up even more.

"Liam helped me hammer it in," Christian said. "After he married Mommy."

"Christian," Andi said, getting close and putting a hand on his shoulder to settle him down. "I need you to tell me the truth, okay?"

His eyes widened like he half expected what was coming.

"Did you use a nail that you took from my office?"

When he didn't answer, Jeff lowered him to the ground, but held onto his shoulders. "Christian!" His tone was sharp, making the child flinch. "The truth now."

Very slowly, he nodded. "I...I...yes."

"From that box I told you not to touch?" Andi asked.

He looked up at Jeff as if he thought he could get him out of it, but his father scowled at him. "Did you use it or not, Christian?" Jeff demanded.

"It...it was...really big. I knew it would work on the board."

"Take me to it." Jeff yanked his hand a little too hard. "Right now!"

Some color drained from his face at the command. "Are you mad, Mommy?"

"Jeff, don't—"

"Is Daddy going to leave again? I'm sorry." Tears welled and spilled as his lower lip quivered as he stumbled under Jeff's powerful hand. "Don't leave, Daddy. Please don't leave again!"

The two other mothers on the bench stopped talking to watch the family drama unfold, and for a moment, Andi almost cried out for help or told them to run for safety. But Jeff had Christian halfway up to the first level by then, pushing him to move faster and looking from side to side as if he expected someone to come after him at any minute.

Only Liam…but where was he?

Rushing to catch up with Jeff and Christian, she stole a glance over her shoulder, willing for Liam to come into sight, but she didn't see him.

"Stay down there," Jeff ordered her, making her heart hitch.

"Why? I can help you."

"Stay down there, Andi," he repeated, his voice tense and nervous as he climbed the rope ladder to the top platform.

Frustrated, she clung to the bottom of the structure, looking up, willing this nightmare to be over, refusing to think about what her son would have to face when Jeff left again. Liam would be there. Liam…

She checked out the entrance to the square again, which felt like a million miles away.

Where is he?

He'd left, of course. He saw her with Jeff and probably took his dog and left, because who would put themselves through misery twice?

"Here it is." Christian's voice was soft and scared, making Andi's chest hurt. He was so confused now. Terrified and thinking he was in trouble. He'd blame himself when Jeff disappeared.

Muttering a dark curse, Jeff got down on his hands and knees, pulling something out of his pocket. Squinting through the spaces in the boards, she realized it was a penknife, and he was digging the nail out of the wood.

She shuttered her eyes and prayed that even if the relic *was* real, God would forgive this particular travesty and let Christian be safe.

"We could get my toolbox at home," Christian said, his sweet offer breaking her heart. "That might help, Daddy."

"Shut up."

She grunted at Jeff's cruel command and the soft sob that came after.

"Let him come down, Jeff," she called up. "Just let me take him, and you can get your nail."

"Not a chance."

She tried to swallow. "Why not?" He didn't answer, and her chest squeezed. "Jeff?"

"Got it!" Jeff stood, giving Christian a shove toward the ladder.

"The slide is faster," Christian said, turning to the opening of the long, twisted tube that delivered small bodies right to the bottom.

"Go down it, Christian!" Andi called. "Get on the slide, honey. Now!"

In one smooth move, Christian flung himself into the tube, but Jeff was right behind him, both gone from sight as they disappeared into the tube. Andi darted to the bottom to grab Christian when he came out, just as the sound of a dog's bark cut through her thumping pulse.

She turned, seeing Jag tearing across the square at full speed, bounding through the air, his focus on that slide. He was still fifty feet away when Christian's feet appeared, but Jeff rolled out on top of him.

Jag barked again, loud and furious, getting Jeff's attention. Without a word, he slammed a booted foot into Andi's stomach, vaulted out of the slide, and swooped Christian up.

"Jag!" Christian screamed as Jeff flung the child over his right shoulder and took off at full speed. "*Jaaaaag!*"

Andi started running, but Jag flew by her and launched himself onto Jeff's back.

His teeth got hold of Jeff's left shoulder, instantly making him drop Christian and fall to the ground, screaming. As Jeff threw his hands over his head to protect himself, Jag barked and slammed his paws on Jeff, holding him down.

"*Zimmer!*" Christian hollered. "*Zimmer*, Jag, *zimmer!*"

Instantly, Jag backed off, and Jeff scrambled to his feet to take off, but as he did, a man came out of nowhere, running directly toward Christian and Jeff, a gun drawn.

As the mothers screamed in horror, Andi threw herself at Christian, covering his body with hers, smashing him into the grass to protect him.

"*Fass*! *Fass!*" The attack order came from behind her in Liam's voice.

Jag leaped at the command, launching toward his victim, directly in the line of the man's gun.

"*Jaaaaa—*" Christian's scream was cut off as Liam threw himself on top of Andi, shielding her and Christian. Under him, Andi could see Jag had the man down before any bullet was fired, coming at him with his full weight and a bite into the arm holding the gun, which went flying.

Only then did Liam roll off them, hopping up in one move. Jag had his teeth in the man's arm, wrestling him to the ground. Liam shouted a command, and Jag backed off as Liam took over and pinned the man with a knee to his chest.

Liam looked at Andi and notched his head toward Jeff, who'd run about sixty feet by now and was going to be long gone soon.

She read the question in his eyes. *Send Jag?* He'd have Jeff down, bitten, and trapped in seconds. And Christian would see the whole thing.

Or they could let him go.

She shook her head and Liam acknowledged her decision with a slight nod, but then his attention was back on the man under him, and she turned hers to the child under her.

"Shhh." She wrapped Christian's quivering body into hers, trying to quiet the sobs. In the distance, she heard sirens, vaguely aware of the other children crying and being swept away by their panicked mothers.

The man Liam pinned was muttering something that sounded like German, and Jag was right in his face, ready to attack again at Liam's command. Andi turned to where Nora had been standing, a witness to all of this, but she was gone, although others in the park were rushing to the action.

"I'm so sorry, Mommy. I'm so sorry. I made Daddy leave. Jag bit Daddy, and I made Daddy leave."

"No, no, you didn't." She stroked his head and tried to get him up and to somewhere safe, although nothing seemed to be safe now. She started to push them both up when her hand hit something sharp.

There, on the ground, was a four-inch-long black

nail that definitely looked like it could be a few thousand years old.

Andi came down the stairs with a completely different expression than the one she'd worn a few nights earlier when she descended that same staircase in white lace. Instead of smiling with joy, she now nibbled on her lower lip, a frown tugging while the heavy sigh of an exhausted mom escaped from her lips.

"How is he?" Liam asked, waiting for her at the bottom of the stairs.

"Asleep, thanks to Jag." She gave him a weak smile. "Let's just say I'm glad the guest room has a king-size bed, or I'd be battling a dog for space."

His heart dropped. So she'd be sleeping with Christian tonight.

"I don't know what I'd have done without you talking to him like that," she said. "It really helped him to understand that Jag was doing his job to go after Jeff. He's having an easier time forgiving Jag than Jeff, but that will come, I suppose."

He nodded in agreement, nudging her toward the kitchen. "Come on. You haven't eaten all day."

"It's the last thing I've thought about, but..." She put her hand on her stomach. "I am starving."

"Crystal left us dinner. Dad's gone up for the night, and so has Gramma Finnie. Darcy's staying with a cousin tonight."

"I really appreciate the offer to stay here...for a while."

"Until they find Jeff."

She exhaled again, this time with frustration, not exhaustion. "He'll be back," she said. "If he thinks I have that nail."

After the police arrived and arrested the man who claimed to be a German tourist, but was surely involved in a European art-theft ring, Liam and Andi had spent a long time talking to law enforcement, taking turns answering questions and calming Christian.

Eventually, they let Christian and Jag go to Waterford with Shane, where the family did their thing, surrounding the child with love and dogs while Andi participated in more interviews at her house. She'd spent enough time with Jeff to be able to fill in many holes for law enforcement.

Paul Batista had been there the whole time, and arranged a phone conversation with the Wytheville PD, who'd handled the investigation of Jeff's "death." Finally, Andi had given Paul the nail and reliquary to arrange a return to the cathedral in Germany through Interpol.

Only then had they been able to put the day's events behind them and concentrate on taking care of Christian, which was when Liam talked to him about forgiving Jag.

Now, at nearly eleven o'clock, Liam and Andi could finally have a private conversation.

He led her to the kitchen table set for two with the cold chicken and salad Crystal had prepared. "Something to drink?" Liam asked.

"Maybe a vat of wine or two."

He laughed, encouraged that she hadn't lost her

sense of humor. "I opened you a bottle already." Pouring a glass, he brought it to her, along with a beer he'd been sipping while he waited. "Here you go, sweetheart."

She looked up at the endearment, uncertainty in her eyes. "A sympathy 'sweetheart,' or did you mean that?"

"If you have to ask, you haven't been paying very close attention to me."

A sad smile flickered. "You're pretty much all I've been paying attention to, Liam, and that might be the problem."

The words twisted inside him as he sat down next to her. "We don't have a problem."

She shot him a look as she lifted the wineglass. "You're kidding, right?"

"I mean, obviously, we have a problem, since Jeff is still out there. And Christian was wrecked by this. But together, we can handle anything."

She closed her eyes and took a deep drink, putting the glass on the table as Liam's words faded.

"We are together, Andi." It wasn't a question. He refused to let it be.

After a moment, she picked up her fork, then put it down again. "I didn't know him," she said softly. "I was with him for more than a few years in Boston, and another one here, and I knew nothing about the man. He was a thief? No, he was a gifted architect with a talent for restoration."

Restoration that included helping himself to valuable artifacts and selling them for a tidy profit. "He clearly got involved with the wrong people over there," he said, hoping that made her feel better.

"Was I madly in love with the guy?" she asked, almost to herself. "No, I never was. But I liked him. I respected him. I thought I knew him. I would have bet anything and everything that he was an upstanding man who loved his son and wouldn't hurt him." She shuddered. "And he tried to use him as a shield."

"Andi." He put his hand over hers, but she drew it away, a move that sliced him, but he understood how fragile she was.

"It's like I don't even know people I think I know."

He sighed. "Don't judge the world by one man."

"I'm judging *me*, not the world," she replied. "How can I not question my own ability to decide who I should and should not have around my son or in my life?"

"Ouch."

"I'm sorry, Liam, but...I'm confounded by the human race tonight."

"Well don't lump me in with the rest of them, Andi. I've never been anything but..." *In love with you.* "Honest," he finished.

She closed her eyes, acknowledging that. "Yes, you have. But I'm reeling, Liam. Christian is wounded by this, and so am I," she finally said.

"What do you need?" he asked.

"I need time," she answered after a moment. "I need to go back to where I was, inching him into the world with love and care and one hundred percent of my attention."

"I can help you."

She sighed and picked up the wine again. "I can't imagine trusting anyone."

"Andi." He took the glass and put it down, then closed his hands around hers. "We're married."

"Are we?"

"You said the words, and so did I."

"It was an act. We did it to stop a custody battle, which I'm pretty sure I won. Along with Christian's inheritance."

He stared at her for a long moment, trying to let this process. She'd walk? The vows meant nothing? He meant nothing? An old and far too familiar weight pressed on his chest, one that started the day she looked at him and told him Christian's father had returned. And now—

Bright headlights of a car pulling into the Waterford driveway flashed into the dimly lit kitchen, pulling their attention. Frowning at unexpected company at this hour, Liam stood to see who it was.

"Paul Batista," he muttered at the sight of the detective getting out of a car.

"Maybe he has news."

The two of them walked straight to the kitchen door to go out and greet Paul.

"We got him," Paul said without preamble.

Andi swayed into Liam. "You do? Is he okay?"

Liam tried not to react to the fact that her first question was about Jeff's well-being. He was and always would be Christian's father.

"He's fine, and so is his sister. They had a fender bender on the highway and the state trooper who showed up recognized them from the alert. And the bastard was bleeding like a stuck pig from the dog bite. He was treated, and both of them are being held without bail."

Liam put his hands on her shoulders, feeling the tension melt away at the news that she and Christian were completely safe.

"Assuming he talks, and we believe he will in order to get a reduced sentence, he's going to be able to help Interpol put a lot of people in jail. This was a real coup, you two."

Andi nodded and turned to Liam. "Thank you," she whispered.

He barely smiled. When was she going to learn he didn't want thanks? He wanted...love. Something she might not ever be capable of giving to anyone but Christian.

Even her husband.

"Oh, and I have some more news for you," Paul said, coming closer into the porch light. "It might actually make this all easier for you, considering..." He looked from one to the other. "That you sort of rushed that wedding for legal reasons."

Denial rose up in Liam, but Andi looked straight at the man as if she couldn't wait to hear what he had to say.

"I did a little digging since..." Paul laughed. "That's what I do. And it turns out that since you applied for the marriage license on Friday and Monday was Labor Day, it hasn't been processed yet."

Liam stared at him, hating the words as they were spoken.

"Not processed?" Andi asked.

"It has to be processed for the ceremony to be official, so if you pull it before nine a.m. tomorrow, you won't have to go through any annulment business. The marriage would be void."

Void.

Now there was an ugly word. But under Liam's hand, which was still on Andi's shoulder, he felt her relax even more. As if this was as much a relief as Jeff being in custody.

All he had to do was get to the town hall by nine in the morning.

"Thanks for letting us know, Paul," he said, stepping toward the man to shake his hand.

"Hey, I'm sorry if I seemed, you know, dubious about all this. Nature of the job, you know. You're a good man, Liam."

Yeah, and look how great that was working out for him. "No worries, Paul."

From the car, Hawk let out a sharp, impatient bark, making Paul smile. "And I still want to go back with a good dog for the force. You have one, right?"

"Not Jag," Andi said quickly. "You wouldn't take Jag."

"Of course not," Liam assured her. "Come by tomorrow morning, Paul, and I'll introduce you to Fritz. You'll love him, and we can do some work together training him."

Paul frowned a little. "Tomorrow morning. Are you sure? Don't you want to go to the county clerk's office and pull that marriage license?"

Liam stood stone-still, waiting for Andi to say they wouldn't do that. Willing her to say it. But she didn't say a word.

"Afternoon, then," Liam said.

"Sounds good." With another shake, and a quick hug for Andi, Paul got back in his car and drove off, leaving them standing in the evening heat on the back porch.

Crickets and cicadas hummed in the Carolina summer air, and the occasional dog barked from the kennels, a sound that was so familiar to Liam, he barely heard it.

Andi sighed, and he sure heard that. And all that it implied.

For once, Liam had no fight left in him. If this was what she wanted, then that's what he'd give her.

"I'll pull the marriage license in the morning," he said softly and headed back into the house, because he couldn't stand there on the porch where his father proposed to his mother and know that the one woman he wanted didn't want him.

"Liam."

He almost stopped at his whispered name. Almost hoped that this would be it, the moment she'd let him in and trust him as the one *certain* thing in her life. Almost took that chance one more time.

I can't imagine trusting anyone.

He could still hear her confession. Just how many times did he have to be hit by the two-by-four? She didn't want what he wanted and he was done begging for scraps of her affection like an unclaimed pound puppy.

He stepped inside the kitchen, but Andi stayed outside for a long time. When she finally came in, she took her wineglass and went upstairs to sleep with her son.

And Liam went out to the kennels to be with the dogs. Because, as he'd always known, people sucked and dogs didn't.

Chapter Twenty-Three

"It's gonna be okay, Jag. Don't you worry."

Christian's soft whisper pulled Andi from a surprisingly deep sleep. She didn't open her eyes, though, or give away the fact that she'd awakened. This was like the old days of listening to a toddler's babble through the monitor in the morning, and the memory warmed her.

"You did everything right. You know that, boy. That's what you were trained to do, and you didn't know that was my daddy. You stopped when I said the code word, too."

Jag's only response was a dog sigh and the soft thump of a tail.

Slowly turning her head, Andi sneaked one eyelid open to see the morning light peeking through the curtains she'd drawn last night, hoping Christian might sleep in. He sat up, Jag's massive head resting in the nest of his crossed legs. The dog's tail moved up and down, patting the bed with the same rhythm that Christian's little hand stroked his black and tan flank.

"Mommy said Daddy had to go away again in a hurry, but you did the right thing, and then you stopped the bad guy. You did your job, Jaggerman. I'm proud of you."

Andi bit her lip to keep from letting out a whimper of her own pride at her son. But she wanted to hear him talk, wanted this sneak peek of the innermost thoughts that he revealed only to his dog.

"I knew Liam would keep us safe."

Her heart rolled around helplessly. He'd gone and fallen for Liam as hard as she had. And yet, she'd literally sat at that table and questioned him last night. Or questioned her own judgment.

How could she do that? Yes, she'd been knocked backward by the shock of Jeff being alive and all the terrible things he'd done. Yes, that had made her question every decision she'd ever made. And, yes, she was fragile but had to be strong for her son.

Yet the one constant in everything was Liam. Until he left her on the porch while she was trying to find the words to tell him *not* to pull that license.

So she'd stood outside and silently cried trying to tell herself that Christian needed her "one hundred percent" even though…that was how much she needed Liam.

"I love you, Jag." Christian leaned over and planted a kiss on the dog's head. "I hope I can keep you and Liam forever."

But Liam was going to the town hall to pull the marriage license this morning. She let out a soft moan at the thought, and instantly, Jag's head was up and Christian turned.

"Hey, bud," she whispered, reaching her hand out. "How'd you sleep?"

He lifted a shoulder. "It's a school day, Mom."

"You don't have to go to school today," she said. "You can stay here at Waterford all day with Jag and me."

"But I want to go to school, Mommy."

"Oh." She pushed up on her elbow. "Really?"

He nodded, looking back down at Jag.

"I thought you'd want to stay here with Jag, and we can talk about what happened with Daddy."

He swallowed visibly and still didn't answer, making Andi immediately sit up to reach for him. "Oh, honey, it's going to be okay. I know that was awful yesterday, but I promise you—"

"I want to go to school," he said. "I made a friend."

She drew back at the quiet admission. "You did?"

"His name is Ryan, and he's really nice and he has a dog, and we were thinking that after school one day, we could play and have both our dogs."

The request was so...so mundane that it shouldn't have sent a shot of joy through her, but it did. "Of course, Christian. You can do that."

"His dog is named Tommy, and he's a beagle." Christian smiled. "He has a picture of him. Can I get a picture of Jag?"

"Yes, yes, of course." She gave him a hug. "And if you want to go to school, you can." Any threat to him was gone now, and she'd planned to keep him here only so he could heal, but it seemed he was on that road faster than she was. "Let's get up right now and get ready, and I'll take you to school."

"With Liam?"

They had gone to school every day together, but that had been for their safety. An escort, a bodyguard, and a husband were no longer necessary.

Nice. Wonderful. Perfect, in fact, but not necessary.

She checked the clock. It was almost eight. Surely Liam was on his way to the town hall to end their "marriage" before the clock chimed nine bells on Bushrod Square.

"Liam might not be here for a while," she said. "I'll take you to school." Since Liam had, in the midst of last night's craziness, thought to ask Molly and Darcy to drive to Vestal Valley College and bring Andi's car here.

"I want Liam to go, too," Christian said, the tiniest whine in his voice. "He makes it fun."

She gave him a playful sad face. "I'm not fun?"

"You're funner when he's around."

Wasn't that the truth? On a sigh, she threw the covers back. "Well, I'll try to be *funner* when he's not." Since he wouldn't be around anymore.

The thought punched her in the gut as she walked into the bathroom, making her close her eyes as it hit hard. Did she even want to go back to life before Liam?

She showered and dressed quickly, while Christian went downstairs for breakfast. When she got to the bottom of the steps, she heard him chattering in the kitchen.

"I don't think your momma would let me do that, lad," Gramma Finnie said in response to a question Andi had missed.

"What's he asking you to do, Gramma Finnie?" Andi asked as she came into the kitchen to find the two of them sitting side by side at the counter, the older woman's laptop open and Christian intently studying the screen.

"Can she put my picture on her blog?" he asked.

"Hmmm. I don't know. I prefer to keep your face off the Internet, bud." Andi peeked over Gramma Finnie's shoulder as she got closer. "What's the topic?"

"Oh, I'm blogging about that lovely memorable event we had here recently. I got some great pictures."

"I'm in one, Mommy!"

Andi froze and inched back, still not having read the screen, but it wasn't necessary. Finnie was going to blog about the wedding?

"Do you think that's a good idea?" Andi asked. Gramma knew what transpired yesterday. Maybe she didn't know Jeff had been arrested, and Andi sure wasn't going to announce that now in front of Christian, but blogging about a fake wedding would be wrong.

"I think it's a grand idea," Gramma Finnie replied. "All those happy people celebrating a moment when life changed for the better. Hashtag joy and new beginnings!"

Andi stared at her, eyes widening with each word. "Christian, honey, can you run upstairs and get your backpack? It's time to leave for school."

"Okay." He seemed a little torn over that, getting off the stool slowly. "Gramma Finnie, can I ask you a question?"

"Of course, but if your mom says you can't be in my post, then—"

"Will you come to my school?"

She hooted softly. "Today? Now? I'm still in my dressing gown, lad."

"No, in October. For Grandparents' Day. My

302

Grammie and Granddad came down from Boston last year, and they might come again, but lots of kids have two grandmas."

October? Andi knew they'd be long past this pretend marriage by then. "Christian, I—"

"Oh, lad." The old woman put her hand around his shoulders, cutting off Andi's protests. "I think you ought to ask Liam's father, too. I would be a great-grandmother."

The Dogfather showing up on Grandparents' Day? That would be…Andi closed her eyes. That would be amazing and impossible.

But Christian beamed. "You are a great grandmother," he said. "I'd like you there, too."

"God bless ya, child." Gramma Finnie gave him a hug, pulling him into her bony bosom. "Now go get your stuff, or you'll be late for school."

As she nudged him away, Andi turned to get coffee, hoping to hide her emotional response to the exchange as Christian ran up the stairs, Jag on his heels.

"You don't seem happy about this, lass," Gramma Finnie said when they were alone.

Looking down at her hand as she reached for the coffee pot, Andi's gaze fell on the rings she still wore. "Jeff was arrested last night," she said quietly. "So…Liam and I don't…" She exhaled. "It's probably best if you don't blog about the wedding that wasn't."

"Oh, I like that, The Wedding That Wasn't. I'd use that for a title, but…" She got off the barstool and put her hand on Andi's shoulder, slowly turning her around. "The big event I was talking about was our recent doggie graduation from obedience training. My readers suck that stuff up with a straw."

"Oh." Andi gave an embarrassed laugh. "I just assumed." She shook her head. "Never mind."

"But now I understand why Liam was moping around here like a mush-faced pug who chewed a hole in his favorite toy."

She managed a smile, but then she realized what she was saying. "He was here already?"

"He stayed here last night." She gestured toward the big sofa in the living room. "But he went out to the kennels early."

"Then that means he hasn't gone to…" She looked out the window toward the drive, her gaze landing on his big Ford F-250 at the far end of the driveway, a ridiculous surge of hope rolling through her. He was still here.

"He's not moving fast," Gramma Finnie said. "More like a man with a broken heart."

Andi let out a little whimper. How many times would Andi break that heart? That heart that she…oh, yes, she *loved* him.

"I know, I know," Gramma Finnie murmured, as if she could read Andi's mind and heard that admission.

"You do?"

Next to her, Gramma Finnie slid a narrow arm around Andi's waist. "The oldest of the Kilcannon clan suffers from a bit of a curse, ya see."

Andi inched back, frowning. "A curse?"

"Oh, we Irish have curses."

"What is it?"

Gramma Finnie bit her lip, her blue eyes twinkling. "Once they find their fated mate, they won't settle for less. It's why I worry about Daniel ever finding love again. But it was true of my Seamus who pursued me with a determination that would curl your hair. Same with Daniel and Annie. Now Liam."

"Liam?"

"Oh, he's loved you from the beginning and, I suspect, will love you to the end. That's the curse."

"It is?" Andi blinked at her, the words tumbling together, but the ones that mattered echoed in her head.

He's loved you from the beginning...will love you to the end.

Just then, she caught sight of Liam crossing the yard, passing the dog training pen, moving with determination and not...a man with a broken heart. If anyone's heart was broken, it was Andi's.

She stared at him, a whirlwind of emotions swirling.

"What are you waiting for, lass?" Gramma Finnie asked.

"I'm not really sure," she admitted on a breathy whisper. "I guess I want to be certain."

Gramma Finnie gave an unladylike snort. "Certain you're a fool if you let that lad go."

She was *so right.*

"Do you think he'll give me another chance?"

Gramma Finnie laughed so loud it drowned out the sound of Christian's footsteps pounded on the stairs.

"I'm ready, Mommy!"

"So am I, Christian. *So am I.*" She gave Gramma Finnie an impulsive kiss on the cheek.

"Hashtag Wedding That Wasn't," Gramma quipped.

Andi pulled back and narrowed her eyes at the older woman. "Hashtag Wedding That *Was*."

Gramma looked down and took Andi's left hand, running her wrinkled finger over Andi's. "That has a much better ring to it, don't you think?"

"It most certainly does."

Liam glanced in his side-view mirror, doing a double take at the sight of Andi and Christian running down the driveway toward his truck. Hitting the brakes, he put his arm on the open window frame and turned to get a better look at that wheat-colored hair flying in the wind and the little boy running just as fast next to her.

"Can you take us to school?" Christian called.

Liam opened his mouth to point out the fact that Andi's car was right there, since maybe she'd forgotten, but he shut it fast when she mouthed, "Please?"

Was she coming, too? She didn't need to be there when he went to the town hall to pull the marriage license, but...

"Sure." He waited until they caught up, climbing out to open the heavy back door for Christian. "How you feeling today, big guy?" he asked.

"Good."

Ah, the resilience of youth. Christian would be fine. He'd never be an extrovert, but that hadn't hurt Liam.

"Gramma Finnie's coming to Grandparents' Day in October," Christian announced.

"She is?" He probably did a lousy job of hiding the surprise in his voice.

"Even though she's a *great* grandma."

"In more ways than one," Liam muttered, looking toward the front seat to see Andi already climbing in and getting situated. So, she was definitely coming along for the ride.

How the hell was he ever going to get over her?

All the way to Jackson Elementary, Andi kept the conversation light and breezy. No talk about the trauma in the square yesterday, which he understood. Christian chattered about Jag and Gramma Finnie and all about his new friend, Ryan. Somehow, Liam got roped into agreeing to have Ryan, his dog, Tommy, Christian, and Jag have a playdate at Waterford Farm later that week.

Andi seemed unfazed by that idea and, in fact, offered to talk to Ryan's mother to make it happen.

Didn't she realize they had to stop this now? The charade was over? Was it to ease Christian "away" so that he didn't get hurt again? Fine. But big boys could hurt, too, as he'd realized during his fitful, miserable night on the couch.

"I'm going to go in and talk to the principal and his teacher," Andi said as they pulled up to the school, and Liam had to decide whether to park or get in the car line, since he was now an expert at car-line navigation.

Fat lot of good that would do him in this lifetime.

"Okay. I'll wait for you. And then…you want me to drop you off at work?"

She looked at him, silent. "I'll only be a few minutes but I have to tell them what happened."

She was more than a few, Liam noted, as he parked and watched the parade of parents and kids stream into school. He waited for the kick of longing for a life he'd always wanted to have, but it must have finally been drummed out of him by his last and final ride down the Andi Rivers Slippery Slope to Misery.

It wasn't supposed to hurt this much, was it? But it did. That damn slope was a knife-edged slide that cut him right in half. Why the hell had he fallen so hard for her? *Twice*?

He closed his eyes and forced himself to think about Zelda. That dog needed him. She needed to be coaxed out of her shell and taught to trust. He didn't know why or how, just that he could do it.

Great, Liam. You can make dogs love you, but not the one and only woman you ever really wanted.

In the mirror, he caught sight of Andi coming back, a lift to each step he already recognized as the way she walked when she was truly happy. He'd seen that tilt to her head and that irrepressible light in her eyes.

This must be the joy of having her ordeal behind her.

Before she got to the truck, he hopped out to round the front and open the passenger door for her.

"Thank you, Liam," she said, then she grinned at him. "And if you tell me not to thank you…"

He nodded and barely smiled, fighting the ache that she was so happy and he was so far from happy that they spoke another language there.

"To work?" he asked when he got back in the truck.

"I thought you had an errand to run."

He glanced at her while he pulled his seat belt back on. "I can do it alone."

"I want to go."

"You want to make sure I actually do it?" he asked with a dry laugh. "Because if I don't—"

"I know what will happen if you don't." She shifted uncomfortably in her seat. "We'd be legally married and need an annulment."

"So, you want to be sure this is done right." He pulled into traffic and headed toward the town hall near Bushrod Square, not looking at her, because it gutted him to see that the light in her eyes hadn't diminished one bit. She was damn pleased about this. Sparkling, practically.

He parked in the small lot by town hall, climbed out of the truck, and slammed the door with a little more force than was necessary, hustling straight toward the wide stairs without waiting for her. He didn't want to walk next to her as she bounded up the stairs to pull their license and end this union.

So he got ahead, moving much faster, aching to get this over with.

"Don't." She grabbed his arm.

"Sorry," he mumbled. "I should have waited for you. But—"

"Don't go in there."

He turned and looked down at her, something in her plea hitting him hard. She was two steps below him, barely at his chest level.

"What did you say?" he asked.

"Don't go in there." Swallowing, she took one step, then another. Not his height, but at least on the same level. "I want to do something first."

"Okay." He scanned her face, looking for a clue, but all he saw was that damned light of *joy* in her eyes. "What is it?"

She glanced at the square. "Here's what we need to do now," she said, the tone in her voice almost sounding like she was reciting something.

He waited for her to continue, frowning a little.

"Come on. With me." She took his hand and tugged him in the opposite direction.

"Where?"

"You'll see."

She pulled him along as they crossed the street, and she still had that little dance in her step. His feet were leaden, but he went along, curious and confused. In the square, she took him to the path, the very one they'd followed the night he walked her home from Bushrod's a few months ago.

"We go to a place where we've never had anything but good memories," she said, still with that cadence to her voice like she was repeating something.

Finally, they reached the middle of the square, near the gazebo and the statue of Thaddeus Bushrod. The very place they'd kissed a few months ago on a hot summer night. That was a good memory, except for the fact that she'd walked away from him.

How many times did that have to—

She spun and looked up. "I can't remember everything you said, but I do remember the part about the bond. You said to establish a bond and show him that you love him completely."

"What are you talking about?"

"What you told Christian about Jag. Remember?"

He blinked as it finally made sense. "Yeah," he

said slowly. "That's how you show your dog everything is forgiven and all is good and you're a team again."

Nodding, she put her hands on his chest. "Does it work for people who need to be forgiven? Like me?"

For a long moment, he had a little trouble catching his breath, probably because his heart was ricocheting around his chest. "I guess it could."

"Because you said if you do that, 'he'll love you back so hard you won't believe it.' Do you remember that part, Liam?"

He nodded, hating the hope that slithered up his spine, but there it was. Full-blown hope, the way he felt every time he climbed to the top of the Andi Rivers Slippery Slope of Misery. "I do remember."

Reaching up, she slid her hands around his neck and threaded her fingers into his hair, sending heat flares down his back.

"Andi," he whispered. "Is that what you want? For me to love you back so hard you won't believe it?" Because he already did.

She pressed his neck harder. "This is where we started, Liam. That night this summer. It could have all been different if I had said, 'Yes, I'll date you, I'll fall in love with you, I'll have a relationship with you.' Instead…"

"We ended up married." He gave a dry laugh, wrapping his arms around her as that hope grabbed hold of his chest and squeezed. "And if we don't go to the town hall before nine, we're going to stay married."

"I'm good with that. Really, really good." She leaned into him, her eyes swimming with tears. "Let's

311

start this whole thing over from the very beginning, and we'll take our time, and we'll fall in love the proper way."

"Andi, we're already married."

"Yeah." She smiled. "So then we know the ending is happy."

He let his head fall so that their foreheads touched, while the wonder of the moment rocked him.

As he lowered his head and kissed his wife, the town hall bells rang on the hour. With each chime, Liam knew the life he'd always wanted was about to start.

Epilogue

"Two months ago, I would have bet all I had that those two couldn't stand to be next to each other, let alone impossible to separate."

Andi nodded in agreement, following Liam's gaze to study the strong muscles and regal carriage of a dog she'd come to love almost as deeply as the man at her side. She couldn't help smiling at the way Jag constantly leaned his head in to get a whiff or touch of the girl who'd stolen his heart.

"Zelda made him work for it, that's for sure," Andi said.

Liam laughed and draped his arm over Andi's shoulder. "Worth the fight," he said, pulling her in. "Watching Jag take down Zelda's walls until she finally realized she didn't want to even be in the training pen unless he was there? Priceless."

"Remember how she snarled at him every time he got near her?"

"Remember? I thought she'd bite his head off the first time they trained together."

Laughing at the not-so-subtle metaphor, Andi slid

her arm around his waist and rested her head on his shoulder, watching the two dogs bound up the hill of Mount Leinster, heading for the box where toys and treasures were stored.

Many treasures, Andi thought with a secret smile.

"But look at them now, Liam. She can't resist him."

He laughed softly and tucked her closer, planting a kiss on Andi's head. "Too bad they can't make little Zelda and Jag babies. I sure would have fun training those puppies."

Unable to hide that smile, she turned her head, pretending to drink in the view. "You were right about the third week in October," she said. "This color rivals anything in New England."

As far as the eye could see, the rolling foothills of the Blue Ridge Mountains were swathed in auburn, russet, crimson, and gold. Above it all, an achingly blue sky was dotted with autumn clouds, warmed by a gentle October sun.

They'd been back to Liam's land at Waterford many times, with Christian and Jag, and then, as Zelda wormed her way into everyone's hearts and became another dog Liam couldn't part with, they brought her along, too. By agreement, no dog training was done here, just play and laughter.

And today, the first of what she hoped would be many trips here for another reason.

Andi had purposely chosen a time while Christian was at school, so it would be only the two of them making this particular memory.

At the top of the hill, Jag trotted over to the "toy box," as Christian called the covered bench, barking to demand one of these people open his trove of tennis balls and rubber chew toys. Next to him, Zelda watched, then joined in on the barking.

"All right, all right," Liam replied, letting go of Andi to hustle ahead and get to the box. But she grabbed his arm to hold him back. She wasn't quite ready for him to open that yet.

"Wait a second," she said, easing him to her.

Jag barked again, but Liam held up a hand, immediately silencing him. Not Zelda, but she wasn't quite as well trained yet.

"What is it?" Liam asked.

"I want…" She swallowed. "To be with you when you open it."

His brows flickered in surprise. "Okay."

She grinned. "Just call me Zelda. Can't let you out of my sight or touch."

For a second, he just closed his eyes. "Not sure what I did to deserve that."

"You were you," she said, wrapping both arms around him and looking up. "Constant, steady, unwavering, unchanged. Liam Kilcannon, I love you so very much."

He shook his head a little. "And I don't think I'll ever get used to hearing you say those words."

"Well, you better." She held up her left hand, where the engagement ring and wedding ring had resided for almost two blissful, delicious months. "'Cause these aren't coming off. Unless…"

"Unless what?"

She laughed at the subtle tone of horror and nudged him to the box. "Come on…open it."

His brows drew in a frown again. "You're up to something, aren't you?"

"Something," she agreed, ahead of him now, pulling him toward the dogs and their toy box. She pointed to it. "Open it, Liam."

Still looking a little perplexed, he unlatched the brass hook in the front and easily lifted the wooden lid with one hand. It took Christian two hands and a noisy grunt. And it had taken some effort by Andi, too, when she'd come up here early this morning and planted her surprise.

As the lid creaked, Jag lost control for a moment and barked, sticking his snout in to make sure no one had sneaked up here to steal his slobbery, fuzzy tennis ball. Of course, Zelda came close to mimic him and nuzzle her nose on Jag's flank.

Liam leaned into the box, reaching for the ball, but stopping as he peered inside. Silent, he didn't even look up, but snagged one tennis ball and tossed it over his shoulder to Jag, who launched after it. He flipped a well-gnawed Nylabone to Zelda, who pounced down for a good long chew. Then he rooted around and produced a gnarled rope, a red rubber ball, and...

"Well, what have we here?" he asked as he drew out the long cylinder of blueprints.

Finally, he looked at her, then took a step closer, sliding her lip out from underneath her front teeth. "Use those lips for better things, Andi Kilcannon," he whispered. "Like an explanation."

She smiled. "You need one?"

Letting out a long, slow sigh, he held the cylinder against his chest. "I guess not."

"You commissioned a house design a few months ago."

"I did?"

"Well, you asked for ideas." She tapped the rolled paper. "These are my ideas for the house that could be built on this land. By us. For us."

He closed his eyes and squeezed the tube a little. "Andi." His voice was a gruff whisper. "I love you."

She laughed lightly. "Most clients wait until they see the house before saying that."

Taking her hand, he pulled her to the grass, slowly rolling the rubber band down the blueprints. "I can't believe you did this."

"Anything can be changed, of course."

"I'm not going to want to change a thing," he said as he smoothed the paper out with his large, skilled, beautiful hands. "When did you have time to do this?"

"I've been sneaking an hour at the office here and there."

"I can't believe..." His voice trailed off as he studied the front elevation that she knew so well she didn't even have to look at it. She knew every angle of every window, the wraparound porch, the shutters and chimneys, and that curved transom over a double front door.

Instead, she watched his handsome features soften into an expression of pure joy as he took in her work. "It looks like home," he whispered.

"It's not a replica of Waterford, but an homage," she said. "Obviously smaller and with some modern touches, and I changed the angles of each dormer, added those doors on the—"

"It's home, Andi." He pressed both hands lightly on the drawing, almost reverently. "Home where I will live with you and Christian and..." He lifted his head, facing the sky, fighting tears. "Home."

"You like it?" she asked softly.

"I love it." He lifted a hand and put it on her cheek. "I love you. I love this home and this life and this place and you and Christian. I love it all."

She angled her face to nestle against his warm palm. "I love you, too."

He leaned forward and kissed her lightly. "It's a dream home."

"You haven't seen the inside yet. Turn the page."

After one more kiss, he did, revealing the first-floor specs that were less detailed, but easy enough for her to walk him through the open kitchen, office, and extra-large dining room.

"That's a guest suite," she said, pointing to a bedroom and bath on the first floor. "So my parents can come more often. They loved Grandparents' Day so much."

"Fantastic," he said. "And this dining room is huge."

"I thought we might start hosting Wednesday night dinners here and give your dad a break."

"Love that idea." He nodded, studying each line. "This is amazing, Andi."

"All the other bedrooms are upstairs," she said, fluttering the page to turn it. "Look."

He trailed his finger over a two-dimensional center hall that joined four bedrooms upstairs, including a huge master, a bedroom and playroom for Christian, and finally, he landed on a tiny room next to it. "Laundry?" he asked.

"No, that's not laundry."

"Second walk-in closet?" He frowned. "No, too big for that. Dog's sleeping room?" he guessed on a laugh. "Jag and Zelda do like to curl up next to each other."

"It's a nursery."

His finger froze, and he slowly looked up at her. "A nursery."

"And if we get this house built sometime in the next eight months, baby Kilcannon can sleep right next to us."

He stared at her, and Andi realized she was shaking a little, wanting him to love this news as much as she did.

"Andi..." His voice cracked.

"Remember that night Christian stayed over at Ryan's house, and we were in the living room and..."

"And on the stairs? I'll never forget it."

She laughed. "We, uh, didn't care about..."

"You said it was fine."

"Oh, it was more than fine." She put her hand on her stomach. "I took the test this morning. To be sure, I made a doctor's appointment for this afternoon, before we pick up Christian. Will you come with me?"

"Are you kidding?" His face lit up from the inside, his eyes wide, his smile wider. "Andi!" He threw his arms around her and pulled her close, throwing back his head to let out a hoot that made both dogs barrel over to see what was wrong.

"It's okay," she told Zelda and Jag as they barked and circled.

"It's better than okay." Liam dragged her all the way down on the grass, kissing her on the mouth while both the dogs tried to get in on the new kind of play.

Laughing into the kiss, Andi wrapped her hands around Liam's neck and pulled him closer. "I take it you're happy about this?"

"Happy? I...I..." He squeezed his eyes shut as if he couldn't contain the emotion. "Andi, I've loved you from the beginning, and I'll love you to the end. Here, on our hill, in our home, with our family."

Every word rolled over her as soft as the grass and as warm as the sun. She managed to find her breath, slow her heart, and put both hands on his face to look at him. "You've changed me from the inside out, Liam," she whispered. "I thought I could only love Christian, but you showed me that my heart has so much room. How can I ever thank you for that?"

"How many times do I have to tell you? You don't have to thank me."

"Then I will love you. Forever and ever, from this day forward..." She held up crossed fingers and very slowly opened them and spread her hand.

Liam placed his hand against hers, palm to palm. "Till death do us part."

As Liam kissed her and the dogs barked and the soft Carolina breeze rustled the trees, Andi knew that this was her forever. She was absolutely certain of it.

Don't miss the next book in The Dogfather series:

Bad To The Bone

The old dog is up to new tricks again! This time, Daniel Kilcannon sets a romance in motion by taking pity on a man who's hit hard times. Daniel sees something fundamentally good in him...and is sure his veterinarian daughter can help the man's sick dog, too.

Trace Bancroft, notorious for being the bad boy of Bitter Bark, has been in prison for twelve years paying for a mistake that cost a man his life. While serving his time, he became a top-level dog trainer, working to help inmates find new purpose through the love of a good dog. Now, he's come back to Bitter Bark, looking to start over, with only his mutt Meatball, who's been by his side for years. When he runs into Daniel Kilcannon, Trace is thrilled to take a job at Waterford Farm in exchange for some medical care for his dog. Of course, that means seeing a woman who has no idea why he left or where he's been. Will Molly Kilcannon remember him? She's probably long forgotten that one crazy night they had before his life took the most unexpected turn for the worse.

When Molly sees Trace Bancroft walk into her vet's office at Waterford Farm, her entire world is rocked to the core. She has kept him as her deepest, darkest secret, telling no one in her family that the bad boy of Bitter Bark is the father of her very *good* thirteen-year-old daughter. She's always had a weakness for Trace, but feels nothing but animosity toward a man who left her high and dry and pregnant at nineteen. She's built a life and a business and a whole world without him and certainly doesn't want Trace near her *or* her daughter. But Molly knows that all it will take is one look at Prudence Kilcannon and a little simple math for Trace to realize the outcome of their passion. And then what will happen?

If you want to know the day BAD TO THE BONE or any of The Dogfather books are available for purchase, sign up for Roxanne St. Claire's newsletter!

www.roxannestclaire.com/newsletter/

I answer all messages and emails personally, so don't hesitate to write to roxanne@roxannestclaire.com!

Fall In Love With
The Dogfather Series...

Watch for the whole Dogfather series coming in 2017 and 2018! Sign up for the newsletter for the next release date!

www.roxannestclaire.com/newsletter/

SIT...STAY...BEG (Book 1)

NEW LEASH ON LIFE (Book 2)

LEADER OF THE PACK (Book 3)

BAD TO THE BONE (Book 4)

RUFF AROUND THE EDGES (Book 5)

DOUBLE DOG DARE (Book 6)

OLD DOG NEW TRICKS (Book 7)

The Barefoot Bay Series

Have you kicked off your shoes in Barefoot Bay? Roxanne St. Claire writes the popular Barefoot Bay series, several connected mini-series all set on one gorgeous island off the Gulf coast of Florida. Every book stands alone, but why stop at one trip to paradise?

THE BAREFOOT BAY BILLIONAIRES
(Fantasy men who fall for unlikely women)
Secrets on the Sand
Scandal on the Sand
Seduction on the Sand

THE BAREFOOT BAY BRIDES
(Destination wedding planners who find love)
Barefoot in White
Barefoot in Lace
Barefoot in Pearls

BAREFOOT BAY UNDERCOVER
(Sizzling romantic suspense)
Barefoot Bound (prequel)
Barefoot With a Bodyguard
Barefoot With a Stranger
Barefoot With a Bad Boy
Barefoot Dreams

BAREFOOT BAY TIMELESS
(Second chance romance with silver fox heroes)
Barefoot at Sunset
Barefoot at Moonrise
Barefoot at Midnight

About The Author

Published since 2003, Roxanne St. Claire is a New York Times and USA Today bestselling author of more than forty romance and suspense novels. She has written several popular series, including The Dogfather, Barefoot Bay, the Guardian Angelinos, and the Bullet Catchers.

In addition to being a nine-time nominee and one-time winner of the prestigious RITA™ Award for the best in romance writing, Roxanne's novels have won the National Reader's Choice Award for best romantic suspense three times, as well as the Maggie, the Daphne du Maurier Award, the HOLT Medallion, Booksellers Best, Book Buyers Best, the Award of Excellence, and many others.

She lives in Florida with her husband, and still attempts to run the lives of her teenage daughter and 20-something son. She loves dogs, books, chocolate, and wine, but not always in that order.

www.roxannestclaire.com
www.twitter.com/roxannestclaire
www.facebook.com/roxannestclaire
www.roxannestclaire.com/newsletter/